CONFESSION

MICHAEL CORDELL

ISBN:
978-1-63161-198-8

Sign up for Michael Cordell's newsletter at
www.michaeljcordell.com/newsletter

Published by TCK Publishing
www.TCKpublishing.com

Get discounts and special deals on our best-selling books at
www.TCKpublishing.com/bookdeals

Check out additional discounts for bulk orders at
www.TCKpublishing.com/bulk-book-orders

1

It was a few minutes past midnight when Cash Dixon sprayed his marble kitchen island countertop with Lysol disinfectant for a second time, despite needing to go to bed. He had a staff meeting at the stadium in six hours but knew he wouldn't have time to clean up in the morning. He also knew he wouldn't want to prepare breakfast on these countertops until they were wiped clean of the night's activities.

A cannonball of a man, Dixon listed his height at six feet, but if he was even 5'10", it was only because he was wearing his thickest-soled shoes and a second pair of socks. He nevertheless presented an imposing figure with his barrel chest and biceps that looked like he'd had DD implants inserted into each arm.

His greying crew cut looked like a moldy Brillo pad, and small droplets of sweat gave the top of his head a sheen like an oil slick. His head often continued sweating long after exercise, even after the rest of his body had cooled down, as if all his internal heat exited out the top of his skull. He used a nearby rag to once again wipe his forehead as sweat trickled toward his eyes.

He maneuvered his hands into a pair of dark purple,

rubber gloves and grabbed a nearby dishrag from a drawer. The marble surface looked clean, but he knew better. He wiped the island down, then threw the rag into the trash as if he had a grudge against it. He wondered whether he should spray the counter down a third time.

Dixon glanced up at the 55" TV on the kitchen wall and saw ESPN replaying a feature story about him. He had already watched it five times throughout the day, but reached over and grabbed the remote to turn up the volume to listen to it a sixth.

The reporter raved about the extraordinary success Coach Cash Dixon was having with his football team this year—as he had the previous four years—and the likelihood that his university was going to be bumped up from Division 2 to Division 1 football, a move that would result in a significant bump in school revenue and, more importantly, his salary.

Dixon noticed a small stainless-steel whisk on the floor, something he always used to make his omelets. He picked it up with his glove and held it out in front of him like a mouse by its tail. Intellectually, he knew the dishwasher would get it perfectly clean, and while it pissed him off to do so, he threw it in the trash with the rags. If he could afford a fourth car, he could afford a new whisk. Still, he always liked that one.

When ESPN moved on to highlights from that night's Laker's game, Dixon once again muted the TV and surveyed the kitchen. Everything back in its place. Tomorrow would simply be another morning.

He heard the soft padding of footsteps in the adjacent living room. Fifteen minutes had passed since they had wrapped things up, and there was no reason for her to still be around.

"Hey, playtime's over," he barked, using his coach's voice out of habit. "If I wanted to hang out with someone, I'd still be married."

He knew that wasn't completely true, since it wasn't his idea to get divorced, but he had since moved on from all that nonsense. It was an old adage that the more successful the coach, the less successful the marriage. Based on that measuring stick, he was one hell of a coach.

When he didn't hear the footsteps heading toward the front door, the gruffness in his voice grew in tandem with his temper. He was used to people following his orders, and quickly.

"Listen, I'm not paying you to be my pal. If you're waiting for an Uber, wait the hell outside. Time for you to go."

Before he had even finished his command, a woman appeared in the kitchen doorway.

"No," she said quietly. "It's time for *you* to go."

Her voice was soft, but the pistol she held shouted loud and clear. He didn't know much about guns, but right now, specifics weren't important. It was enough to see she was holding one.

"Now hold on just a minute," he stammered, almost indignant. He tried summoning the force of his personality, usually enough to make a 350-pound lineman cry. "Nothing happened here I didn't pay for. I paid a lot of money—a *hell* of a lot of money. That's the way these things work."

"Well, apparently things don't always work out the way they're supposed to," the woman said. She walked up to the opposite side of the island from Dixon and picked up the TV remote from the sparkling clean countertop.

"Well, okay," Dixon said, now softening his tone. "I understand. Look, I'm sorry. I know sometimes I get carried away. I have a stressful job, but that's no excuse for what I did. But I can make things right…"

He reached for his wallet, but she shook her head.

"You can't make things right with money."

Dixon slowly put his wallet back in his pocket and nodded in agreement, looking for a civilized way— actually looking for any way—to resolve this.

"Then tell me what I can do to make things right."

"You can die," she said, as if offering a helpful suggestion that had suddenly occurred to her.

She looked at the gun as though noticing it for the first time, then turned up the TV volume to a blasting level, making communication impossible, but Dixon had already come to the realization that communication time was over anyway.

The woman pointed the gun at his chest and stared at him for a long uncomfortable moment, her eyes looking every bit as dead as the barrel of the gun. He knew it would be about a minute before his eyes looked as dead as hers.

Turned out, it wasn't even five seconds.

2

"This brings me back to my earlier question: why are you here?"

A simple question, but one Thane still didn't know how to answer. Was it to try to find a sense of direction? A path forward? Or did he simply need to talk to someone about his struggles, even though he knew he wouldn't be able to talk openly with this woman anyway?

"My wife thought it would help to talk with a therapist," he offered.

Thane knew this was a cop-out and was sure the therapist knew that as well. He appreciated her not laughing out loud, although when she looked up from her notebook, she couldn't hide a slight smile.

Jenna Kennedy's office was exactly as Thane thought it would be—a simple room with a wooden floor, lighting resembling a sunset, barely audible ambient music, and a thick Moroccan rug that looked more comfortable than the bunk he slept on while serving time in Forsman Penitentiary. A large fish tank bubbled in one corner of the room, the fish enjoying its own lighting and noise machine.

Thane didn't know how Jenna could work in this space without falling asleep. He sat on a plush, sapphire-blue sofa with a couple of throw pillows he figured some patients hugged when conversations got tough. It was all he could do to not close his eyes and take a nap. If she had designed the room to help her patients relax, she had accomplished this, although he felt there was a fine line between relaxing and nodding off.

"So, you're doing this for your wife?" Jenna said in a tone that showed she was in on the joke.

"No, not exactly. I know she's right."

While her office met his expectations, Jenna herself wasn't what Thane had envisioned. For whatever reason, he imagined someone in their early 60's, with gray hair, horned rimmed glasses and sensible shoes. Jenna, on the other hand, appeared to be in her late 20's, and sat curled up in an overstuffed chair, not wearing any shoes at all. It didn't take long, though, for him to feel like she knew her stuff.

"So again, I ask, why are you here? It's been well over two years since you were released from prison. Don't get me wrong, there is no right timeframe for seeking help, especially for someone who went through something as horrific as you did. It would just help me do my job better if I had a stronger understanding of why now? What made you feel now was the time to talk to a therapist?"

Thane pretended to think about her question. He knew what he wrestled with, but he didn't know how much he could—or should—share. He understood patient confidentiality laws protected what he told her, as long as he wasn't planning on hurting himself or others, and that's the last thing he wanted to do, if for no other reason than there wasn't anyone left he felt he needed to hurt.

"I'm having trouble moving forward," he finally offered, since this was true without getting into specifics. "I took some steps I thought would give me some peace, but I find the anger remains. I thought I would be better by now."

"What you went through had to have been unbelievably traumatic. Spending five years in a prison for a murder you didn't commit. Are you comfortable sharing with me what sort of steps you took that you thought would help you move on from such a horrific experience?"

Thane shook his head. He wasn't yet ready to explain that he had figured out who had actually killed Lauren McCall, the murder for which Thane was wrongly convicted. He had also learned who had hired the killer and set up Thane to take the rap.

When he didn't answer, Jenna ventured a reasonable guess. "I know from following your first case that the man who killed the McCall woman later died during a home break-in. Do you suppose your anger stems from the fact that the person who hired that man and framed you got away with it? You resent someone you can't identify, and that's what's causing your inability to find justice?"

But Thane had been able to identify the two men, and he believed justice had been delivered. Both of those two men were dead because Thane had orchestrated their murders. He didn't actually pull the trigger—the father of the woman who was killed had done that—but Thane set the whole thing up. He was also able to prove that Bradford Stone, L.A.'s District Attorney at the time, had known Thane was innocent during his original trial, but still let him go to prison. Once exposed, Stone had no choice but to resign in disgrace. Thane wasn't proud of how he had managed to elicit a confession from the man, but he also hadn't lost any sleep over it. The important thing was he had gotten it done.

Once the men behind the murder had been punished—albeit with a vigilante flavor of justice—and the D.A. had been exposed, Thane thought he would be able to move forward with his life. But not long after, the police charged an innocent man with one of the murders Thane had set up, so he had to focus on getting that man freed, something he accomplished by once again painting outside the lines of how the legal system operates, although this time with no one getting hurt.

But now all of that was over. He knew he wasn't totally in the clear just yet, not with one of L.A.'s finest detectives still working one of those murders, an investigation that could lead back to Thane. That investigation explained his concern about once again losing his freedom, but he didn't understand why he still felt the anger. He had thought exacting his own form of justice would have freed him from that. But it hadn't.

"I don't think it's about the person who hired the murderer still being free," Thane said. He paused, wanting to tell her everything, but not feeling comfortable doing so. "I'm sorry I'm not more forthcoming," he finally added. "Five years in a place like Forsman has made it difficult for me to open up about what I'm thinking or feeling. You learn not to do that in prison. To not trust anyone."

"Do you have anyone in your life now who you totally trust?"

Thane didn't have to think about that. "My wife,

Hannah. I trust her." He did trust her, but that wasn't the same as feeling like he could confide in her. He resisted telling her what he had done for fear of losing her. "I also did time with someone in prison. Gideon. He now works with me at my firm. I trust him. He helped me survive in there."

"Have you opened up to either of them?"

Thane could only shake his head. He felt he was wasting her time.

"Do you believe it's anger you feel, or fear?" She looked at Thane for a long moment, as if she could hear the game show-style bell dinging inside his head signaling a correct answer from the contestant. The woman might be young, but she was astute. "You mentioned worrying about not being the man you used to be before going to prison, but again, what you went through was traumatic. I can see why it would be hard to simply go back to being that same man. I'm not sure you've given yourself enough time."

Thane knew prison had changed him. After being released on a technicality, he had set up two murders. One of the victims was not only a friend and mentor to him, but also the man who had set him up. Thane had done a number of other things he never could have considered doing before he'd gone to prison, but he executed his plans to perfection after he got out. He had felt justified doing what he did, although he never let himself believe that it was morally sound.

None of this represented who he was before prison. Who he was when Hannah married him. But what did it mean now? Could he find his way back to being the kind of man Hannah deserved?

"And you said there's a baby on the way. That can

bring anxiety in the best of circumstances."

And these weren't the best of circumstances. Hannah saw Thane's fear of being ripped away from his family again as an understandable remnant of having been falsely imprisoned the first time, but she also saw it happening again as all but impossible. But Thane knew it was far from impossible. If his role in the two killings was revealed, this time he would not only be taken away from his wife, but also his daughter. He wouldn't survive that. He couldn't survive that.

And if he did get away with it, what sort of role model would he be for his child? Would he keep working under the premise that the ends justified the means? But if that was true, where did the anger come from? Shouldn't it be gone, now that all of the guilty parties had been taken care of?

Jenna tried outwaiting his silence, but she likely hadn't dealt with many ex-death row inmates. Thane could stay quiet for as long as it took.

"I don't expect you to trust me after only one session," she finally said, "but I'm hoping you'll come back, and perhaps, after a while, you'll feel more comfortable opening up a little more. But it's a process. It can take time."

Thane wanted this to work, but didn't yet feel comfortable sharing what was going on with him, despite knowing he had to do something. His wife could sense him struggling, and at some point she would demand some answers. If he wasn't willing to open up to her, he knew his marriage would be in jeopardy.

He needed to find a way to move forward. He needed to find his way back to the man he used to be before all that betrayal and revenge had changed him.

3

Kristin had put off this meeting for months now, even though she was the one who had reached out to Hannah and really wanted to talk with her. Now that the meeting was taking place, however, she felt her insides tightening.

They had crossed paths a couple of times before, in the courtroom, and when Hannah had visited Thane at the office, but they had never spent any time one-on-one. But now that Hannah was settled into her new position as Director of an L.A. women's shelter, Kristin had sought her out. And now here they were face to face in Hannah's office.

"Has your new job lived up to your expectations?" Kristin asked as she glanced around Hannah's exceptionally small, but warmly decorated, office. It was the sort of space Kristin associated with working for a non-profit organization.

"It's exceeded them," Hannah said. "I found myself getting envious of the difference that you and Thane were making in the lives of people who needed help. It made me want to do something more fulfilling with my life."

Kristin understood. Barely a year and a half out of law school, she had already worked on two extremely high-profile cases with Thane that she knew made a difference.

At the same time, she now found herself wondering if she needed something more.

"I volunteered here before being offered this position," Hannah continued, "so I'm happy to try to answer any questions you might have. I mean, if you're still interested in volunteering."

"I am. Or at least I'd like to learn more about it. Can you tell me how many women stay here on average?"

"Somewhere between 15 – 20, with an average stay of around three to four weeks. And about a third of the women have at least one child with them, so it can be an active place."

"And are most of them trying to get out of abusive relationships, or are some trying to recover from a different type of traumatic event?"

Kristin saw Hannah was now looking at her a little more gently than previously, although she may have been imagining that. Or at least she hoped she was.

"Most have been in abusive relationships, but some have simply found themselves in situations or cycles they're trying to break. There's no one story here."

Kristin nodded, suddenly finding herself having trouble making eye contact with Hannah. She wished she had waited a little longer before reaching out. For someone who prided herself on being strong and confident, Kristin was surprised to find she wanted nothing more than to excuse herself and ask to reschedule, but she wasn't going to give in to that.

"When I got here this afternoon," Kristin said, "I saw a couple of women in the kitchen area, and I wanted to give them a hug. I didn't even know their story, but I wanted to hold them and tell them everything was going to be alright." She surprised herself by saying that out loud. She was also surprised by the truthfulness of the statement. She had always cared about others, but never thought of herself as being very touchy-feely. "Is it hard for you to not want to try to fix everything, even those things beyond your control?"

Kristin glanced back up at Hannah and now clearly saw the look of sympathy she was hoping to avoid. Apparently, her usually reliable poker face had abandoned her this morning. She wondered if her eyes were even tearing up, although her sight didn't seem blurred. Just the same, she again reproached herself for not holding it together.

"I'm assuming Thane told you about me being physically threatened in my apartment during our last case?" Kristin asked.

Hannah nodded. "He didn't tell me everything, but it sounded like a terrible experience."

Kristin didn't know how to respond, other than reflexively clenching her fists. She had yet to find the words to describe what she had gone through, although 'terrible' was a good starting point. Something closer to a beast than a man had forced his way into her apartment and threatened her with unspeakable violence if she involved that animal's brother in a case she was working on. Intellectually, she knew she was fortunate the encounter hadn't crossed the line into something worse, but nothing about the experience felt fortunate. It remained too fresh in her mind to think about it much.

"It was rough, but I'm okay now," she lied. "And that's not really why I'm interested in volunteering here," she lied again.

A longer than comfortable silence filled the room before Hannah finally spoke again. "Can I ask you a personal question?"

Kristin wanted nothing more than to avoid a personal question. She hated personal questions. "Of course," she said, forcing up a smile.

"Have you talked to anyone about what you experienced?"

Kristin shook her head. "No. I suppose I should, but I'm actually a pretty strong person. I've always been quite self-sufficient and taken care of myself."

Hannah nodded, as if pretending that what Kristin had just said made sense. "Between you and me, I've been trying to get Thane to talk to someone about his experience in prison, but he's avoided it so far. I understand, though, everyone needs to follow their own path."

The problem was, Kristin wasn't sure where her path led—only that it often seemed to run alongside a steep ravine. But she also knew that sometimes these things get better with time. Or at least that was her hope.

"What I would suggest," Hannah said, "is to give it a little more time and then let's see what sort of volunteering opportunities we might have. I'd love to have you help us here. Thane speaks so highly of you, and I think your experience would provide you with an understanding and empathy that would be helpful, but my gut feeling is that you should focus on yourself a little while longer before you try helping others. But that's only my sense. If you feel otherwise, we can certainly talk about opportunities right now."

Kristin was surprised at how easily Hannah read her, although she had always struck Kristin as being insightful. And Hannah was right. If she was being completely honest with herself, she saw volunteering as an opportunity to find solace for herself, as if helping others would bring healing to her, but deep down she knew it didn't work that way.

Kristin looked down at the floor for a long moment, then nodded. "You're probably right. Maybe a little more time should pass, but I do look forward to talking more with you down the road."

A tap at the door saved Kristin, as a young woman leaned in through the doorway.

"Excuse me, Hannah, but we have a new resident who arrived a few minutes ago, whenever you have a chance."

"Thanks, Wanda."

Kristin welcomed the opportunity to end their conversation, standing immediately and grabbing her briefcase. "I appreciate you taking the time to talk. And I'm glad to finally get the chance to get to know you a little better."

"Me, too," Hannah said. "And I meant it when I said Thane is so effusive about the work you do and, more importantly, the kind of human being you are. I'm happy you reached out."

They walked out of Hannah's office and into the front foyer, where Hannah gave Kristin a firm handshake, probably recognizing that a hug might break Kristin's last bit of resolve.

"Please stay in touch," Hannah said. "We would be so incredibly lucky to have someone like you helping us out, even if you were only able to give us a few hours a month. Every little bit helps."

Kristin glanced down at Hannah's stomach, anxious

to shift the attention off herself. "How much longer?"

"Due date is still two months away and I'm telling you, it can't come soon enough, although Thane might need another two years before he's no longer scared at the thought of being a father."

"You guys are going to be great. I'm very happy for both of you."

Kristin promised to follow up, and watched as Hannah started down a long hallway. As Kristin turned to exit, she saw Hannah's assistant leading a slender, young woman across the hallway, disappearing into a room at the end of the hall.

Kristin flinched without knowing why, although this wasn't unusual lately. She had frequently been seeing possible threats where there weren't any, and she often felt like she recognized someone who represented danger, only to find they were a total stranger simply out living their life. Just the same, she wasn't quick to dismiss feelings of potential danger. She had learned that lesson.

She picked up her pace as she left the shelter.

The elevator to her condominium complex opened and Kristin glanced down the brightly lit hallway in both directions before stepping off and walking toward her front door.

She had purchased this place in part because it was new, in a good neighborhood, and appeared safe. Until recently, it had lived up to her expectations. But ever since the man who went by the ridiculous name Stick forced his way into her condo, she saw the building as a source of danger.

Kristin knew her business with that man was over. The case that Stick had inserted himself into was finished, so there was no reason for any future interaction, but that didn't take away the trauma or the fear that someone new might be waiting for her. She wasn't someone who had ever lived in fear, but now she had discovered firsthand the fear of the unknown, which was possibly the worst kind.

She noted the new Ring doorbell that provided her with video of whoever might be out in the hall, and she looked forward to the day when it didn't serve as a reminder of why she bought it. She removed a small, yellow sticky note from the door, something she'd asked her housekeeper to place there to let Kristin know when she'd been in her condo.

She punched in a six-digit code on her new digital door lock, then used her key to unlock a second dead bolt before entering. She stepped into her apartment and quickly shut and secured both locks before surveying her apartment.

The place had been freshly cleaned. Kristin wasn't messy, but her apartment never looked more pristine than when her housekeeper had been there. Vacuum tracks ran along the carpet like a miniature railyard, all surfaces were dust free, and the magazines on the glass coffee table were arranged in an orderly fashion.

The one thing her housekeeper had forgotten to do, as usual, was re-close the curtains before she left. It wasn't a big thing, but it also shouldn't be a difficult thing. As she walked over to draw the curtains, she tried figuring out a way to make this simple request again without sounding obnoxiously privileged.

Kristin walked into the kitchen to start making dinner. She had some important paperwork to review while eating, which meant she couldn't have anything messy like pasta or soup. She'd just make a sandwich.

As she pulled a couple of slices of bread from her freezer and put them in the toaster, she glanced over at her kitchen table. The same table that the violent man with the stupid name had pressed her against as he threatened every part of her.

She still debated whether or not to buy a new kitchen table. She wasn't sure if it would help her forget that part of her experience, or if it would only remind her in a different way—adding insult to injury knowing she'd been forced to buy something new that she didn't need, all because of that man. She didn't want to give him that power over her, even though he had made it clear that day that he already had that power.

She wondered when this memory would stop shadowing her every thought. She hoped it would be soon. She feared it would be never.

4

Thane sat behind his desk, savoring the fact that he was no longer in the middle of a contentious case. He had resided squarely in the spotlight ever since being released from Forsman, and welcomed the reprieve of not having the press constantly swarming around him like flies at a picnic. It was time to find new cases to take on, but he was confident none of them would bring the sort of attention experienced with his previous cases. Or at least that was his hope.

The city funded Thane's law office as part of his settlement over his wrongful imprisonment lawsuit. Being able to show that the previous District Attorney had known Thane was innocent when he sent him to prison resulted in the city of Los Angeles paying him handsomely.

Per his agreement with the city, Thane used a large portion of that settlement money to represent people he believed were innocent but who were being persecuted unfairly by the powers that be. He knew criminal lawyers normally didn't concern themselves with their client's guilt or innocence, nor should they for the system to work. Those lawyers represented everyone, because everyone deserved a fair trial, a sentiment Thane supported. But he nevertheless approached his clients differently.

Originally a real estate development lawyer, not a criminal lawyer, Thane's main goal now was to keep other people from going through the same thing he had—spending time in prison for a crime they hadn't committed. As a result, he could be particular when choosing the type of case to take on. Given the publicity he had garnered over his previous two cases, in part because of his unexpected victories in both of them, there was no lack of people requesting that he represent them.

He glanced at his watch: a couple of minutes before 8:00. His colleagues would soon be joining him for their Tuesday morning team meeting, which almost always started with Letitia making a comment about trees.

A few seconds before 8:00, Kristin walked in and said good morning before sitting at the small conference table where the team met. Always punctual, she brought agenda items to cover during that morning's meeting. A few seconds later, Gideon lumbered in and lowered himself into the chair opposite Kristin. He never arrived before her and, other than a trash-can-size cup of coffee, never brought anything with him, especially not agenda items.

Letitia entered right after Gideon and tossed the morning's L.A. Times on Thane's desk.

"Another tree gave its life so that you wouldn't have to read this on your tablet," she said.

Thane nodded. "Thanks" He glanced at the front page of the paper. "Will you be saying that every time you bring in the paper?"

"Not unless you also start getting the Sunday paper. Then I'll note you're killing two trees."

"Fair enough."

Thane looked at the huge headline at the top of the paper and skimmed the article.

"Did you all hear someone murdered the coach of ULA's football team?"

"Yeah," Letitia answered for the group. "We all heard because we don't get our news delivered by the pony express."

"I didn't know," Gideon said.

"Sorry," Letitia said. "I forgot we had another member of the Forsman Penitentiary graduating class of 2020 in the house."

"That's too bad about the coach," Gideon said, ignoring Letitia. "The team's been having a good year."

"Yes," Kristin jumped in. "That's what makes it a shame. If only the team had been struggling this year."

"That ain't what I meant."

Thane walked over and joined them. "Let's go ahead and get started. I don't know about you guys, but I've been loving the quiet that has come these last few weeks. But I suppose we need to start working through the requests for help we've been receiving. I would, however, like our goal to be to keep the firm out of the news for a while. We've gotten enough press coverage for a lifetime."

"Amen," Gideon muttered.

"Kristin, what's up with Skunk's settlement?"

Thane's first client had been Scotty "Skunk" Burns, a thief Thane and Gideon had known in prison. He had been arrested for the murder of a former L.A. detective, and Thane had been able to show that, once again, the D.A. had known a man was innocent but was still willing to let him go to prison, as he had done with Thane. Kristin had been negotiating with the city over a settlement for Skunk.

"We're almost done," Kristin reported. "We finally settled on a payment of $750,000."

"Whoo-ee," Gideon said. "My new best friend Skunk is going to be living high on the hog."

Thane couldn't help but smile. "And he's still open to you helping line him up with a financial counselor?"

"He's onboard with it," Kristin said. "I've warned him to be wary of any of his old prison friends reaching out to him." She looked over at Gideon and grinned.

"Oh, best friends he never even knew he had will be coming out of the woodwork," Gideon said. "Better tell him to be sure to bring any requests for money or get rich schemes to you first."

"I've already blocked your number on his phone."

The rest of the meeting went quickly. They talked about some of the requests they'd received for legal help, but many of them were from men Thane and Gideon knew from their time in prison, men they were quite confident were guilty as hell.

Thane asked Letitia how law school was going, and she said she was staying afloat. She tried putting in as many hours as she could as the firm's receptionist and administrative assistant, and she appreciated everyone's support as she tried juggling these two parts of her life.

The meeting broke up after about twenty minutes. Kristin and Gideon headed back to their offices, while Thane asked Letitia to stay a moment.

"How's Lawrence doing?" Thane had managed to get Letitia's brother released after spending almost nine years in prison on a trumped-up charge. During their case,

Thane had put a spotlight on the questionable practices of the L.A. detective who had put Lawrence away all those years ago. Granted, Thane's method of exposing the detective wasn't exactly legal, but it resulted in an innocent man being set free, so Thane was comfortable with that.

"I don't know," Letitia said, sounding disheartened. "He's obviously glad to be free, and the entire family is grateful for what you did to get him out, but I worry about him. He seems a little broken. And angry."

"The anger might be with him for a while. Give him time."

Letitia nodded and started out the door.

"Hey, Letitia? If it would help, I'd be happy to talk with him. I've been where he is, and maybe talking about it with someone who gets it would help. But only if he wants to. I just wanted to make the offer."

"Thanks. For a tree killer, you're actually an okay guy. I'll let him know. I hope he takes you up on it. I worry he's going to end up back in jail as a result of how he responds to all this."

Thane had the same concern for himself, an ever-present guillotine blade hanging over him.

5

Hannah reviewed the Power Point presentation for her first Board presentation since becoming the head of the women's shelter. It had been years since doing any sort of formal presentation, going back to her days at Wharton Business school, but she was confident.

As she prepared to run through it again, her assistant Wanda all but fell into her office, looking panicked.

"Hannah, there's a guy trying to take our new client out of the shelter. You better come because I don't think she wants to go."

The location of the shelter was a well-kept secret, although every once in a while one of the occupants told a friend or relative—or worse, their abuser—its location. Hannah jumped up and quickly followed Wanda down the corridor. As they passed by the kitchen, Hannah saw a young woman looking like she was going to cry. A number of women staying at the shelter had been through different types of trauma, and any sense of conflict could bring back the instinct to run.

"It'll be okay, Sheila" Hannah said to the woman. "Go back to your room and we'll take care of this. You'll be fine."

Hannah then dashed down the hallway to catch up

with her assistant who hadn't slowed down to wait for her.

As they neared one of the private bedrooms, Wanda abruptly stopped and pointed to the open door, letting Hannah know she'd be going no further. A young security guard who looked like this could be his first job out of high school stood half in, half out of the room. He looked torn between trying to do his job and running away, perhaps explaining on his way out that no one had discussed any of this during his orientation program. As Hannah approached, the young man all but let out a sigh of relief.

A man in his mid-20's who looked like he'd just stepped out of a wanted poster stood in the room of the new client who had arrived the previous day. His loose clothes looked like they were worn by the week, not the day, and he had a heavy silver chain hanging between his back pocket and one of his belt loops. Hannah didn't care to know what was on the other end of the chain.

The young man had several scars carved across his forehead and left cheek, as if someone had played an impromptu game of tic-tac-toe on his face with a knife. He had the air of someone who had been in far more than his share of fights over the years and, scars notwithstanding, had likely won most of them.

The thug glanced back over his shoulder toward the theoretical security guard.

"I'm telling you for the last time, boy, take your cereal box badge and get the hell out of here or you ain't going to be walking right for the next few years. I'm not playin'." He turned back to the young woman on the other side of the room. Hannah could tell that if the woman left the shelter, it wouldn't be by choice.

"I said pack your shit, Boo, or I'll drag you out of here without it," the man continued. "We're leaving."

The woman, who was at least a foot shorter and a hundred fifty pounds lighter than the man, stood frozen. Hannah sensed their client had some fight in her but knew the odds were stacked against her. Just the same, Hannah felt the young woman was still weighing her options.

"No, she's not leaving," Hannah said, calmly stepping into the room and standing in front of the much-relieved security guard. "Not unless she wants to." The young woman barely shook her head no, enough to confirm to Hannah that she wanted to stay. "All right, then, you need to leave the premises."

"And you need to keep the hell out of this or I'm going to hurt you. This don't involve you none."

"It does involve me. This woman is our guest, so I have a responsibility for her safety."

"It's your safety you should be worried about."

Hannah was already worried about her safety, but she thought her best option was to appear calm. "Sir, I need to ask you to leave."

"There it is. 'Sir.' Damn, how come the only time anyone calls me sir is if they want something or they're pulling me over?" the man said, as if becoming weary. "Listen, we can squabble all afternoon if you want, but Boo's coming with me."

"Actually, we can't argue all afternoon because the police will be here in about..." she glanced at her watch, "two minutes."

The man looked at her and all but guffawed.

"Seriously?" Hannah said. "You don't think a place like this has a panic button to summon the police when there's an emergency?"

The man studied her before shaking his head with as much confidence as he could muster. "You're bluffing."

Hannah brought her Apple watch up to her mouth and pressed the crown on the side of the watch. "Set timer for two minutes." She looked back at the man. "Betcha a dollar I'm right."

The man continued trying to stare her down, but Hannah didn't falter. He coughed up a laugh, but Hannah could tell it was forced. He turned back toward Boo. "You better leave his name out of your mouth, you got me, else that's the last thing you'll be sayin'. You know he don't fuck around. You know what he can do."

Boo nodded nervously as she pressed against the wall, as if trying to pass through it like a ghost.

The man turned and walked toward Hannah and the doorway. When he got within a couple of feet in front of her, he made a quick jerking movement, as if charging at her, then stopped, but Hannah didn't flinch. The security guard, on the other hand, jumped back a couple of steps, causing the man to laugh.

"Lady, you need to stop recruiting your security guards from the playground 'cause trust me, you may be needing quality security soon."

He casually strutted out of the room and down the corridor. Hannah spoke softly to the guard.

"Petey, make sure he leaves the building, but no need to follow him too closely," she added, unnecessarily. "And when he's gone, see what we need to do to get our panic button fixed. How in the world have we not gotten that repaired by now?"

"Yes ma'am," the guard said as he cautiously made his way down the hall.

Hannah walked over to Boo. "Are you okay?"

Boo nodded and tried acting like it wasn't a big deal, but Hannah could see her hands shaking.

"If you remember, one of the ground rules we went over when you first got here is that the shelter's location has to remain confidential, even from other family members and friends. It's for everyone's protection."

"I didn't tell anyone," Boo said defensively. "Believe me," she added, apparently having noticed Hannah's look of skepticism, "I'm not looking for anyone to know where I am. I don't know how he found me, but the guy he works for pretty much knows everything. If he wants to find someone, they're going to be found."

"And who is it wanted you found?"

Boo started to speak but caught herself before a name could slip out. "He's the one been pimping me out. I can't go back to that life. I won't go back to that life."

"I'll help you," Hannah said. "It'll be okay."

Boo smiled sadly and looked at Hannah as if amused by her naivete. "I'd like to believe you, but I'm a little too old for fairy tales."

"You might be surprised," Hannah said.

"I'm betting you'd be more surprised."

After a bit of back and forth, Hannah pulled some of Boo's story from her. In her job running the shelter, Hannah had heard numerous stories that tested her faith in mankind, but Boo's was one of the toughest.

Boo eventually retreated back inside herself, as the sound of hard shoes coming down the hallway grew louder. The footsteps ended when a man in a sports coat and khakis appeared in the doorway, accompanied by two police officers. It pleased Hannah to know Wanda hadn't been so nervous that she didn't think to call the police.

"Thanks, officers, but the man already left. We're safe, now."

"Glad to hear it," the detective in the jacket said as he brought out a pair of handcuffs, "but I need you to please step aside."

He walked around Hannah and up to Boo.

"Bonnie Cruise, you're under arrest for the murder of Coach Cash Dixon. I'm going to need you to come with me." He turned her around, gently but with authority, and pulled her arms behind her and cuffed her.

Boo had been right. Hannah *was* more surprised.

6

"So, the Spence family tree is gonna have its first college kid," Gideon said, looking across the diner booth at his nephew.

Gus grinned before stuffing another fork full of eggs into his mouth. "Yeah, and with a full scholarship, too. No way I'd be getting to USC otherwise."

"Glad the city come through for you."

"No, you guys came through for me. You didn't give them much choice. Guess they couldn't come out and say they did me wrong, but I'd rather have the scholarship than an apology anyway, although both would have been even better."

Gus had spent over a month in jail awaiting trial on a bogus drug charge. The arresting detective had tried pressuring Gus into lying in a drug case and was willing to let him go to prison if he didn't cooperate, but Thane and Kristin had been able to shine a light on his situation. Thane had also suggested to the city's new District Attorney that a scholarship for Gus would help avoid a lawsuit. It was a small price for them to pay.

The month that Gus had been in jail had been one of the longest of Gideon's life. Gideon had spent more years of his life in prison than out, and he knew he deserved every one of them. But his nephew was different—a good kid who studied, played sports, and wasn't a total asshole. And Gus's mother—Gideon's sister, Pearl—had done all the right things in raising her son, so seeing Gus locked up for refusing to lie absolutely gutted Gideon.

Today, though, Gus looked good, dressed in a cardinal red polo shirt and a pair of clean jeans which had rips in the legs that looked like they had been professionally added. Gideon wasn't sure if the easy-going attitude his nephew displayed was an example of his resiliency or evidence of him being good at not showing when something bothered him.

"How you doing after all that?" Gideon finally decided to ask. "You able to put it behind you?"

"Not sure it'll ever be totally behind me," Gus said, looking hard at his plate of food as if he had just spotted a shard of glass in his eggs. "You can't forget something like that, but I have no interest in having it define me, either."

"Good man. Anger landed me back in jail a whole lot of times. Used to follow me around like a damn shadow. Not that it doesn't still pop up every now and then, but I'm trying, and I like to think I'm doing better. Guess time will tell. You know what you're going to be studying yet, college boy?" Gideon asked, looking to shift the conversation away from himself.

"Not sure yet. People always ask me if I'm going to study something that will help stop the sort of thing I went through, like law, or social work, or something like that, but I have no interest in ever seeing a courtroom or jail again."

"Can't blame you there. You leaning toward one thing or another?"

"I've been thinking a lot about studying oceanography, or maybe marine biology." Gus glanced up at his uncle, who nodded approvingly.

"You'd be great at that."

"Thanks." Gus said, before adding, "You know what those are?"

Gideon laughed as he shook his head. "Nah, I never was any good at any of them 'ologies. I just figured you'd be great at anything you wanted to do."

Gideon shoveled in the last bite of his Double Lumberjack special, which consisted of four eggs, three strips of bacon, hashbrowns, white toast with jelly, and a side of sausage, the latter something he added to make sure he didn't get hungry before lunch. It was his go-to breakfast at the Blue Bird diner, a local favorite a few blocks from his apartment. He liked its down-to-earth feel and the constant hustle and bustle of the place. Plus, the staff was nice.

"How about you, Uncle Gid? You still doing good out here roaming free?"

Gideon shrugged, but also offered up a hint of a smile. "I've never been out this long between stints before. Normally I would have been locked up long before this. Don't get me wrong, I'm not getting all cocky and saying I've got it all figured out, but it is kind of feeling different this time around. For one thing, it's amazing what a real paycheck can do for you. That, and having people in your corner."

He looked up at Gus as the young man finished his breakfast. He never imagined sitting across from family and having a meal together. Never imagined having a real job or colleagues who actually seemed to care about him. He knew that, for most people, that sort of thing wasn't unusual. But until the last couple of years or so, his current situation was like how he thought of the lottery: he read of people who had done it, but it didn't seem like the sort of thing that would ever happen to him.

A 40-something waitress displaying dark blue mascara and a smile suddenly appeared at their booth, carrying a slice of bright yellow coconut cream pie, the meringue topping as tall as her index finger.

"Fresh out of the oven for our lunch crowd," she said as she placed a piece in front of Gideon. "Figured I'd save you the trouble of ordering a slice."

"Alice, how'd you know?"

"But it's still breakfast!" Gus exclaimed as he watched Gideon position his piece in front of him.

"That's why I didn't bring you a piece," Alice said. "You look like you eat like a normal human being." She tilted her head toward Gus as she looked back at Gideon. "This your son?"

"Do I look like someone who could have a kid this smart or good looking? Nah, this is my nephew, Gus."

"Well, Gus, if you'd like a slice, just let me know, but if you do, I suggest you keep it close. Might want to keep that knife handy too, in case he finishes his piece first. Otherwise this guy here will make it disappear like a magician."

Alice looked back at Gideon and offered up one more mega-watt smile before resting her hand on his shoulder for a second and turning to head on back to the counter.

"Uncle Gid's got a girlfriend!" Gus sing-songed once Alice was out of earshot.

"What are you talking about? I just come here a

bunch."

"Ah, come on, unc. First of all, your piece of pie is like twice the size of a normal piece. And the way she smiled at you and touched your shoulder, you should ask her out."

Gideon turned his attention to the pie. "You crazy, boy. I'm not asking no one out. Those teenage hormones of yours are affecting your brain. Waitresses are nice because they want a big tip."

"I'm telling you, she was flirting with you. She likes you. What do you have to lose by making a move?"

"I ain't asking her out. I don't know nothing about women. I ask her out, she'd probably call security and have me thrown out, and then I lost a real good place to come and eat. Ain't gonna happen."

Gus shrugged. "Suit yourself, but I don't know what you're so scared of."

"I ain't scared," Gideon said, as he inhaled almost a quarter of his pie in one bite. "I'm what you call practical."

7

Thane refused to admit defeat, but started to suspect it was a definite possibility. Maybe even likely, although he wasn't ready to go there just yet. He had overcome enormous odds over the past couple of years and always managed to make it through in one piece, but ironically, this time around it was the number of pieces that concerned him.

He tried calming himself by closing his eyes and taking a deep breath, then he took another stab at the problem at hand, but his emotions finally won out.

"Oh give me a damn break!" he shouted.

Thane immediately regretted his outburst as soon as he heard footsteps coming down the hall. Hannah leaned into the room and found him sitting on the floor amongst far too many items that, at least theoretically, could be turned into a baby crib.

"I hope you know you're not going to be able to swear like that when the baby arrives," she said.

"I like to think by then I'll finally have this thing put together, although that may not be a sure bet. I wonder if a nice baby sleeping bag would work?"

"I take it the directions aren't overly helpful?"

"Given that they're written in Chinese, yeah, not so helpful."

"Oh, no! Are you serious?" she asked as she grabbed

the instructions from the floor. "We can always send it back and..." She paused as she looked up from the instruction manual.

"Okay, so technically they aren't in Chinese," Thane said, "but they might as well be."

"And you've actually read them?" She looked at Thane in a way that let him know she already knew the answer to that. "Sorry, I forgot, you're a guy."

He picked up a long, narrow piece of wood and tried fitting a bolt into one of its holes, but it didn't fit. He sighed and leaned against the wall of the baby's bedroom. "I don't know that I can be a parent."

"Well, it's a little late to be deciding that now, mister, so time to buck up." Hannah lowered herself to the floor and scooched over until sitting close to Thane. "But personally, I know you're going to be a great father. Maybe a lousy handyman, but a great father."

"I'll be of no practical use to her. I'm going to have to resort to bribing her for her affection."

"Now that is one thing I do worry about. You can't be a pushover with our daughter. I worry you're going to make me be the disciplinarian and you'll give her anything she wants."

"Well, not if it's something like heroin, but if it's a pony or something like that, then yeah, I probably will."

Thane stared at the assorted pieces of wood and metal. "This is like one of those medieval challenges that the knight has to complete in order to unlock the door to the treasure."

"Would you rather try removing a sword from a stone?"

"I'd probably just cut myself."

He leaned back and took in the baby's room. Hannah had painted it a light blue, adding small, white, puffy clouds along the top of the wall. A rocking chair that once belonged to her grandmother had been refinished and would be placed next to the baby crib, assuming, of course, there would ever be a crib.

"You know we're going to have to figure out her name pretty soon," Hannah said.

"I still like the name 'Mesa'," Thane said, holding back a smile.

"Mesa's not a name! It's a flat-topped hill. It's not the name for a little girl."

"But it sounds like it should be a name. Besides, she wouldn't need to worry about there being other Mesa's in her class."

"If that's the goal, let's name her 'Horseradish'. I'm sure there wouldn't be two of those either."

"You have any idea what sort of nicknames she'd be called if we named her 'Horseradish?' That's not practical."

Hannah punched him in the shoulder and shook her head. "We're not calling her Mesa. But I do still like the name Logan."

"Logan is a boy's name."

"It used to be, but it's not anymore. There are a number of girls in Scotland named Logan."

"Are we planning on moving to Scotland?" Thane asked.

"Are we planning on moving to a flat-topped hill?" Hannah looked at him with an 'I rest my case' expression. "I'm simply saying I like the name Logan."

"Logan is Wolverine's name in the Marvel comics, so

that could be a problem."

"Seriously? You had to tell me that? Thanks a lot."

"I thought it best you make an informed decision."

"Although I do sort of like the idea of our daughter being a complete badass. But okay, we'll keep thinking. But if you could try limiting your search to actual names, that'd be terrific."

Hannah leaned her head on Thane's shoulder. There were few things that brought him inner peace like having Hannah close to him. He could breathe slower and deeper when they were together. Times like these made him want to tell her what he had done in the hope that she could forgive him. However, times like these reminded him of what he never wanted to risk losing. They were what kept him alive.

"Speaking of female badasses," Hannah said, "we had a young woman in our shelter who's in trouble, but I feel deep down she's a good person. I believe there are men around her who have forced her into a life she normally wouldn't have taken. In fact, a guy showed up today, trying to make her leave through threats. What is it about men and their need to resort to violence to get their way?"

Thane knew she wasn't including him in that generalization, but he, more than most men, had done that to an extreme.

"And then the police came and arrested her."

Thane glanced down at Hannah, whose head still rested on his shoulder.

"Does she need a lawyer? Is that where this is heading?"

She lifted her head and looked at him. "Could you at least meet with her? I feel like she's been dealt a raw deal and she's trying to turn her life around. That's the sort of person you're wanting to help, isn't it?"

"You don't have to talk me into it, babe. I'm happy to reach out to her tomorrow and see what I can do. I take it she doesn't have a family who will be providing her with a lawyer?"

"I don't believe she has family. At least no one she's still connected with. Also…" she paused for a moment, "I already told her you would talk with her."

Thane smiled, but not out of surprise. "Then I'll talk to her. In exchange, you can put together the crib."

Thane leaned over and picked up the instruction manual, holding it with two fingers as though it might be contaminated. "Do you know why she was arrested?"

Hannah paused, looking at him sheepishly. "They claim she murdered that football coach."

Thane slid a bit further from her in order to get a better look at his wife's face. "Seriously? You couldn't have led with that?"

"I wanted to see if you'd talk with her before that came up."

"Aren't you always telling me I need to stay out of the news for a while?"

Hannah shrugged. "Yeah, I know."

Thane pulled her back close to him. "Not as easy as it seems, is it?"

8

Thane and Kristin made their way toward Los Angeles's Twin Towers Correctional Facility, the sprawling jail located between Chinatown and the Los Angeles River. When Thane first told Hannah he'd be happy to talk with the young woman, he assumed it would be a quick conversation about some sort of misdemeanor. After hearing the charges against his potential new client, he knew he wanted Kristin alongside him.

Kristin had joined Thane when she was still in law school and he had just taken on the case that led to where his firm was today. Since that time, Kristin continued growing in her confidence, her intuition, and her legal acumen. She was also committed to doing things the right way, and still viewed the law as a noble profession. Thane used to feel the same way, and wanted to get back to that belief.

"I thought you said you wanted to keep a low profile for a while," Kristin said, as they neared the jail. "And yet, I seem to recall reading something about this murder," she added, deliberately understating the wall-to-wall coverage that had blanketed the city.

"I told Hannah I'd talk to the young woman. With any luck, we can keep this low profile."

"Yeah, because you have a great track record doing that."

Despite giving Thane a hard time, he knew Kristin enjoyed the bright lights that accompanied a controversial case. Or at least that used to be true. She had been a bit more circumspect this past couple of months. But when Thane told her about this case, and how their potential client had been the victim of sex trafficking and physical abuse, he knew there was no way she'd be left out of it. The violence she had experienced in their previous case left a mark on her, and he knew she was not going to sit on the sidelines with their new client.

He pulled into the public parking lot for the jail. The Twin Towers was considered the world's largest jail at 1.5 million square feet and housing over 3,000 inmates at a time. Even though they had arrived at the facility, it would take another 45 minutes to make their way through the building to their ultimate destination.

When they were finally directed into one of the jail's interview rooms where lawyers and their clients could talk, they waited for Bonnie Cruise to be brought to them.

Thane and Kristin had both spent a lot of time at this jail over the past couple of months, in rooms just like this one—though with different clients. Kristin had taken the lead role representing Gideon's nephew, Gus, who had been unfairly placed here, while Thane had met several times with Kilo—the man accused of killing Thane's former boss and friend, the very boss whose murder Thane himself had set into motion. He obviously didn't tell Kilo that part.

After a long wait, the door to the interview room opened and a young, black woman in her early 20's entered the room. At little more than five feet tall and less than 90 pounds, at first glance she looked like someone you'd see in a high school hallway. But as soon as Thane took in the look of steel coating her eyes, he knew she was no pushover, regardless of her size.

After the guard left, the woman reached out to shake Thane's hand. She had a solid grip for such a slight person, as if daring someone to underestimate her. She hesitated a split second before accepting Kristin's extended hand, while avoiding making direct eye contact with her. Maybe she thought she was more likely to be judged by a successful young woman, or maybe because Kristin seemed to be studying their new client, as if trying to place the face.

"So, Bonnie…"

"Call me Boo," she told Thane. "Nobody calls me Bonnie anymore."

"Alright. Can you tell me about your relationship with Coach Dixon?"

"Relationship?" Boo looked at him as if he had just gotten off the Good Boat Idiot. "There wasn't no relationship, although if you asked Dixon that question, he'd have probably said our relationship was that of master and slave. He paid money, and he got to own me for a while. He got off at the thought of owning another human being. He was born a couple hundred years too late, although I guess if you got money…" She ended her thought with a shake of her head.

"He paid for sexual relations."

"Man, you gotta move away from that word 'relations.' Shit. He paid his dollars and thought he could do anything he wanted with me. Anything. He didn't care if it hurt, or if I begged him to stop. In fact, he seemed to like it better when I tried to get him to stop because that showed he had all the power. There weren't any relations, unless your relative is a sick, sexual predator. The man was a sadist, but he thought it was okay because he paid for it. Like he deserved getting his money's worth."

Boo gave examples of what had been done to her over a series of nights during the past three to four months. She had been sent to his house on numerous occasions, always dreading what the night had in store for her. He raped her, he struck her, he even inserted kitchen utensils inside her. A wooden spoon. A pair of tongs. A stainless-steel whisk. And finally she decided it had to stop. She kept asking him to let her go, and he wouldn't, and she didn't see how the abuse would end except for the action she took.

"Could you have just stopped taking the money?" Kristin asked, although Thane figured she already knew the answer to this.

"I didn't go through all that to make money. I was sent there by someone who didn't give a damn what the man did to me so long as his money was good. And it was good money. The guy whoring me out viewed me the same way that that coach did, like his property. I didn't have a choice." Boo looked over at Kristin and glared at her. "And I swear if you say something like 'you always have a choice,' I'm going to reach over and punch you."

"I wasn't going to say that," Kristin said, unconvincingly.

"My wife said a man came to the shelter and told you to leave another person's name out of your mouth," Thane said. "Was he talking about the man trafficking you?"

Boo shifted in her seat, appearing uncomfortable for the first time since their conversation began. She obviously didn't want to travel too far down this road. "Yeah."

"Can you tell me the name of that man?"

Boo looked at him for a long moment, as if trying to decide whether or not she could trust him, but eventually she shook her head.

"It's best we don't talk about him. He could make me disappear, even in here with me all locked up. Wouldn't be good for your health, either. Trust me on that. I'm not going to talk about him."

Thane noticed Kristin's body stiffen, as if she'd just seen a rattlesnake slithering across the floor toward her. He watched her lean back a bit from the table as she studied Boo.

"It's Stick," Kristin finally said. "The guy pimping her out is Stick." She didn't take her eyes off Boo.

Boo sat up straight, looking defiant toward Kristin.

"This is the woman who got me to open my apartment door the night Stick threatened me," Kristin continued, her voice sounding like it had come out of the freezer. "She told me she had information about Gus's case, but she only wanted me to unlock my door so Stick could come inside. She helped him."

Boo broke eye contact and looked down at the table, as if trying to figure out the best way to respond.

"How could you do that to me?" Kristin said. "How could you do that to another woman?"

Boo shook her head slightly. "I didn't have a choice."

"On this one I disagree. You did have…"

"I didn't have a choice!" Boo shouted. "What do you

think I could have done? Said 'I'm afraid I'm going to have to pass?' Stick tells you to do something, you do it."

Kristin shook her head, as if trying to understand.

"Don't you be shaking your head at me, princess. You were with Stick for five minutes," Boo continued. "You feel like you had a choice? Why didn't you call the police? Why didn't you tell him you weren't going to do what he wanted and ask him to leave? Why didn't you fight back?"

Thane knew these were questions that haunted Kristin, but before he could intervene, Boo answered her own questions.

"Because there's no choice with Stick. You stayed in your apartment and were intimidated and scared within a minute. Imagine what it was like for me. I was around Stick for months, and I saw what he could do, whether to women who pushed back or men he viewed as enemies. If he told me to do something, I damn well better do it or my face might get slashed, and that was only if Stick was in a good mood. And he was rarely in a good mood."

"Do you know how many women Stick traffics?" Thane asked. "I encountered him a few months ago and he tried offering me women. Girls, actually. He said he had girls as young as fourteen."

"He has 'em younger than that," Boo said. "He probably figured you were too respectable to go younger than fourteen. As for how many, there's too many to count. And there's more connections with the athletic department than just the coach. Unfortunately, I was Dixon's favorite." She turned back to Kristin. "You're wondering why I didn't push back after all the abuse I suffered? Well, I feel like shooting that son-of-a-bitch made for a pretty damn strong push-back."

Thane told Boo he would be doing what he could to help her. She looked at him, then glanced at Kristin as if trying to decide whether or not their history would make it unlikely that she could get a good defense, but in the end, she appeared to trust Thane. He told her that given the evidence he had heard—and the fact that she admitted to the police that she had shot Dixon—their best strategy would be that of self-defense, although they didn't need to make that call yet. They would be talking again soon.

Kristin didn't speak on their way back to the car. She hadn't made eye contact with Boo as their client was led back out of the interview room. Once in the car, Thane tried gauging where she stood on this case.

"I'll understand if you don't want to help on this one. It's fine if you'd rather focus on something else."

"I'll help. I know what she meant about not having a choice with that psycho. She actually helped me a little."

"It's possible we might end up having to cross paths with him again. If there's a way of avoiding it, I will, but if he was pimping her out to Dixon, we might have to run up against him."

"That's fine," she said coldly. "In fact, I hope we do. I hope we can expose him for what he is. Even get him put away for a while."

"I understand," Thane said, "but you can't be taking on this case to try to get back at Stick. Everything we do will need to be with the goal of helping Boo, not exposing Stick. Plus, he's a dangerous man. It will be safer for everyone if we don't have to go up against him."

"I get it," Kristin said. "Believe me, I get it. I want to help Boo. She may have set me up with Stick, but we have more in common than not, at least as far as that asshole is concerned. My focus will be on getting her freed." She turned and looked out her passenger window. "But if any of this does end up blowing back on Stick, I won't object to that. That will be gravy."

9

Thane and Kristin turned into the parking lot to the small office building that included their law office. When the mass of reporters staking out the building's entrance saw them, the men and women holding tape recorders and video cameras scrambled, looking like ants swarming toward a half-eaten apple. It was a familiar site for Thane.

He recognized several of them from his first case after being released, where he received almost universally hostile coverage until the end of the case, at which point he had been vindicated and suddenly became the media's darling. The press often loved the underdog story, even when they were the ones who had put the person in the underdog position.

As he got out of the car, the tenor of the questions thrown his way showed that the pendulum had begun swinging back the other way. Apparently, a person could only be a media darling for so long before the press once again began chipping away at the pedestal.

"Is it true you're representing Coach Dixon's killer?" one reporter shouted, her shrill voice rising up over the others.

"Are you a football fan?" an older reporter hollered. "Do you have any idea what the coach's murder means to the team's chances this year?" Several of the other reporters looked at the man asking this question, as if he had embarrassed the rest of them.

Thane encouraged Kristin to go on ahead, but she remained by his side. When she first joined him, he would have assumed she stayed for the publicity. But now, he knew she was there because they were a team and she had his back.

"I don't have any comment at this time," Thane said to no one's surprise. "I'm not yet representing the young woman charged with this crime. If she does become my client, you'll be the first to know, but right now there's simply nothing to say."

Despite the cacophony of questions following him into the building, Thane didn't look back. As they entered the entrance to their offices, Letitia was wrapping up a phone call.

"If something changes, I'll be sure to give you a call. Yes sir, I'm writing down your number as we speak," she said, miming the act of writing something down with her empty hand. "Yes, I have it. Thank you."

She hung up the phone and looked at Thane quizzically. "If this is your idea of a quiet case, can you tell me what an unquiet case is, because the phones haven't stopped ringing for the past hour." As if on cue, the main number rang. Letitia looked at the phone and sighed. "Seriously, dude," she said, looking up at Thane.

"Let it go to voicemail. I'm calling a team meeting in a couple of minutes."

Thane turned to go into his office. If nothing else, at least this time Hannah couldn't blame him for being in the news.

Letitia and Kristin walked into Thane's office and sat at his conference table. Both looked exhausted. Dealing with the media and bad memories could take it out of a person. Gideon dragged himself in a couple of minutes later and headed over to the table.

"I thought you was going to be low-key for a while," he said to Thane.

"Sorry, but everyone here has already used that line."

Thane joined them at the table and leaned back in his chair, as if looking for talking points on the ceiling before sitting back up.

"As you've been able to deduce, this morning Kristin and I met with the young woman accused of killing ULA's football coach. Here's where things stand, best I can tell: the much-loved Coach Dixon was a sleazebag."

"In other words," Letitia noted, "a guy."

When Thane described some of the things Boo said Dixon had done to her, Letitia shook her head, disgusted. "Okay, so worse than just a guy. That motherfucker!"

"From what I've learned so far, the police have the video doorbell footage showing Boo going into the house. It also shows her breaking the doorbell later with a hammer."

"Why'd she do that?" Gideon asked.

"She told the police she thought that would get rid of the online video footage."

"Hell, even I know that ain't true, and I don't know nothin' about all this new tech shit. It turns into a cloud, or something." Gideon turned to Kristin and asked quietly, "I'm right about that, aren't I?"

"About breaking the doorbell not getting rid of the video, or about you not knowing anything?" When

Gideon glared at her, she nodded. "You're right on both counts."

"It doesn't really matter because she admits she was there and that she killed the coach," Thane said. "They also found a piece of her clothing that had her blood on it, and her fingerprints are all over the house. The question doesn't appear to be who did it. What we need to explain is why she did it."

"Self-defense?" Kristin asked.

"Too early to decide for sure, but my gut tells me that's the direction we'll be heading."

When Thane gave them more background to the situation, Gideon raised an obvious problem.

"If she shot him in the kitchen when he was in there cleaning up, that's going to be a harder defense to go with."

"Constant abuse might warrant that defense," Kristin said coldly.

Gideon held up his hands as if Kristin was about to throw a punch. "Hey, I'm not saying the asshole didn't deserve it. I'd be open to shooting him myself if I thought he wasn't already dead enough. I'm just saying that for a jury, shooting someone after the abuse took place may not be so open and shut."

"You're right," Thane said. "You're both right, but that might still be our best chance. Now, regarding the fingerprints, the police didn't already have her prints on file, which surprised me, since it seems she's been living this life for a while, but maybe she's not been busted before. That might help in terms of how the jury views her."

Thane took a long pause before providing the rest of

the story. "The other thing I need to mention is that Stick is involved in this."

Letitia glanced over at Kristin, who didn't display any emotion. Gideon also looked over at her, then looked back at Thane.

"Turn over just about any rock with blood on it and you'll find that cockroach under it," Gideon said.

Kristin told Gideon and Letitia about Boo being the woman who helped Stick get into her apartment. She said it wasn't relevant to the case. She only wanted them to know the whole story.

"You willing to help her out, given what she done to you?" Gideon asked.

"She's been victimized by him far longer than I have."

Gideon nodded, satisfied. "Yeah, shared hatred does have a way of bringing people together."

"Here's where I want to start," Thane said. "Kristin, do some research on other cases where repeated abuse was used as a defense in a murder trial. I know there are some out there. Find the ones where it worked, as well as any where it didn't work, and see if you can figure out why they might have failed. Letitia, dig around and see if you can find anything in Dixon's past that might help show a pattern of abusive behavior. If he's ever been charged with anything like solicitation, abusive behavior in a past relationship, anything that might be relevant. Boo said she wasn't the first woman sent to him, so I'm guessing there's a pattern to this guy. There usually is."

Thane paused, studying Gideon for a long moment. Gideon decided to help him make a decision.

"I promise not to hurt nobody."

Thane smiled. "Okay, as long as you promise. I'd

like you to ask around and see what you can find out about Stick and his sex trafficking activities. And by 'ask around' I don't mean confronting Stick and beating the information out of him."

"I said I wouldn't hurt nobody."

"I wanted to be sure you knew that meant not beating up Stick."

"They say if you want information, it's best to go to the source."

"Not this time. Not yet. I'm not looking to poke that hornet's nest yet, for Boo's sake as much as anyone's. But I want to know how extensive his trafficking ring is, and then hopefully someone else can help confirm Boo's story."

"You told the reporters you weren't representing Boo yet," Kristin said. "Does this mean we're taking her case?"

"We're taking her case."

"Well," Letitia said, closing her iPad. "It was a good couple of quiet weeks." She saw someone enter their reception area and got up to intercept them. "That better not be a reporter. I told them not to come into the office."

Thane looked up and saw Detective Vince Struthers standing at the reception desk, looking at Thane and his team through the open office door. The site of the detective working the murder of Thane's friend always caused his heart rate to bump up a few beats per minute.

"He's not a reporter. He's here for me."

10

Letitia escorted Detective Struthers into Thane's office and shut the door. As always, Struthers showed up dressed in a sports coat, dress shirt, and tie. His polished black shoes reflected the overhead fluorescent light, making it look like he was being lit from below. Thane wondered if the detective's meticulous manner of dress stemmed from a previous stint in the military, or if Struthers felt he had to go above and beyond as a black man, or if it was simply an expectation of the Los Angeles police department that few members tried to achieve.

"Sorry to stop by unannounced, Mr. Banning."

"Please, call me Thane," he said, knowing the detective would never address him in anything but the most formal manner despite Thane's frequent requests.

"I did try calling, but it looks like you were in a meeting."

"It's not a problem. Please, come on in and have a seat."

Thane always tried acting at ease with Struthers, even though he knew he'd be more comfortable encountering an unchained pit bull. Struthers was one of L.A.'s finest detectives, and Thane was confident the man would pick up on most anything that didn't feel right.

Thane also sensed the detective knew there was more to Thane's story than met the eye. But one skill Thane had acquired during his time at Forsman was the ability to hide his emotions. Whenever he was around Struthers, though, he always wondered if he had learned that skill well enough. Ex-cons almost always thought they were more clever than they were, which is why so many of them ended up back in jail.

Struthers took a seat across from Thane's desk, sitting up straight, rather than letting himself relax in the cushioned chair. Thane quickly glanced at the items on his desk, as though perhaps he had left a murder weapon or a written confession out in plain sight. Struthers had a way of stirring Thane's paranoia, although, as the saying went, was it paranoia if someone really was out to get you?

"Now that your client was found to be innocent in the murder of your former boss, I'm going to once again be taking on the case."

"I assumed you would but I'm glad to hear it. I'd hate to think of Joseph's murderer going free."

"But that's not why I stopped by. I'm also taking the lead role on Robert Gruber's murder, and wanted to ask you a couple of questions about that."

"Oh," Thane said, surprised. "I assumed you were already working that case, given your testimony at that trial."

A few months after Thane had been released from death row on a technicality, he represented Skunk, an ex-con he knew from his time in prison. All evidence in the murder of former detective Gruber pointed to Skunk, but that's only because Thane pointed the evidence toward him. While Thane's former friend and mentor, Joseph, had arranged to have Lauren McCoy killed, ex-detective Gruber had been the trigger man. Gruber, still a detective at the time, also framed Thane for the murder. For those sins, Thane set things in motion for Lauren's father to get justice by killing Gruber.

"My partner at the time had the lead on that case," Struthers explained. "I only testified at Mr. Burns' trial because my partner had just had his appendix out. But new evidence has been uncovered which resulted in the Chief asking me to take the lead on both investigations."

"What evidence is that? If you're able to share, of course." Thane immediately wondered whether he should have waited to see if Struthers told him. Thane tried going with his gut instinct on what he should and should not ask, otherwise he could get too caught up worrying whether asking certain questions would make him appear anxious, or if not asking a question that most any innocent person would have asked would strike the detective as suspicious. Such was Struthers' ability to cloud Thane's head.

"That's actually what I wanted to talk with you about," Struthers said. "Do you know if your boss Mr. Crowell knew the victim?"

"Detective Gruber?" Thane asked, as if trying to make sure he understood the question. "I don't believe so, but I can't say for sure. I do remember talking with Joseph the morning after the murder and he didn't mention ever having met the man, which I would have thought he'd have done if they had crossed paths. Joseph never missed a chance to name-drop when he had a connection with almost anyone in the news, regardless of the reason."

Struthers jotted something down in a notebook.

Thane would have given big money to have the chance to look through that book. He feared his name appeared more often than he wanted.

"I assumed that would be the case, but I wanted to be thorough."

"Do you believe there was a connection between the two men?"

"Actually, there was. When Gruber left the force, he worked for a local security agency that Mr. Crowell used from time to time. I have established that he worked directly with Gruber on occasion."

Thane noticed that Gruber was one of the only people Struthers referred to on occasion by last name only, not adding a 'Mr.' or 'Detective' in front of it. Given that Thane showed in his first case that Gruber had killed Lauren McCoy, Struthers apparently didn't want to continue connecting the man to the police force.

"Mr. Crowell knew Gruber," Struthers continued. "Gruber killed Ms. McCoy. Years later—you had obviously been paroled shortly before then—Gruber was murdered, followed by Mr. Crowell a few weeks later. I'm not saying there's a connection between the three murders. I'm just saying there's a whole lot of connections here, which is a bit unusual, so naturally I wanted to talk with you."

"Why 'naturally'?"

"Because you knew all three of these individuals. You're the one common link. I was hoping you might be able to shed some light on Mr. Crowell's connection to Gruber, although I didn't really expect you'd have anything to share. But like I said, I do try to be thorough."

Struthers closed his notebook and slid it into his

sportscoat pocket as he slowly rose. Thane got up from behind his desk, but Struthers motioned for him not to bother seeing him out.

When the detective reached the door, Thane called out to him.

"Detective, I wonder if I could ask you a question about the murder of Coach Dixon the other night?" Given Struther's professionalism, Thane knew there would be no way in hell the man would share anything with him beyond saying he couldn't comment on an ongoing case, but like the detective, he tried to be thorough.

"What would you like to know?"

Once again, the detective surprised him, which immediately got his guard up yet again.

"Well, I'm assuming you're working this case." Thane paused and could tell Struthers was simply going to wait for him to ask his question. The man was all business.

"I'm wondering if you had any other suspects you were looking at for this murder?"

Struthers shook his head. Again, he assumed the detective would say he couldn't share that sort of information, but it turned out Struthers was simply answering Thane's question.

"Off the record? No, there are no other suspects. The young woman admitted to killing Mr. Dixon. Even if she hadn't confessed, physical evidence shows she was there at the time of the murder."

"The coach was shot. Is that correct?"

"Shot once in the chest. Killed instantly, at least according to our coroner. There didn't appear to be a struggle beforehand, or any attempt to flee, all of which is consistent with the victim knowing the shooter, as opposed to a break-in."

Struthers appeared to wait for any further questions, but Thane wasn't sure what to ask at that moment. Struthers nodded his head toward the main entrance to the firm.

"Given the mob of reporters out front, is it safe to assume you are representing the young woman charged with the murder?"

"I am."

"May I ask how you ended up with this case? I'm assuming given your recent high-profile cases, you're the person people call first when they're in trouble?"

"Actually, my wife runs the shelter where the young woman was arrested. She asked me if I would help her."

Struthers appeared to consider this for far longer than Thane would have expected, before nodding.

"If you have any more questions about the case, please don't hesitate to give me a call."

Struthers turned to leave. Before opening the door, he turned around one last time and looked at Thane with a plaintive expression on his face.

"Please tell me you didn't also know Mr. Dixon."

11

As Kristin was escorted down the long, sterile corridor, she couldn't shake the feeling of being in enemy territory, even though that's not how she saw it. Her tremendous respect for the legal system was one of the reasons she wanted to be a lawyer. Even though the prosecution and the defense were adversaries, each played an essential role. Neither side was the bad guy.

Knowing that intellectually, though, didn't totally put her at ease as she was being led to L.A. District Attorney Angela Day's office. Thane had, on numerous occasions, expressed a great deal of respect for the new D.A., which helped ease Kristin's guilt for having reached out to her. But it didn't help to feel the eyes of several nearby workers looking at her, perhaps recognizing her as part of the team that had made the D.A.'s office look bad on two occasions. Actually, more than bad.

When Kristin finally arrived at her destination, Day warmly greeted her, as if they were old friends finally having a chance to catch up.

"Ms. Peterson, it's so nice to see you again. Especially outside the courtroom."

Kristin immediately felt at ease with her. Although she guessed twenty or so years separated them, Day spoke to Kristin like they were colleagues on equal footing.

"I appreciate you taking the time to meet with me. I know you must be very busy."

"Not at all. It's my pleasure. Anytime a lawyer with your skills and intellect expresses an interest in working on our side of the courtroom, I'm happy to take the time. Please, have a seat."

Day's office was the size of Thane's, Gideon's, and her offices combined, and decorated far more elegantly. Kristin figured the scale of the office may have been larger than Day would have picked on her own, but it came with the job. On the other hand, she knew Day had to have overcome a tremendous number of challenges to reach that position, especially as a black woman, so perhaps she did appreciate the trappings of her office.

Day led Kristin over to a comfortable, padded wingback chair in a sitting area that had been arranged on one end of the expansive office. After offering a bottle of water, she asked Kristin what she could do for the young lawyer.

"As you know, I haven't been out of law school very long…"

"And yet already you've been part of two exceptionally complex and significant cases. Both of which were found in your favor."

"Nevertheless, I'm still trying to figure out what I want to do career-wise."

Day nodded as if she knew exactly what Kristin was talking about, and knowing her, she probably did. "My sense is you began your career on the defense side for a reason. Has it not lived up to what you thought it would be, or has something changed?"

"It has been good. I feel like I've made an important difference in people's lives."

"You certainly have. So why are you thinking about working for my office?"

Kristin had been working for several days on trying to figure out how to best answer this question, which she knew she would be asked, but she could never settle on a response that would satisfy Day and still be truthful.

"Sometimes I see some of the people out there who are doing heinous things, and I feel like I would also be helping society by putting them away. That also feels important to me."

"It is," Day said. "But again, you have been able to keep innocent people from going to prison. That is also exceptionally important. I'm sure you are familiar with the writings of William Blackstone."

"It's better that ten guilty persons escape than one innocent suffers," Kristin said, quoting the British jurist.

"I don't disagree with that philosophy."

"Neither do I," Kristin said. "And it's been rewarding to me. But I still sometimes wonder if I'm making as big of a difference for society as a whole as I would be by getting truly bad guys off the streets."

Again, Day nodded thoughtfully. Kristin wondered if this was what it would feel like to talk to a therapist. She found herself wanting to open up to the older woman, even though the D.A. was simply asking questions and listening to Kristin's responses.

"They're both important," Day finally said.

"I don't mean that keeping an innocent person out of jail isn't important. It might be the most important thing. But putting away a hardened criminal could keep him from inflicting pain and suffering on scores and scores of people, so the overall impact on society could be greater. I don't know that I'm expressing myself well, but I guess that's what I'm trying to figure out."

Day took a long drink of water, then leaned back in her chair. "I'll tell what I think, and as you get to know me, you'll know I'm a straight shooter. I think having a woman of your capabilities would be a tremendous asset to this office. We have some sharp women working here, but not enough. The legal system would benefit by having more women in positions of power. But I also believe you need to think long and hard about your true reasons for wanting to work in this type of setting. What you say about our impact on society is true, and it's what drew me to want to work on the prosecutorial side of things."

She paused and took a long look at Kristin, as if trying to decide how candid she wanted to be.

"But I know you also had to deal with some extremely unsavory individuals in your last case. One of your witnesses was killed, and we both have a pretty good idea who did that. If that's the sort of person you want to go after by working in the D.A.'s office, then that's understandable—it just can't be personal. You can't be making your decision based on revenge."

Kristin wondered if she had managed to hide the flinch that ran through her body when Day referred to all of this being personal. As much as Kristin told herself it was bigger than that, she didn't always believe it. Not only was she afraid it was personal, she knew it was a lot more personal than the District Attorney realized.

Kristin also knew that wasn't the right reason to move over to the prosecutorial side of the aisle. Or at least it shouldn't be the only reason, and right now she wasn't sure if she was trying to rationalize her decision by talking about the impact on society.

"But whatever your motivation," Day continued, "I trust you'll make the right decision. And I'll be happy to talk with you at much greater length sometime if you want to continue batting this around a bit. I look forward to watching your career regardless of where you land, but my understanding is that Thane is likely going to be taking on the case of the young woman accused of killing Mr. Dixon, and I feel like it would be more appropriate for the two of us to talk about your future after that case is over. You and I both know we would be professional about it, but sometimes you have to be aware of the possible appearance of things, especially as women."

Kristin understood. If she was the First Assistant on their case, meeting with the D.A. might be a part of her responsibility, but being the junior member of the team meant she shouldn't be doing anything that wasn't focused on helping Boo win her case.

"I appreciate that," Kristin said as she stood. "I made this appointment before we took on this case, but you're correct that now's not the right time."

"But call me when this is over and let's talk more. I'd enjoy that."

"So would I." Kristin picked up her bottle of water and turned toward the door, but stopped.

"Can I ask how you're doing in terms of the upcoming special election?"

Los Angeles's special election for District Attorney was scheduled in the next few months. The resignation of the previous District Attorney—a resignation brought about following Thane's initial case out of prison—had brought about the need for a special election.

"Too early to tell," Day said. "Unfortunately, so much of my job is politics rather than law, but that's the nature of the beast. I'm sure our new shared case will bring out the worst in some people, given the publicity that Mr. Dixon's murder will generate, but again, that's the business I've chosen. I would, however, appreciate your vote come election day."

"You already have it. Thane has expressed a lot of positive things about you, which is no small thing given his previous experience with this office."

"Fortunately for me, it was a different D.A. But I appreciate you telling me that. I find your boss to be an interesting man. It's also safe to say some of my colleagues are not relishing the thought of going up against you and him again."

Day walked Kristin over to the door and shook hands once again.

"Seriously, please call me after this case is over. I'm interested in seeing what you decide you want to do."

Kristin was also interested because, as of that moment, she had no idea.

12

Thane leaned back on a sofa that looked like it belonged on the cover of Architectural Digest. In fact, the entire office felt like it had been designed and curated by one of L.A.'s top designers. Thane didn't believe the University of Los Angeles's Chief Development Officer did this himself, although he had to admit, the man's choice of suit and tie also reflected a sophisticated sense of style.

"Preference for type of gin? I have Tanqueray, Plymouth, and even some Hendrick's—which, if you haven't tried it, is really something special."

"Whatever you're having is fine," Thane said.

"In that case, let's go with the good stuff."

Thane didn't usually drink in the afternoon, but if there was a possibility of ULA's head fundraiser getting a little tipsy from gin and tonics, Thane would take the chance. He guessed, however, that this man was a professional—drinking with potential donors was likely near the top of his job responsibilities.

Silver handed Thane his glass.

"Thank you, Mr. Silver."

"Please, call me Sterling."

"Alright, Ster…" Thane paused as he put it together.

Silver laughed heartily. "Yes, my parents named me

Sterling Silver, but before you stereotype me, let me say it was more aspirational than providential. My father drove a truck and my mother cleaned houses, so there was a bit of irony growing up in a household like that with a name like mine, but to their credit, maybe the name helped me end up where I am today."

"And you appear to be doing quite well for yourself," Thane said, once again taking in the opulence of the office.

"Well, the university is doing well, so I guess that means I'm doing alright too."

Thane took a sip of his drink. It really was a damn good gin.

"Are you ever concerned potential donors will come into an office like this and decide your school might not need more money?"

Silver again offered up a boisterous laugh. Apparently, he and Thane were starting to become best of friends, probably another important part of Silver's job description: make everyone feel like best buds.

"I like your candor, Thane, and it's an excellent question. I'll let you in on a little trade secret. I also have a smaller, much more spartan office where I meet a certain type of potential donor. If I'm meeting someone who has slowly built up a sizeable portfolio through hard work and being fiscally conservative by living modestly, I usually hold the meeting there. On the other hand, there are individuals who want to feel as though they're donating to a winning organization, and they would rather be in an environment like this."

"Did you have to decide where to talk with me?"

"No, not really. I'm not asking you for a donation, so

I figured why not be more comfortable. Of course, with the money the city gave you for your settlement, if you'd ever like to talk about sending a portion of that our way, I'd be happy to meet with you in my other office."

"Too late," Thane said, as he took another drink.

"Just as well. To be honest, I try to spend as little of my time as possible there. It's quite dreary."

A knock on the door interrupted them and a fit man in his early 60's with distinguished gray hair and a high-quality suit leaned in. If Thane hadn't already recognized the man, he would have assumed a politician running for higher office had just entered the room.

"Excuse me, Sterling, do you have a second?" The man noticed Thane and shook his head. "I'm sorry, I didn't realize you were in a meeting. I can come back."

"No, no, please come in." Silver stood, so Thane did the same. "I'd like you to meet Thane Banning. Perhaps you've heard of him." Silver offered up another laugh, as if he found it impossible to believe anyone hadn't heard of Thane. Given the publicity that had accompanied Thane's last two trials, it wasn't an unreasonable bet.

"Mr. Banning, it's nice to meet you," the man said as he crossed the room in a surprisingly few number of steps. "I'm Kenneth Albrecht, president of this fine university."

Thane shook hands, surprised at the firm grip offered up by the university's president. It was like getting his hand shut in a car door, and probably a point of pride for the man.

In prison, Thane had to learn how to read people and their intentions, as that sometimes meant the difference between life and death. He had quickly learned how to tell when someone pretended to be surprised. Thane had no doubt Albrecht was acting like he didn't realize Silver had a visitor, but that was fine. He'd let them play out their game.

"I understand you're representing the young woman who confessed to killing Coach Dixon. A real tragedy, for everyone involved. Including, of course, the young woman."

"Of course," Thane agreed.

"Well, I didn't mean to interrupt. I'll let you two go back to your conversation, and Sterling, I'll catch up with you later."

Albrecht again reached out to shake hands, even though Thane was just starting to get the feeling back in his fingers from the last manly handshake.

"But I'm glad to have had the chance to meet you in person. If there's anything you need from me pertaining to this case, I hope you'll let me know. Of course, I'm sure our legal counsel will be telling me what I can and can't talk about, but if I'm allowed to help you in any way, I'm happy to do so."

Albrecht turned and headed back out of the office, pausing right before opening the door, exactly when Thane knew he would. These things were usually meticulously scripted.

"Mr. Banning, I want to say, if I had become aware of anything untoward going on involving Coach Dixon, I wouldn't have allowed it to continue. It does appear as though the man wasn't above paying for sex, which came as a huge surprise to me, but I'm sure that sort of thing does go on. But as for the reports I've read about accusations of sadistic sex and violence, well, I just don't believe that to be true. Coach was a good man. He instilled discipline in the young men who played for him."

"According to my client, he tried distilling discipline with her as well."

Albrecht began to respond, then apparently thought better of his initial reaction.

"Like I said, this whole thing is a tragedy. But apart from paying for sex, which isn't something I would ever condone, I refuse to believe he was a violent man."

Thane nodded, acknowledging the president's position. "In that case, I'll be sure not to accept you as a juror for this trial."

Thane smiled as Silver laughed a little less heartily this time, as if trying to strike a balance between placating his guest but not embarrassing his boss. Albrecht nodded at Thane, then turned to leave.

Thane and Silver sat back down after the office door closed, followed by a long quiet moment as each man took a drink of their cocktail.

"What I can do for you, Sterling?" Thane finally asked, deciding the introductory niceties had been achieved.

Silver took another drink before looking again at Thane, as if trying to gauge the man.

"May I be candid with you?"

Thane shrugged. "I don't know. Let's find out. Did your boss really not know I was here, or was that planned?"

Silver seemed to be rapidly working through the calculations on that question before offering up a slight smile.

"It was planned."

"In that case, apparently you can be candid with me. So tell me, what's on your mind?"

Silver took another long drink from his glass, keeping

the bottom of the glass tipped upward until nothing was left except the clinking ice cubes. He got up to make himself another one, glancing at Thane's glass to see if he needed another as well. Thane still had more than enough.

"I wanted to let you know that President Albrecht wants to resolve this case as quickly as possible. Whether Coach Dixon crossed the line or not—and I believe, as does our president, that he did not—the publicity is still not good for our university. We want parents to feel comfortable sending their children here. And on the off, off-chance the coach wasn't always who he presented himself to be, the fact remains he's dead now, so in a way justice will have already been served."

"Although perhaps not served to my client."

"With all due respect to your client—and I don't say this to be adversarial in any way—but she apparently accepted money from the coach on several occasions. In other words, she kept going back. And there were other steps she could have taken. She could have called the police. She could have simply turned down his money. All sorts of things she could have done, but I'm hard-pressed to believe self-defense when the man was cleaning his kitchen, for god's sake."

Thane was confident he would be hearing this line of argument from other people as well. Silver could have written the prosecution's opening statement.

"Apparently I guess I need to cross you off the list of potential jurors as well. But just out of curiosity, what makes you say she accepted money from him on numerous occasions?"

Silver paused before answering. "I believe I heard that

on a cable news show the other day, so let me say it before you do: don't believe everything you hear on cable news. I apologize. I usually pride myself on knowing the facts before forming an opinion, and not blindly accepting what I've heard second hand."

"Maybe what you heard comes from a reliable source."

Silver sat back down across from Thane, his drink now refreshed. He let Thane's theory go unanswered.

"I'm simply saying I'm not sure your client is the victim in all of this, even though claiming to be the victim seems to be the new pumpkin spice in this country lately. But that aside, if there's anything the University can do to help your client, I'm open to seeing what we can do, even if it's in the background. If her family needs financial assistance after she goes to prison, for example, that's a possibility. Or if she needs help getting an education after she gets out of prison, that's also a possibility. I understand it's hard getting back on one's feet after serving time in prison." Silver paused, and all but shrugged. "Present company excluded, of course," he said, once again referencing Thane's settlement with the city.

"She'd likely be in prison for a long time."

"Not necessarily. The point is that if there's something we can do to help make a plea deal more acceptable, don't hesitate to include me. You might be surprised at the influence I have in certain circles."

Thane actually wouldn't have been surprised. Silver dealt with money, therefore, making influence almost a given, especially in politics. He nodded over at a poster board image of a stadium sitting on Silver's desk.

"I understand ULA is in the process of fundraising

for a new stadium."

"Yes," Silver said, cautiously. "It's been in the planning phase for a couple of years now."

"I read the other day that your office is being inundated with donations to help fund the stadium following the coach's murder. I guess that falls under the 'every cloud has a silver lining' category."

Silver shook his head. "I'll never look at a man's murder as anything but a tragedy."

"But donations are up."

Silver nodded.

"And revelations of the coach's behavior—if they turn out to indeed be true—certainly wouldn't help your fundraising efforts."

"In the interest of continuing my candor, no, it wouldn't. Mr. Banning, my priority is the University and what's in its best interest. I'm assuming your priority is your client, and what's in her best interest, so if there's a place where those interests align, I'm simply saying I hope you'll feel comfortable reaching out to me."

"Hey, Banning!" a husky voice bellowed as Thane walked toward his car outside Sterling Silver's office. It immediately brought back memories of prison, where everyone called him by his last name. Since being released, most people called him 'Thane' or 'Mr. Banning.'

Thane turned and saw a short man in a tight-fitting suit barreling toward him. His body resembled a set of Russian nesting dolls, with a large midsection that made him look like he would rock back and forth but not fall over if pushed slightly. He appeared to be in his mid-60's, but his tight, gray crew cut and flapping jowls made it difficult to pin an exact age on him with certainty. But the man obviously recognized Thane and had something on his mind. Thane also thought he had seen this man somewhere before.

Just as Thane could tell the university's president didn't just happen to be passing by Silver's office, he was also certain this encounter wasn't simply a coincidence.

The man walked up and extended a sweaty hand. "Luther Fournier. I own a string of Lexus dealerships across the city. You know, 'Loony Luther'? Luther bugged his eyes and shook his head violently back and forth like a horse. Thane realized that's where he recognized the man: his obnoxious commercials polluted the airwaves.

"Sorry. Not familiar with the name, but it's nice to meet you." He wanted Luther to feel a little foolish, although after having seen the man's commercials, he doubted feeling foolish was in his repertoire.

Thane turned to continue on to his car, but he knew escape wasn't going to be that easy.

"Whoa, whoa, whoa, hold on a second, pardner. I got a meeting here on campus and saw you and didn't want to let this opportunity slip by. I'm a big supporter of ULA. Almost went to school here myself, but decided to jump right into business. I'm more of a 'get to it' sort of guy rather than waste a few years reading books. But I'm still a big supporter. Also a big booster of the team. Shame what happened to Coach Dixon. Hell of a man. They don't make many like him anymore."

"That's my sense as well," Thane said.

Luther nodded in solidarity before pausing and

looking at Thane as if uncertain how to interpret that remark.

"Listen," Thane said, "I'm afraid I'm meeting someone in a few minutes, so I need to…"

"The team was having a hell of a year before Coach got killed. Hell of a year. Hope they can keep it up. You know, win it all for Coach. Anyway, I know you got to represent that black crackhead who killed him. You defense lawyers don't have a choice as to who you represent, right?"

"Actually, those of us in private practice do have a choice. I've chosen to represent her."

Luther shook his head as if this didn't compute.

"Well, I'm not sure that was the best decision, but far be it from me to tell another man how to do his job. I will note, though, that you're not exactly in private practice. The city is funding your office."

"Funding that is part of the city's settlement for sending me to prison for a murder I didn't commit, so I'm comfortable using that money how I see fit."

"And that's noble. Very noble. And I wanted to let you know there are a number of boosters like me who could help give you more funding so you can help out more crackheads, if you're interested."

"And what would you be looking for in return?"

"There's a lot of people interested in having this case get resolved without all of the mudslinging and inuendo that's already been appearing in the papers. If you could get your client to take a plea, or even just lighten up on talking 'bout the coach's so-called bad behavior, it might work out best for everyone."

"I'm afraid that's not how it works."

"Aw come on, you and I both know it works however people like us say it works. Dixon was a hell of a man."

"So you said."

"That's 'cause he was." Luther's face flushed and the top of his head started to glimmer in the sun. "Listen, if you think people are going to believe some whore who got her feelings hurt instead of all the people who are going to testify about the coach's character, you're deluding yourself."

"In that case, you don't have anything to worry about."

"You know that's not true. There'll be enough folks out there who'll believe anything someone like your client says because they want to be woke. Poor little black girl, let's give her money because she's upset about something. The coach built a damn good team here and did a hell of a lot for this university. What did your client ever do for anyone?"

Thane studied the man for a long time until he saw the sweat from the top of Luther's head start making a run down his forehead. In prison, Thane learned that often times not saying anything was the best way to make an adversary uncomfortable.

"Just do me a favor," Luther finally said, desperate to end the silence. "Think about it."

"Alright, but in return perhaps you can do me a favor."

Luther's face lit up. "Name it."

"If you're one of the people who testify on behalf of the coach, when you're sworn in and asked to state your name, can you do that thing where you shake your head back and forth like a horse? That would make me so happy."

Thane's cell rang, keeping Luther from responding.

The name appearing on the phone surprised him.

"Sorry, I have to take this." As Thane turned to walk away, he paused and looked back over his shoulder. "You really are loony, aren't you?"

Walking away from the sputtering car dealer, he answered the phone call.

"Please don't tell me you're already in trouble again," he said, partly kidding, totally hoping it wasn't true. He listened for a moment before a pained look crossed his face.

"I'll be honest, I'm not a fan of public speaking." He knew before he said it that he would lose this argument, but he wanted to get out of this. "Yes, I know I'm a lawyer, and…" He hung his head. "Tomorrow? I may not be free then. Hold on, let me check my calendar." He pulled up his calendar on his phone and sighed.

"OK, I'll be there, but don't make a habit out of this. I can't be doing things like this just because you…hello?" Thane looked at his phone and confided to it as if it was an old friend.

"I am so going to regret this."

13

Thane entered the Starbucks on La Brea and scanned the packed room. Half the people sitting at tables were staring at their laptop screens, likely working on a screenplay, with the other half doing something with their lives.

As the barista called out names, Thane once again surveyed the mob until he saw Sheri Omernik seated across the room, waving him over as she spoke on the phone. A public defender, Sheri had been helpful to him on his previous case. When he reached her table, she motioned for him to sit down while holding up one finger—the international sign for 'just a minute'—then rolled her eyes as she tried to end her call.

"Listen, Wilbur, you can either..." She listened, shaking her head as if the caller could see her. "No, I'm not going to call you Mad Dog, because that's the last thing I need to be calling you in front of a jury or, to be honest, in front of anybody. So again, Wilbur, you can either let me represent you, or you can keep hitting on me, but if you choose the latter you're going to end up in jail, so you have to ask yourself, what's more important to you?"

Thane smiled at her. He had no doubt she got hit on by at least every other client. Sexism impacted most every female in the public defender's office—and pretty much any law office—but Sheri had movie star looks and always stood out even on the streets of LA where people were unusually obsessed with beauty. Given that a lot of the guys she represented probably thought of themselves as smooth rollers, Thane assumed she had conversations like this every day.

"I have to go, but you need to let me do my job, okay, and quit being such a dick."

She hung up and looked at Thane, sighing. "Just another day in paradise."

"Mad Dog? With a nickname like that, I'm assuming you go into this figuring he's guilty."

"Let's just say I don't represent a lot of doctors named Mad Dog."

"I appreciate you talking with me this morning," Thane said.

"Are you kidding?" Sheri said. "After what you did for Lawrence, I owe you. Not to mention getting Detective Asshole suspended. That alone grants you permanent status on my 'happy to help' list."

Sheri had previously represented Letitia's brother, Lawrence, and helped when Thane tried freeing the young man.

"Do you stay in contact with Lawrence?" Thane asked. "His sister works with me, and I hear bits and pieces, but I was curious if you knew how he was doing?"

Sheri shook her head. "He's happy to be out, but resentful as hell. That was a hell of a lot of years to spend locked up for something he didn't do. You can only imagine how…" She paused and looked at Thane, breaking into a smile. "Well, fine, I suppose you're someone who can do more than just imagine. Regardless, he's at least talking to me, so I'm hopeful. But I'm guessing you might have a harder time helping your latest client. By the way, she gave me permission to talk to you about her."

"Bonnie?"

"She let you call her that?"

"No, I just feel a little silly calling an adult 'Boo.' But when I saw you'd represented her in the past, I hoped you could give me a sense about her."

"I can try, although she's a bit of a mystery to me."

"How so?"

"I don't know, exactly. I guess that's part of the mystery. A lot of women in her position have had a hard life and they never rise above it, but Boo strikes me as being someone coming from a much stronger foundation. That's not to say I haven't represented young women who come from solid homes but ended up getting caught up in drugs or prostitution, but I don't know if that's Boo's case."

"You said earlier you had represented her on at least three occasions. Is it a fluke you caught her case that many times? Aren't your cases assigned randomly?"

"Usually, but we can also ask to represent certain individuals if they end up getting arrested again. I don't do that with too many people, but Boo is different. She is..." Sheri struggled for the right word.

"A mystery?"

She smiled and finished off her cup of coffee.

"I'll tell you another mystery," Thane said. "The police didn't have her fingerprints on file. Given her rap sheet, they should have had them multiple times."

"That one's not necessarily all that mysterious. I've

won more than one case because of the LAPD's sloppy paperwork."

Thane glanced at his watch and rose. "I know you said you had a packed day, so I'll let you get back to it. But I appreciate your thoughts."

"I hope you can help Boo. These women far too often end up getting lost in the cracks of the system. They're the ones who do the time while the men who take advantage of them usually skate on with their lives."

"I'll do my best." He looked at her coffee cup. "Since you didn't charge me for your time, at least let me buy you another cup."

"Deal. Regular coffee. Black."

"No special spices or creams or goofy names?"

"Just coffee."

"God bless you. No wonder Wilbur is hitting on you."

Thane walked over to the counter and placed Sheri's order.

"Name?" the barista asked, marker in hand.

"Mad Dog."

14

Thane entered his reception area that morning dressed in a too tight three-piece suit from his previous days as a real estate lawyer. He had added on quite a bit of muscle while behind bars and still needed to take some of his suits to a tailor. He only wore this particular suit because he thought it looked the most 'lawyerly', which was his instruction for the day.

Skunk made his way out of Kristin's office. She had her arm around his shoulder, which caused Skunk to both beam and blush. Kristin looked happier than Thane had seen her in several months. She led Skunk into the middle of the reception area and turned him toward Thane.

"May I present to you Mr. Scott Burns, newly minted wealthy person."

Thane walked over and shook Skunk's hand. The small man looked overwhelmed, possibly the result of the large settlement, but just as likely from Kristin's attention and support. Skunk had never exactly had a support system, probably from the time he was a baby.

"You deserve every dollar the city is paying you, Skunk," Thane said. "Or do I need to start calling you Mr. Burns now?"

Skunk all but giggled as he shook his head. "I've

gone by Skunk almost fifty years so I don't see no need to change it now. But maybe I can start dressing a little better," he said as he took in Thane's suit.

"Yeah, what's up with that?" Kristin asked, curious.

Thane sighed. "I don't usually dress like this," he told Skunk, "but I'm supposed to give a talk today and it was requested I show up in my 'full-lawyer' outfit. Trust me, I'm not a big fan of public speaking."

"I'm with you there," Skunk said.

Thane turned to Kristin. "And congratulations to you as well. Good job on this."

"She's the best," Skunk added, looking as though he wanted nothing more than to propose to Kristin on the spot.

"Good seeing you, Skunk," Thane said. "And seriously, call Kristin or me if you have any questions at all. And listen to her when it comes to financial advice."

"Oh yeah. She knows lots more than I do. Probably everybody knows more about money than I do. I ain't never had none before."

As Thane turned to go into his office, Skunk called out to him. "Hey, Thane? You got a minute I can talk to you about something else?"

"Sure. Come on in."

Thane led Skunk into his office and leaned against the desk as Skunk followed him in. Before Skunk could speak, Gideon leaned into Thane's office.

"Thought I smelled a Skunk in the house."

"Hey, Gid!"

The two men shook hands. Gideon towered over Skunk and would have been able to pull the small man's arm out of its socket if he wanted to.

"Dinner better be on you, next time," Gideon said.

"You got it, man."

"Didn't mean to interrupt. Just saw you and wanted to say hey."

"That's okay," Skunk said. "I just wanted to tell Thane that that detective who testified against me at the trial tracked me down the other day to ask me questions, and he sort of made me nervous."

"Which detective?" Thane asked. "You mean Detective Struthers?"

"Yeah, that's the guy. Smooth-talking brother made it sound like he was only shooting the shit about the weather. I wanted to see if you thought he still liked me for that Gruber murder. Do I got anything to worry about?"

Gideon jumped in before Thane could answer.

"Listen, Skunk, don't forget you got all that new money of yours because of this man."

"Gideon," Thane said, "you don't have to…"

"I know that, Gid," Skunk said, looking caught off-guard by Gideon's harsh tone. "That's why I'm here, to give him a heads-up. I got a strange feeling about it."

"Alright, then," Gideon said. "I'm just saying you better do right by this man."

"Gid, all I'm doing is…"

But Gideon turned and walked out of Thane's office, closing the door behind him. Skunk turned back to Thane with a puzzled expression. "What's up with him?"

"You know Gideon. Social skills were never his strong suit. What kind of questions did Struthers ask you?"

"Just weird shit, like did you and I spend much time together at Forsman. Did I ever talk to you about the jobs

I'd pulled in the past. Did I trust you. Things like that."

Thane struggled to keep his emotions in check. Struthers obviously suspected Thane had some sort of involvement in Gruber's murder, or at least was involved in Skunk being set up for the murder, both of which were correct. And the detective had to know Skunk would tell Thane about his visit, so that was sending another message.

"Do I got something to worry about?" Skunk asked. "Anytime a cop starts asking me questions, I usually end up back in jail."

"You're fine, Skunk. Seriously. Struthers is just working the case. He talked with me about it as well. He's simply being thorough."

"But why ask me questions about you and me?"

"Who knows how cops think? But trust me, Skunk, you have nothing to worry about. Do me a favor, though, and let me know if he talks to you again and what he asks you, alright?" Thane knew Skunk had done enough time in prison to know when something didn't sound right, but the man didn't press it.

"'Course. I was hoping it was nothing, but my track record with cops ain't been too good." Skunk shoved his hands in his pockets. "Anyway, I'll let you get back to work. Just wanted to say hey."

Skunk turned and walked out of Thane's office. Thane wanted to rise off his desk and go sit in his chair, but his legs were unsteady. Struthers was obviously working this case hard and, unfortunately, he appeared to be on the right track.

15

Shortly after Skunk left, Thane and his team convened in his office for a morning update. They would have to start having more of these as they moved further along with this major case.

This was the first case of Thane's that didn't involve the murder of his former boss, Joseph, or the death of the detective who framed Thane for killing Lauren McCoy—both cases where he had held the upper hand. He knew with this case he would need all the help he could get from his team.

"Mind if I go first?" Letitia said, "In case any of those greasy reporters start trying to come into the office?"

"Any signs of it letting up?" Thane asked.

"If anything, it's getting crazier. So as far as an update, I'm still digging, but I did learn Dixon abruptly resigned from an assistant coaching position about eighteen years back, when he was pretty much an unknown. The details are a little sparse, but it appears one of the team's cheerleaders accused him of being…" Letitia checked her notepad. "A neanderthal."

"Sounds about right," Kristin said.

"But she didn't shoot the guy," Letitia said. "She reported him."

Letitia looked down at her notes again, but Thane thought she did that as a way of avoiding an argument as opposed to actually looking for something she'd written down.

"Do you have a concern about our case?" Thane asked.

"We work the cases we're given," Letitia said. "Our job isn't to try the cases ourselves. Our job is to defend the client."

"True, but if you were a member of a jury?"

"I'm torn. I'm all about justice being served. I mean, I'm going to law school to fight for the disadvantaged, but I'm not sure I equate vengeance with justice. A lot of black people get killed by white people who feel threatened. If I don't like that, it's a little hard for me to support the reverse."

Thane recognized this as the same question he wrestled with constantly.

"If she had shot him while he was abusing her," Letitia continued, "then sign me up. And I'm not even sure I disagree with her shooting him after the fact. It just feels like more of a slippery slope." She paused, looking at Kristin. "I'm surprised you don't feel the same way. I would have thought you'd be the first to have concerns about a killing that feels more like revenge than self-defense."

Kristin shook her head with more confidence than Thane assumed she truly felt.

"Like you said, it's not our job to determine guilt or innocence."

Thane interrupted the discussion before it went too far. He knew Letitia had a point. In the past, Kristin would have made a comment about the ethics of what Boo had done, even though she would still defend their client as expected. But with this case, she seemed to be more comfortable supporting Boo, not only from a legal standpoint, but also from a moral one.

"Do you know if charges were brought against Dixon in that previous job?" Thane asked.

"No. It looks like something done off the books. Or it's a coincidence he quit after the young woman's complaint, but I doubt it. Assholes like Dixon keep getting jobs because H.R. departments don't share negative information for fear of being sued."

"Keep digging. That's good work." Thane turned to Gideon. "You come up with anything yet?"

"I've been asking around. I hear Stick's name more often than not when I say I'm wanting to get it on with a girl and am willing to pay. Rumor has it he provides girls to members of the football team, and a couple of guys said there's an assistant coach or two who are on speed dial. They tell me that like it's some sort of Amazon review."

"Wouldn't surprise me if there are others on the staff doing this. The leader of an organization often sets the tone."

"Does that mean you think I might start subscribing to the physical newspaper?" Letitia asked.

"One other thing," Gideon said. "When I got a couple of them talking about the team, I was told that college girls were sometimes called in to help 'entertain' top football recruits. Sort of a ULA Welcome Wagon kind of deal."

"Kristin, any chance you know anyone at that school who might be able to give you insight on that sort of thing?"

Kristin thought about it. "I can't think of anyone off the top of my head, but I was in a sorority at USC…"

"Of course you were," Letitia said with a partial smile.

"And there's a chapter at ULA. I could see if anyone there knows anything."

"Do that. If the sorority grapevine is anything like the prison grapevine, maybe you'll get lucky. And Gideon, poke around a little more and see if you can find out more about Stick's prostitution ring. But again…"

"No blood," Gideon said.

"If you don't mind." Thane closed his notebook, signaling the end of the meeting. As everyone rose, Letitia spoke to Kristin.

"Hey, who are you talking to at the D.A.'s office about moving forward with this case?"

Kristin looked at her with a puzzled expression on her face. "I don't know that they've assigned the case yet."

"Oh, sorry. I saw you coming out of the D.A.'s building the other day and I assumed it was about this case. I wasn't trying to pry."

Kristin turned red as she became flustered. When no one said anything, she looked over at Thane.

"It wasn't related to the case."

"I wouldn't have thought it was," Thane said, but no one turned to leave. All eyes were on Kristin, and she finally succumbed to their questioning expressions, if for no other reason than to show she had nothing to hide.

"I had a meeting with Angela Day. I always like to know what options I have career-wise."

"You thinking you might want to work for the D.A.'s office?" Letitia said, incredulously.

"I don't know what I want to do. Like I said, I prefer to know what my options are."

Gideon inserted himself into the conversation. "If you worked for the D.A., you could have been assigned Gus's case. You might have been in charge of trying to put him away for something he didn't do. And Skunk, too. Bet you could have sent him to the electric chair."

Kristin's eyes narrowed. "I'm just learning about options. Besides, it's not that simple. The D.A.'s office also puts away truly bad people. Murderers, and child molesters, and…" She stopped and took a deep breath.

"And rapists," Letitia said, her tone softened.

"Hey, I'm still here, aren't I? How about you all give me a break?"

"Come on, guys," Thane said. "Let's focus on the case at hand."

Letitia looked out at the reception area and saw someone who looked like a reporter with a small video camera on his shoulder standing at the reception desk, looking around.

"And the circus begins," Letitia muttered, as she looked at Gideon. "Want to help me convince him it's in his best interest to leave?"

"That's my specialty." As they walked out of Thane's office, Gideon raised his hand partway up. "And I know: no blood."

Kristin stayed behind. "I wasn't trying to do anything behind your back."

"I don't ever worry about that. You should always know what your options are. But if you're ever unhappy doing what you're doing here, I hope you'll feel comfortable talking with me about it."

"It's not that. It's just…" She paused, as if unsure how to explain.

"Don't worry about it. For selfish reasons I'd love for you to stay here until I retire in thirty years, but we all have to follow our own road."

Kristin nodded her appreciation but didn't turn to leave. Finally, she asked, "I'm right about not trying to determine the morality of what Boo did, aren't I?"

"Of course. We're her lawyers."

Kristin nodded. "I don't want to come off like I support vigilantism. I like to think I would have handled it differently than Boo, but that doesn't mean she doesn't deserve representation." She paused again, looking like she wanted to leave, but still had a question.

"Did you ever want to get revenge for what happened to you?" she finally asked.

Thane wondered if she had suspicions of what he had done, but it seemed to him like she was wrestling with her own emotional reaction to Stick's attack on her.

"Of course I did. I think that's a natural reaction."

"But what's important is we don't follow through with that reaction, right?"

Thane knew the right answer to that question. He just wasn't sure what the non-hypocritical answer was.

"We do the best we can. That's all we can do."

Kristin nodded in agreement and turned to leave his office. He thought he could just catch the words she seemed to be saying more to herself than to him.

"But what if that's not good enough?"

16

Thane was once again comfortable leaving his office building through the front door, now that the media understood he wasn't going to comment on the case. That hadn't stopped them from volleying questions his way, but it was usually done half-heartedly, without the normal effort to provoke a response.

About half a block away from his office building, however, a familiar voice coming from behind caused him to regret not having slipped out the back.

"Banning. Jag Colter, American News Network."

Thane already wanted to punch the guy before he finished calling out to him. Jag Colter had cornered Hannah in the courthouse hallway during Thane's first trial after his release from prison, peppering her with questions about Thane and trying to bait her into losing her temper.

Instead, it was Thane who had lost his temper. After years of not being around to protect Hannah, Thane overreacted, lifting Jag up by the collar and slamming him into a wall. Footage of Thane picking up the reporter had made the news that night. Thane knew it was his own fault for getting angry, but he still had no interest in interacting with this sleazebag again.

"Banning, wait up."

If anything, Thane picked up his pace, but Jag caught up with him nevertheless and hopped in front of him.

"No comment."

"I haven't even asked you a question. What if I was simply going to ask about the weather?"

"Then I would tell you I have no comment on the weather. Now get out of my way."

Thane stepped around the reporter and continued down the sidewalk, with Colter following beside like an eager little brother.

"I don't know why you should be mad at me. I should be mad at you. I got fired because of our last encounter."

"No comment."

"Those snowflakes at the station said they received too many angry calls claiming I was rude to your wife, and the cowards ended up getting rid of me. Fortunately, I ended up getting a job at this new cable network that is a much better fit for me."

"From what I've read about their ratings, it seems like a much better fit for the public, as well. Not a lot of people are going to see you."

"Also, the last time we met, you were extremely violent toward me. You could have killed me."

"If that's your idea of extreme violence, you've led a very sheltered life. And if I had wanted to kill you, you'd be dead."

"Because you learned how in prison, right?"

Thane stopped so abruptly that Colter jumped back a step as if he thought Thane might take a swing at him.

"What do you want, Colter?"

"I want to know if you're planning on presenting

some sort of 'woke' defense for your client when the fact remains a prominent and well-respected man was killed by a black woman who is rumored to have ties with Antifa."

"A rumor I'm assuming your network started. Are there any connections to Antifa other than the fact the woman is black?"

"I'm only reporting what I heard."

"Yeah, because that's the basis of good journalism."

Thane again tried walking away, hoping against odds Colter would leave him alone, but he knew he'd have better luck buying a Powerball ticket.

"Are you hoping character assassination of the coach will force the city to give you more money to represent murderers, rapists, and illegal immigrants?"

"I'll tell you what, if I decide to pursue character assassination, I'll consult you first."

"Oh give me a break. You know as well as I do that when a white person kills a black person, there are riots, but when a black person kills a white person, it's crickets."

"Other than the sound of a prison door slamming shut."

"Then what's your strategy with this case, Banning? Make the jury feel sorry for the poor woman because the coach didn't give her a big enough tip? Or are you going to play on white guilt and make the jury feel like it's their fault this woman had to turn to violence. God forbid anyone take responsibility for their actions. Being a victim is the new pumpkin spice of society nowadays."

Thane stopped and looked at Colter. The reporter again took half a step back, in case he needed to turn and run.

"Why do I get the feeling the University has recruited you to do a little character assassination of its own?"

Colter shook his head, unconvincingly. "I don't know anything about that."

"That's the second time I've heard that pumpkin spice analogy. Did you think Sterling Silver only used it on you?"

It didn't surprise Thane that the University would take advantage of media contacts to try to present the murder in a positive light for them, but it surprised him they were stooping to work with a cable station like American News Network. On the other hand, they were likely the only network willing to go to that extreme. Either way, it was naive to think ULA wouldn't pull out all their weapons. Silver's fancy office and job title didn't mean he was above fishing in the sewer.

"I'm going to lunch now," Thane said. "If you continue to follow me, I will hurt you."

"Is that a comment after all?"

"No, that's a promise."

17

Thane entered the sports bar and looked around but didn't see who he was looking for. The place was starting to fill up but was by no means crowded yet. A couple of TVs above the bar were blasting a soccer game being played overseas. Not a lot of other options for live sports that time of day in L.A. He scanned the place one more time before seeing the back of Lawrence's head in a booth near the corner.

Thane had told Letitia he'd be happy to meet her brother for lunch. He would have been happier if he thought the young man was doing better, but if anyone could understand what he was going through, it was Thane. He walked over to the booth and slid in, keeping Lawrence from feeling as though he had to stand up and shake hands.

Lawrence was in his early thirties and had been sent to prison nine years earlier because he wouldn't testify against a friend who he knew was innocent, despite pressure from a detective who played fast and loose with the rules. As a reward for standing up for what he thought was right, Lawrence had been sentenced to thirty years in prison. It was only because Thane had played fast and loose with the rules himself that the detective's questionable practices had been exposed in court, and

Lawrence had been set free.

"Sorry I'm late."

Lawrence offered a no-big-deal shrug of his shoulders and picked up the menu. Thane wondered if it had been a mistake setting up this lunch, and if perhaps Lawrence was only there at the insistence of his sister. If that was the case, Thane thought it best to wait until Lawrence was ready to talk about anything of substance.

"Anything look good?" Thane asked as Lawrence finally put down his menu.

"Compared to that crap in the joint, roadkill would look good."

"And fresher." Thane smiled. Forsman Penitentiary was known for a lot of things, but culinary excellence wasn't one of them. Actually, it wasn't known for anything positive, at least not from the perspective of its occupants. Thane's five years there had almost killed him, and Lawrence had been there almost twice as long.

The waitress came over and brought two glasses of water, took their order, and darted away, a woman on a mission. Thane watched Lawrence stare at his glass of water.

"I know your sister was hoping it might help to talk," Thane said, deciding that outwaiting Lawrence wasn't a great idea. "But I also know you need to work on your own timeframe. People who haven't gone through what you and I went through don't understand. And we don't have an automatic understanding of each other's experiences either."

"Yeah," Lawrence muttered, "like I was there almost twice as long as you."

"And I was on death row."

Lawrence looked up at Thane and made true eye contact with him for the first time. Apparently, Thane had scored a point reminding the younger man of the severity of the time Thane had served. Whatever their many differences were demographically, they each went through something few people had.

"I know," Thane said, "that loved ones feel we should be skipping up and down the streets with glee upon getting released. And obviously it was a wonderful thing to get out of that hell hole, but if you're anything like me, joy was elusive at first. It couldn't compete with the anger and bitterness that had built up."

Lawrence only nodded, as if he wasn't ready to talk about himself yet.

"I'd like to say it gets better with time, but I suppose that depends in part on the individual."

"And whether you get a large payout from the city."

Thane understood why everyone believed that getting millions of dollars from the city in recognition of what had been to him would make everything better, and it did make a difference, but it didn't gloss over the memories of what Thane had endured. It didn't replace the five years he had lost with Hannah, or living in constant fear that each day in prison would be his last, or experiencing days where he wished they would be his last.

"The payout was nice, but it didn't take away the bitterness. That's not the sort of thing money can do for you."

Again, Lawrence just nodded. Thane could almost feel the man's anger radiating off him.

"We don't need to talk about any of this if you don't want to. We can shoot the shit over a burger and not talk about anything more serious than what you think the

Lakers are going to do this year. Or we can call it an early lunch and you can tell your sister you met with me. But if there's anything you'd like to bat around, I'm also up for that. It's your call."

Lawrence took a long drink of water, looking around the bar as if thinking of getting up and leaving. But instead, he leaned back and appeared to lower his guard by a degree or two.

"First off, I want to say I appreciate what you did for me. Seriously. Hopefully that's obvious, so don't take anything I might say as me being ungrateful, because I'm not. I wasn't expecting to get out of there alive, so to be back around family is a blessing I didn't think I'd ever see, and I know that was 'cause of you."

"I understand."

"But at the same time, I was innocent. The papers covered you like you was a hero for getting me out, but I was supposed to be out. I hadn't done nothing. Again, I do appreciate it, but at the same time, someone should have gotten me out of prison. Know what I mean?"

"Are you feeling like the city should have acknowledged what was done to you more than they did?"

Lawrence shook his head at first, but it quickly shifted into nodding. "I don't know. I'm not saying they should have given me millions of dollars like they gave you, but they should have given me something. No offense, but it's like the white lawyer gets done wrong and they say here's a bag of money, but a black man gets done wrong and the best they do is tell me they're doing me a favor by letting me out. Why can't they tell me they did me wrong?"

"Because it would be more likely you could sue them."

"Then maybe I should. Why not?"

Thane understood. After all, he had helped orchestrate a murder and had been able to publicly expose the then District Attorney, all with the goal of clearing his name. And for vengeance. He wanted to get even with those who had done him wrong. Lawrence was looking for the same thing.

"Frustrating as I'm sure it is, letting you out is about as close to admitting they were wrong as it's going to get."

"But how can they get away with that?" Lawrence said, the anger in his voice growing with every syllable.

"Because Detective Mahone caught you with some drugs. Where he crossed the line was trying to pressure you into falsely testifying against your friend and threatening you with a maximum prison sentence for the drug possession charge if you didn't testify. But he never put any of that in writing, and the sentence you were given was within the guidelines, albeit the severe end of them. In my case, I got the D.A. to admit what he had done, but you don't have that sort of leverage."

"So you don't think I could win if I sued?"

Thane leaned back and considered how much he could level with this man. He didn't feel comfortable sharing everything with him, but at the same time he didn't want him to get so lost in his anger that he ended up back in prison.

"I don't think you'd win, but not just because we don't have an admission of guilt."

Lawrence sat back further, waiting for more.

"Mahone didn't play by the rules with you. He didn't fight fair. When I took on your case, I didn't fight fair either. I rigged the fight to help get you off. That would be hard to prove, but not impossible, and if what I did was discovered, you'd run the risk of having your parole revoked."

Lawrence took all of this in and nodded, looking at Thane as if seeing him in a new light. Thane knew this man had also lived through the dynamics of prison life which often involved doing whatever needed to be done to get by.

"You set him up."

"I didn't say that," Thane said quickly.

"Not out loud. And you're not saying you didn't. But I getcha."

"I'm saying you need to focus on moving forward with your life. I can tell you that holding on to the anger and resentment is only going to hold you back. If you can't find a way to move beyond that, you're wasting the freedom you've been given."

"Did getting the D.A. to admit you were wronged enabled you to move on?"

After everything Thane had set up, he had assumed he would be able to move forward, but that hadn't proven to be the case. At least not to the degree he had hoped.

Meanwhile, across town, Gideon studied the greasy cheeseburger like it was a work of art, which was pretty much how he saw it. As it neared 1:00 p.m., more customers were leaving the diner than entering, so Gideon was more comfortable making his call. He shoved a fistful of fries in his mouth and took out his phone.

"Yeah, I was told you was the person to talk to about

lining up girls," he said, scowling as he listened, frustration starting to build. "What the hell does it matter what my name is? Money is money no matter my name, but sure, you need a name, then Joe Smith. How's about that? Does that work for you? Now you got any girls or not?"

He waited to make sure the person on the other end had, in fact, hung up on him, then put his phone back in his pocket. Looking up, he noticed Alice standing next to his booth, holding a pot of coffee to top off his cup.

"That wasn't what it sounded like. I'm working a case and had to pretend I—ah, never mind. But I know it sounded bad."

"I read about you and your friend representing that young woman accused of killing that coach, and I admire you for it. Was that coach as bad as some of the news is implying?"

Gideon nodded. "I can't talk much about it, but yeah, he was a cockroach."

"I've known my share of those," she said as she topped his coffee. "Fact, I was married to one."

"But you ain't no more?"

"No, it was long enough as it was, so I hope you're able to do right by that girl. Even if she did kill the son-of-a-bitch."

"I appreciate you believing I wasn't really looking to buy a girl."

"Honey, I've been waitressing for over twenty years now. You get a strong sense of people, and you strike me as being one of the good ones."

Gideon shook his head and looked back down at his cheeseburger. "You might need to get your sense fine-tuned a little more."

Alice laughed and put her hand on Gideon's shoulder. "No, my sense is just fine. You may have gotten into trouble in the past, but that doesn't mean you're bad."

"I appreciate that, Alice, almost as much as I appreciate the cheeseburgers here."

"You a big cheeseburger fan?"

"Yep, I'm big, and I like cheeseburgers."

"Well, I make 'em even better at home than they do here at the diner."

Gideon nodded as if being told a piece of trivia, but his insides tightened. Was he supposed to say he'd like for her to prove that sometime? Was she sending a hint, or simply stating a fact? If she had any idea who he really was, she'd be hightailing it away from him.

"Is that a fact?" he finally offered up.

"It truly is." The manager called her name, so she turned to leave. "Let me go grab you a piece of your pie before we run out."

She walked back to the counter to grab a couple more plates of food. Gideon thought he'd rather be confronted by an inmate with a rusty shiv than think about asking someone out. But all of that was ridiculous anyway. She was just doing her job, probably looking for a bigger tip. He was not the kind of guy women flirted with.

Just the same, he looked forward to her coming back with the pie, and not solely because he was still hungry.

18

Thane sat near the front of the sterile room, off to the side, under the harsh fluorescent lights and the ugly tiled floor, while being introduced. Usually when he did any sort of public speaking—which he tried doing as little as possible—the event organizer asked him for something they could use by way of introduction. In those instances, Thane tried to keep it as brief as possible, but this time no one requested any input from him. That didn't surprise him, but it did worry him.

He had worked on this talk longer than he usually did, but he still believed Vegas would list the odds of a successful talk as being a long shot. For one thing, he didn't think his usual talk would work very well, and second, he'd never spoken to a group of fifth graders before.

"As most of you know," Cricket said, standing at the front of the room, "I don't have no daddy. That snake slithered off when I was just a baby, so I can't be bringing him to talk about what he does for a living, since I'm guessing he doesn't do much of anything anyway, other than maybe dealing or whoring."

"Cricket!" her teacher said.

"But even though I haven't got a daddy," Cricket

continued, ignoring her teacher, "I got something better, since let's face it, most of the daddy's we've had come talk to us have been boring as turtle turd. I mean, come on, Stevie, if your dad told us one more accounting story, I thought I might have to jump out the window."

"Cricket," Mrs. Winslow, her teacher, said again. Thane wondered how many times the woman had to say that name during the average school day. He guessed at least a dozen.

Thane had helped Cricket a few months earlier after she got in trouble for hacking into the city's cable system. The young girl was, without a doubt, a prodigy when it came to computers and electronic systems, which he ended up taking advantage of on another case he had been working on. He knew it was wrong to ask a fifth grader to help hack into a system, but desperate times called for desperate measures. In exchange, he agreed to help her out in the future if she needed it, and he had the feeling she would need it. The best he could hope for was that she would use her powers for good.

"Anyway," Cricket continued, ignoring Mrs. Winslow's admonition, "my speaker needs no introduction. He's living on the front page of every newspaper and been the lead story of most every newscast for the past couple of years. He's also my own personal mouthpiece and, as such, he's here to talk about what it's like to be a lawyer for the stars because, baby, I'm a star."

Cricket nodded to Thane like he was a circus pony, and it was time for him to do his tricks. Thane walked to the front of the room as Cricket retook her seat. She beamed her 1,000-watt smile at him, nodding for him to go ahead and begin.

"As Cricket so colorfully put it, I'm a lawyer, but I've been in the news more than is usually the case in my profession, in part because there are different types of law. There is contract law, and real estate law, and corporate law, and…"

He could see the class was already losing interest. Cricket's eyebrows furrowed as she shook her head and spun one upright finger in a circle as a signal to get to the good stuff. Thane realized he wasn't there to do career counseling for the kids. He was there to tell a good story.

"And, of course, there are lawyers like me who represent innocent clients who have been charged with murder."

And with the word murder, he had regained their attention.

"Not that that's why I represented Cricket here."

He spent much of the rest of his talk focusing on his most recent couple of cases, and a few kids even clapped when he got to the point where his clients were found to be innocent.

When it came time for questions, a couple of the kids asked about the murdered football coach and were disappointed when Thane said he couldn't talk about an active case, although they were more understanding when he explained it was super top secret. The kids seemed to appreciate the sanctity of super top secret.

Another boy, who appeared to have something specific in mind, asked if Thane was taking on new clients, and what he charged. The boy said he might be in need of a good mouthpiece. Thane glanced over at Mrs. Winslow who, through a subtle nod of her head, suggested the boy would indeed need a lawyer at some point in his life. Thane said that unfortunately his client list was full at the time. The boy said he'd give his contact information to Cricket in case Thane's caseload lightened up.

When the class ended, the few students who weren't grabbing their backpack to race out of the classroom gave him a polite round of applause. When all of the students had left the room, Cricket's teacher came over and thanked him for coming.

"I have to be honest, when Cricket said you were her lawyer and were coming to speak to the class, I was a wee bit skeptical, to say the least. She sometimes has a tendency to embellish."

"Do tell," Thane said with a smile.

"If you really are her lawyer, I hope you've blocked out large parts of your calendar because I'm guessing she could end up being a little time consuming. Don't get me wrong, she's one of the brightest students I've had in quite some time, and I really do care for her, but you know…"

"I can't imagine what your job must be like. I'll light a candle for you this evening."

"Won't help, but I appreciate the gesture."

Thane walked out of the classroom and found Cricket leaning against a locker, waiting for him.

"Can't believe you tried weaseling out of this, Thor," she said, shaking her head disapprovingly.

"Like I said, I'm not a fan of public speaking."

"That wasn't public speaking! It's a group of fifth graders."

"I was afraid they might all be like you."

"Baby, there ain't nobody else like me," Cricket responded as she struck a pose. "Come on, I'll walk you out."

She took his hand and escorted him down the hall. It made Thane imagine what it would be like walking his own daughter down the hallway of her school in the years to come. As they passed a couple of younger kids looking at them, Cricket nodded toward Thane.

"My lawyer," she said. The kids looked impressed.

"So how's the Mrs.? You naming the baby after me?"

"We thought about it, but like you said, there ain't nobody else like you. Since you're one of a kind, I can't see there being another 'Cricket' hopping around."

"I can understand that. Plus, it'd be unfair to make her try to live up to the name. That's a lot to ask of anybody."

"That's what we figured."

When they reached the door with the metal detector and the sleepy looking security guard sitting on a stool, Cricket stopped.

"This is as far as they let me go, unless I tell them you're my daddy, in which case we can go get some ice cream or something. Might help soothe your nerves after this ordeal."

"I'm not sure that would work."

"You don't think they'd believe you're my daddy?"

"I'm guessing I appear too relaxed to be your daddy."

Cricket grinned and shook his hand with a firm grip before turning and sashaying her way back to the classroom.

Thane hesitated before calling out to her. He wasn't comfortable once again asking Cricket to do something illegal. This was another thing he was trying to get away from: doing whatever it took to get justice. He took whatever solace he could find in the fact that this was pretty small potatoes compared to some of his other actions.

"Cricket, hold up. I've got a question for you."

The young girl turned and apparently could read Thane's expression without missing a beat.

"What's it pay?"

19

As Thane walked into his reception area, he noticed Letitia nod hello, then watched her eyebrows furrow as she looked behind him. He glanced over his shoulder and saw Stick plodding through the door, following him.

At 6'4" and 250 pounds of malevolence, Stick was a man who could kill someone in the morning and not even have it cross his mind by lunchtime. Thane knew everyone had a different reaction to frustration. He had no doubt Stick's first reaction was violence. It was probably his only reaction.

Thane turned toward him, not wanting Stick anywhere near him, let alone in his law firm.

"What do you want?"

"I wanna talk."

"That's why they invented phones."

"This is best said in person. You're gonna want to hear what I have to say, and I need you to understand I'm serious."

Thane knew Stick wasn't going to go anywhere without an argument, so he decided to take him into his office before Kristin encountered him, but he didn't move fast enough.

Kristin walked out of her office and headed toward Letitia, her attention focused on a document she was holding before stopping when she saw the man who had threatened her a few weeks earlier.

"Whoa, lookie here," Stick said with a malignant grin on his face. "My own real life Barbie doll. What up, girl? You don't call, you don't write."

Kristin collected herself, walked over to Letitia and handed her the document.

"If you don't mind, could you include this information with the rest of Mr. Burns' file?"

As she turned to walk back to her office, Stick called after her.

"Ah, come on, sweet pea. Don't be like that. I thought we had something. You didn't feel any sort of connection there at your kitchen table?"

Thane held up his hand. "Stick, come into my office, or get the hell out of here."

"I'm surprised," Kristin said, turning back toward Stick, "that you're actually willing to approach me when other people are around. You strike me as being the kind of guy who can only threaten women when it's just you and them."

"Threaten? How'm I threatening you?"

"First, let's start with your breath."

Stick laughed, although his expression didn't reveal any sort of amusement. "I don't need to be alone with anyone to threaten them, 'cause I ain't scared of no one."

"You should be." Gideon stepped out of his office, looking like he had updated his to-do list to include breaking something over Stick's head.

"Would you look at that?" Stick laughed, turning to Thane. "I didn't know your office was dog friendly. I would have brought my mutt, too. Our dogs could have played together."

Thane put his hand on Stick's shoulder and directed him toward his office. "You want to talk, then let's talk, but if you want to just stand around pretending you're the toughest guy in the room then quit wasting my time, because we all know that's not true."

Stick looked back at Kristin and smiled. "'Till next time."

Gideon began to follow, but Thane shook his head. "It's fine. I've got this."

"Obviously your boss wants to hear what I have to say without anyone else around."

"No, I just don't want to have to deal with your blood on my office carpet."

Thane finally got Stick into his office and shut the door.

"What do you want, Stick?" Thane walked over and sat on the edge of his desk, not offering Stick a seat. He had no interest in being around the man any longer than necessary.

"I saw you coming out of that grade school earlier. You already trying to pick out a school for your young'un? If so, I would have thought you could afford something a lot better than that one?"

"You following me? Or were you looking for another child to pimp out?"

"No, I got all the young girls I need. I just wanted to talk."

"So talk."

Stick walked over and lowered himself into one of the chairs across from Thane's desk. He bounced up and down a couple of times as if checking out the chair cushion's padding. He nodded, approvingly.

"Don't get all high and mighty with me, counselor. You may have everyone else fooled with your 'white knight' reputation, but you and me, we ain't so different."

"Are you under the impression I deal drugs, murder innocent people, and pimp out young women?"

"No, but you did have me threaten a witness to testify the way you wanted in that last case of yours. I didn't go to law school, but I'm pretty sure that's not the way you're supposed to do those things. At least I ain't never seen that on any Law and Order episode."

"Stick, what do you suppose the odds are of you coming to the point? Less than 50-50?"

"The point is this: you need to make sure my name don't come out of Boo's mouth, or your mouth, or Barbie's mouth. There's no connection between her and me, understand?"

"Are you afraid it will hurt your reputation as an upstanding citizen?"

"I know it will hurt your reputation if people learn you had me threaten that punk into lying on the stand for you. In fact, I imagine it could even get you disbarred."

"I'm not sure you're the kind of person who could hurt my reputation."

Stick reached into his pocket and pulled out his phone.

"It's not a case of 'he-said-he-said.' It's more a case of 'he said on tape.'"

Stick pushed something on his phone screen and Thane's voice came through loud and clear. "I'm going to ask three questions of someone, and these are the answers to those questions."

The tape continued replaying the conversation Thane had had with Stick a few weeks earlier, when he tried to find a way to get his client from being convicted for a murder that Thane had helped put together. He had run out of other options and finally decided that if the detective pursuing that case was willing to lie and intimidate to get the answers he wanted, then Thane would do the same. He should have known, however, that doing business with someone like Stick wasn't a good long-term plan.

"I'm going to do what's right by Boo, whatever that takes," Thane said, once Stick turned off the recording.

"No you're not," Stick said. "Not if you don't want trouble raining down on you."

"You need to play that tape for someone, play it. Let me know how that works out for you."

Stick rose and stood uncomfortably close to Thane, who thought the man smelled like leather and whiskey.

"I believe you understand from last time that I don't play nice. Remember that other witness you had? How'd things work out for him? Oh, that's right, he got himself killed. Wonder how that happened."

"It's in your best interest to leave now."

"Not before I'm sure you get what I'm sayin'. If my name comes up in Boo's case, you might find someone else being hurt mighty bad, and this time, it won't be no witness. Could even be someone closer to home. Someone who would actually end up being a two-fer."

Thane rose slowly, causing Stick to take a step back. As confident as the thug could be, even he had to have realized he might have pushed things a bit too far. He also might have remembered that Thane wasn't just another lawyer: he was a man who had survived five years on death row in a maximum-security prison.

"You ever do hard time in prison, Stick? I don't mean spend a few nights behind bars, I mean spend a few years in a place like Forsman?"

"Nah. I ain't never been dumb enough to get caught. I don't get caught."

"That's what I thought. Not the part about you not being dumb, but I can tell the people who think they're tough, and those who actually are."

"What, you going to sick your big dog on me now?"

"I don't need anyone else to make you bleed."

Thane picked up a fountain pen and looked at its sharp nib.

"You have any idea how much something like this goes for in prison? Something this simple is gold. A man with a fountain pen could kill another man at least four different ways in a matter of seconds. And that's just a pen."

Thane held up the pen in front of Stick's face so he could see the pen's sharp point.

"If I even sense you're breathing the same air as my wife, I will gut you like a fish."

Stick tried smiling, but it looked forced.

"In that case, all you got to do is keep my name out of Boo's case. That's all. For a guy who hires other people to intimidate witnesses, that doesn't seem like too much to ask. Then we can all go our merry way."

"Do not threaten my wife again, Stick. And also keep away from Kristin. I'm sure it's easier for you to threaten women, but it's not very impressive."

"Technically it wasn't only your wife. I mean, not if you believe life begins at conceptio..."

Thane's free arm shot under Stick's armpit and reached over and across the front of the big man's neck, pushing his head back so that it faced the ceiling, making it impossible for Stick to find his footing. With his other hand, Thane pressed the tip of the fountain pen hard against Stick's jugular.

"Don't threaten her again, Stick." Thane's voice left no question as to his seriousness.

"I thought you didn't want to get blood on your carpet, counselor," Stick managed to croak out the words.

"We don't always get what we want."

"Well, I sure as hell better."

Thane knew Stick wouldn't back down in his office, and that he wouldn't back down anywhere else, either. The best he could hope for was Stick getting the message and deciding it wasn't worth the risk, but he also knew Stick's brain wasn't wired right, so doing what made sense wasn't a given for him.

Thane slowly removed the pen and let go of his neck, giving Stick an opportunity to take a full breath again.

"My name better not come up in Boo's case," Stick said one last time. "That ain't asking too much. After all, you owe me. And if you decide you have to come after me, then come on after me, but you're going to need a hell of a lot more than a pen."

Stick turned to leave, then looked back at Thane.

"And you best not try grabbing me like that again, counselor. You get one freebie. Next time, I'll rip your head off and use it as an ashtray."

20

Stick plowed out of Thane's office and through the firm's main entrance, paying no attention to the glare being delivered by Letitia. Thane had met far too many men like Stick while in prison: men who, for whatever reason, grew up doing whatever they wanted, and taking whatever they wanted, with no thoughts of possible repercussions, due to the fact that they were usually the ones doling out the repercussions.

Kristin and Gideon both came out of their offices as soon as Stick left and beelined it to Thane's office. Thane wished he could have had a couple of minutes alone to make sure he had regained his composure. Even an implied threat against Hannah, and their child, had him wanting to grab a tire iron and go after Stick.

"What did that asshole want?" Kristin said in an accusatory tone, as if Thane had been responsible for her earlier encounter with Stick.

"Apparently the branches we're shaking are causing some things to fall out. Stick wanted to let me know he'd appreciate it if his name didn't come up in Boo's case."

"Yeah," Gideon said. "I'm sure that's exactly how he phrased it."

"Well too bad for him," Kristin said. "I hope his name ends up on the front page of every newspaper."

Thane nodded, but didn't want anyone to take Stick too lightly. "We'll do whatever it takes to help Boo, but I'm not looking to go after Stick just to go after him."

"I'm not scared of him," Kristin said, almost sounding as though she meant it.

"It's not an issue of being scared of him. It's a matter of poking a sociopath for no reason. If we need to involve him to help Boo, then we'll involve him. Otherwise, we steer clear of him."

"And he better steer clear of us," Gideon said.

"What's wrong with that guy?" Kristin asked Gideon. "How does someone get to be like that?"

"Sometimes the good Lord gives some people the soul of a rabid dog."

Letitia leaned into Thane's office. "Excuse me, but the detective working Dixon's murder is on the phone asking to speak to you."

"Thanks." Thane went over to his desk as Gideon and Kristin left his office, both unsatisfied.

"Detective Struthers," Thane said. "What can I do for you?"

The briefest of pauses followed Thane's question before a voice came over the phone. "Sorry, this isn't Struthers. I'm Detective David Hawkins. I'm the lead investigator on Coach Dixon's murder. I'm hoping we might talk sometime soon about this case. Do you have any free time in the near future?"

Thane drove to LAPD headquarters on First street, just south of L.A.'s Chinatown. The 500,000 square foot building itself was an architectural work of art, looking more like a museum than a police headquarters.

Thane had been surprised to learn Struthers wasn't the lead detective on Dixon's murder. Not that he expected the man to get all of L.A.'s high profile murders, but Struthers himself had made it sound like he was the man in charge when he told Thane to contact him if he had any questions about the case.

Thane always felt like he was running two steps behind Struthers in everything the detective did. He wondered if Struthers was somehow working to turn Thane's involvement in this case into something that would expose his involvement in either Gruber's or Joseph's murder. Or both. But he couldn't figure out what he was up to. So even though Thane was there to meet with Detective Hawkins, he knew he always had to keep an eye open for Struthers' fingerprints on this case.

Thane was directed to a small meeting room and brought out his phone to check emails. He was used to detectives keeping lawyers waiting, perhaps in an attempt to establish their authority, or simply because they didn't like lawyers, but Hawkins entered the room right on time.

Detective Hawkins struck Thane as being former military. His hairstyle wasn't exactly a crew cut, but it was tight and clean. His shoes were polished, and his tie was neatly knotted—unlike many detectives, who wore theirs loose unless they were in court.

In his mid-30's, the man looked all business, but didn't come across as the sort of guy trying to impress anyone. Instead, he conveyed himself as someone who believed his results would do the impressing. Thane rose to shake his hand.

"Mr. Banning, I'm Detective David Hawkins. Good to meet you."

"Please, call me Thane."

"Alright. Please have a seat, Thane."

They sat across from each other at a small table as Hawkins let out a small chuckle.

"I suppose I better tread carefully around you, seeing as how you got Detective Mahone suspended."

"For the record, Detective Mahone got himself suspended. As long as you're not breaking the law, you should be fine."

"Yeah," Hawkins said, leaning back in his chair. "I should be okay in that regard. I'm guessing I fall somewhere between Struthers, who I believe you know quite well by now, and Mahone."

"How so?"

"I view Struthers as being an idealist. Everything by the book. Every law and regulation followed to the letter. Whereas Mahone was more of a nihilist. He paints himself as trying to do the right thing, and I'm sure he even believes it, but he's fine ignoring rules and regulations if they get in the way of what he's trying to do."

"And you're somewhere in-between."

"I'm more of a pragmatist. I'm as dogged as Struthers when I work a case, but I'm willing to stretch the rules, as long as they don't break. My particular skill is being able to go right up to the point where the rule is about to break."

"And that's where you stop?" Thane asked.

Hawkins smiled and all but shrugged. "That's always the goal, yes."

"Good to have goals," Thane offered.

Hawkins laughed and nodded in agreement. "Similarly, I believe there is a wide range between what former D.A. Stone would do, and what our current D.A. will do. Everybody falls somewhere on the spectrum between rules and no rules. Chaos versus order. Do the ends justify the means, or are the means what's most important?"

"I'm sure you're right."

"Let's take you, for example. I may be wrong, but my sense is you paint from a far, far broader palate than I do. Definitely a broader palate than most other lawyers. That's another reason why I feel I should watch my step around you. The last thing I want to do is make you mad."

Thane wondered what exactly Hawkins was trying to imply. Did he suspect something wasn't completely kosher with how things went down with Mahone getting suspended? Or could the working theory around police headquarters be that Thane had been involved in two murders stemming from what the two men had done to him?

Paranoia was a helpful thing to hold onto in prison, because often someone truly was out to get you. And while Thane wasn't sure if he carried too much of that with him in his current life outside prison, he knew he had every reason to be on alert, given the stakes if he was found out.

"I have great respect for the law," Thane offered. "I've seen first-hand what happens when people start justifying illegal acts as being for the greater good."

"Agreed," Hawkins said. "But I've also seen what happens when good people feel like they've been dealt a terrible wrong. Sometimes vengeance short-circuits their moral code. But I don't know how we've gotten so far off topic here. Obviously, what I want to talk with you about is your client and the murder of Coach Dixon."

Thane worked hard to once again focus on his current case. He knew he could read all sorts of things into Hawkins' comments about vengeance, but he couldn't afford to be thrown off his game if, in fact, that was Hawkins's intention.

"So, what can I do for you, Detective?"

"I have some questions for your client, but now that she has a lawyer, she's not answering anything without you present, which I understand and can appreciate. So instead of going through the hassle of trying to set up time to meet with you and her in jail, which is usually a pain in the ass to pull off, I figured I'd ask you the questions and if you're going to advise her not to answer them, then I won't be wasting my time."

"Fire away."

Hawkins pulled a small, worn leather notebook from his sportscoat's breast pocket and flipped through a few pages until he found what he was looking for.

"I'm not sure I understand why your client broke the video doorbell when she left."

"Didn't you ask her that?"

"Yes, and she said she thought breaking the doorbell would also destroy the video that it captured. If I was dealing with my grandmother then I would understand, but a woman Ms. Cruise's age would know better."

"I don't want to answer for my client, but I don't

believe she comes from a world of video doorbells and nice homes. It doesn't surprise me she's not familiar with how they work. Either way, it sounds to me like you've already asked her that question and she has answered it."

"Then I guess we'll just have to go with that." Hawkins had trouble suppressing a small smile as he looked back at his notebook. "Next, your client made a call to what appears to be a burner phone. I'd like to know who it is she called."

"Yes, I would advise her not to answer that."

"As I assumed. There was also a second call after the gunshot, but I'm sure you'd have the same answer for that one. I do know, however, that Ms. Cruise claims to have been sexually trafficked by a known drug dealer and pimp, and people like that do tend to use burner phones. She wouldn't give us his name, but I'm pretty sure I know the man. Perhaps if your client was willing to implicate him, it could help her during her trial."

"Depends if she lived to see the trial. If not, giving up that name wouldn't help her all that much. Either way, that seems like something the prosecutor in this case would offer, not the investigating detective."

"Just wanted to toss that out there. Something to think about." Hawkins closed his notebook. "Guess I was right to not go through the hoops of setting up a meeting if you wouldn't let your client answer anyway."

"Which I'm assuming you knew."

"I did, but again, I hate to assume."

"It's also a conversation we could have had over the phone."

"Again, true, and I apologize for dragging you down here. Truth be told, I really wanted to meet you in person.

You're getting quite the reputation around headquarters."

Thane once again didn't like Hawkins' phrasing, although he also knew he had recently won two high-profile cases—and gotten a detective suspended—so it's not as though Thane wasn't getting a reputation in many parts of the city. He just would have preferred it to not be at police headquarters.

"I appreciate you reaching out," Thane said. "If you have other questions, don't hesitate to let me know, although, again, feel free to consider a phone call. But now that an arrest has been made, I'm assuming most of the future questions will come from the D.A.'s office."

"Probably, but if there's a way I can strengthen my case and help the prosecutor, that's what I'll do. The thing about me is that once I have a suspect in my sites, that person is going down, regardless of how long it takes me. That's one way Struthers and I are similar. We're both relentless, and the more personal I can make it, the more determined I become."

"Have you found a way to make this case personal?"

Hawkins' expression shifted from friendly to all business. Even his posture straightened, as if reflecting his commitment.

"I was a huge fan of Coach Dixon, and of the football team. He was a winner. What your client did cannot be justified, even if whatever bullshit story she's spinning is true."

"You don't believe Coach Dixon could have abused a young woman?"

"Maybe he hired someone to relieve the stress, but the scale of abuse that Ms. Cruise is claiming? No, I don't believe it. I'm not saying he wasn't without flaws, but let he who is without sin throw the first stone."

"If you were a woman, you might prefer he threw a stone than use a kitchen utensil to violate you."

Hawkins' lips tightened. "I don't believe the Coach did that. I believe your client let him do what he wanted if it meant more money. She's a whore, after all."

"Let he who is without sin."

"And my sense is you know a lot about throwing stones. Even a couple of big ones." Hawkins looked like he immediately regretted saying that and held up his hand as a silent apology for having gone too far. He stood and studied Thane for a long moment with curiosity rather than accusation.

"Again, sorry I wasted your time. Next time I'll be sure to call." Hawkins turned and walked out of the room.

Thane sat there, almost tired of the veiled accusations constantly lobbed his way. The police obviously believed Thane knew more than he was letting on, and he didn't want to do anything stupid that would expose his role in the previous two murders, but he also felt frustration doing nothing while the threat of incarceration seemed like it kept getting closer. He learned in prison that being passive often meant being the victim, but he also knew reckless action could be worse.

As if reading his thoughts, his phone vibrated. Caller ID displayed the name of Rita McCoy, the wife of the man who actually did carry off the murders that Thane set up. He paused before answering, then took the call.

"This is Thane."

He waited through a long pause before Mrs. McCoy's uncertain voice could be heard.

"Mr. Banning, Rita McCoy. Do you have a few

minutes sometime for us to talk in person? It might be important."

21

Kristin saw their client pause before being led into the small meeting room set aside for prisoners and their lawyers, probably because Boo saw it was just Kristin in the room. But she only hesitated for a moment before walking in and sitting across the table from Kristin, already putting forth an air of defiance. He was far more comfortable with that conversation than one about children.

Kristin looked at the questions she had entered on her iPad, but she wasn't reading them. She just wasn't ready to make full eye contact with Boo quite yet. She found it ironic that she was the one who didn't want to look at Boo. Boo should have been ashamed of her actions, but instead she leaned back in her chair, looking indignant and waiting for Kristin to speak as if Boo's time was being wasted.

As soon as Kristin was at least somewhat confident she could speak without venting her anger, she looked up at Boo.

"Thane asked me to see if we could get the names of any other women who Stick might have provided to Dixon. Or at least any who would be willing to talk."

"I can't."

"You can't because there aren't any, or because there were others but you don't know their names, or because you're not interested in trying to help us out?"

Boo looked at Kristin with a 'so-that's-the-way-we're-going-to-play-this' expression and shrugged her shoulders.

"I can't because if Stick knew I gave you names, those women would likely end up dead."

Kristin's anger toward her client dropped a couple of degrees at her display of concern for other women.

"Are you concerned for your own safety?"

Boo all but laughed out loud at Kristin's question.

"You seriously need to ask me that? To be honest, I'm amazed I'm still around to be having this little chat with you. I already had some brain dead chick threaten me in here to keep my damn mouth shut. Who do you think gave her that message? That's why I'm wanting to have this trial as soon as possible, otherwise I might not live long enough to be around for it."

Boo didn't seem scared about her situation; instead, she looked tired, or simply resigned to her fate, as if death wasn't all that bad of an outcome if it got her out of this life. At the same time, Kristin could already tell Boo was a fighter. She just didn't seem to believe this was a fight she could win.

"One thing you have in your favor," Kristin said, "is Stick knows you didn't have to give up his name for me to make the connection. He knows I'd recognize you from my apartment."

Boo sat up a little straighter, ready for a fight.

"I can't keep apologizing for what I did," Boo snapped.

"I didn't ask for an apology. But on a side note, you haven't apologized at all, so you're not exactly at risk of having to say you're sorry too often."

"I haven't apologized because Stick made me. It's not like I woke up and decided to turn your life upside down because I didn't like you. I did it because if I didn't, he would have cut me. Where I live, it's every person for themselves."

"That's not true."

"Probably not where you come from," Boo said, "but a lot of women don't have your life."

"I say it's not true because you said you wouldn't give me the names of other women because it put them at risk. If you believed in every woman for herself, you would have given me names."

Boo started to respond, then paused. "In that case," she finally said, "you know what? I'm sorry. Okay? I'm sorry your perfect little life had to be exposed to this sort of ugliness. You dealt with Stick for five whole minutes, but that has been my life for the past couple of years. And the other women whose names you want me to give, some of them have lived with that longer than me."

"We could keep what they tell us confidential."

Boo sighed. "There's nothing confidential when it comes to Stick. He'd be able to smell it on them the next time he saw them. He can tell them what they dreamt the previous night. There's no secrets with him. He knows. He just knows."

Kristin closed her iPad and gathered her things. She paused and looked at Boo.

"Can I ask you something?"

"You're going to ask me whatever it is you want

anyway, so go ahead."

Kristin looked at her for a long moment before asking the question she'd wanted to ask all along.

"Instead of shooting Dixon, why didn't you shoot Stick?"

Boo nodded slowly, the hint of a smile appearing on her face, but the smile quickly disappeared as she answered.

"Because I'm convinced you can't kill that son-of-a-bitch. I swear he's not human. There are well-adjusted humans, screwed up humans, totally fucked up humans, and then there's Stick. He's like those killers from the slasher movies. You can shoot 'em, stab 'em, take a flame thrower to 'em, but they just keep on coming. But I understand why you asked the question. And, looking back, I'm thinking I should have at least tried."

"I sure wish you had," Kristin said, before smiling. Boo chuckled, then the two women sat in silence for a long moment.

While Kristin truly did wish Boo had shot Stick, at the same time she recognized that that simply would have made Kristin's life easier. She wasn't taking action against Stick either. She could have filed a complaint against him for breaking into her apartment and threatening her, but she knew that would have only made him mad. Instead, she sat there wishing someone else had shot him dead.

Kristin called for the guard who came to escort Boo back to her cell. When Boo stood, she stopped and turned back to Kristin.

"I am sorry. I'm sorry you had to go through what you did. Nobody should have to experience that."

As Boo turned and walked out of the room with the

guard, Kristin knew she was now all in when it came to trying to help her client.

22

Rita McCoy answered the door seconds after Thane knocked, as if she had been standing at the window, watching for his arrival. She ushered him into the house quicker than she had the first time he visited, when he came to talk with her after being released from prison for the murder of her daughter, Lauren.

She had been nervous during that conversation, at least at first. She had been used to seeing him as evil incarnate, as the man who had taken her daughter from her. But by the time he stopped by to talk, it had been proven he was innocent, which made her emotions all the more difficult to sort out.

As he did during his previous visit, Thane took a seat on the sofa while Rita sat across from him in a wingback chair. She couldn't have been older than mid-50's, but she looked at least 70. She also looked smaller. The loss of her daughter, followed by the death of her husband just a few months ago, had diminished her significantly.

"Mr. Banning," she finally said, "the last time we spoke, I told you I was concerned perhaps Russell had been involved in something bad. Something that weighed on him heavily as a man of faith."

"I remember."

"I thought he had finally had time to properly grieve our daughter's murder once the man who had killed her was dead. But earlier today, a Detective Struthers came to the house and confiscated Russell's computer. He also asked for his phone, but I had already donated that to an organization that helps the poor."

Rita looked at Thane as if hoping he would finally tell her what he was hiding from her, but when he didn't, she asked him directly.

"Mr. Banning, what is it I don't know?"

Thane understood her desire to know what had so bothered her husband, but he also knew for certain it would not help her to know that her husband had killed the two men who arranged and then carried out the death of their daughter. He also knew it definitely wouldn't help him for her to know.

"Mrs. McCoy, all I can tell you is Detective Struthers told me the other day that they have made some sort of connection between the man who killed Lauren, and my friend, Joseph Crowell. The detective asked me if I knew of the connection, which I did not. Given Joseph's murder, I'm sure the police are simply trying to figure out if they're related."

"But how does that involve Russell? I told you the last time we spoke that he was out the evening your friend was murdered. I told you I feared he had accidentally killed your friend, thinking it was you, but you told me that wasn't the case."

"And I still believe that. Your husband knew I was innocent. He had put aside any animosity he had for me, I promise you. He wouldn't have tried to kill me, which means no one would have been killed by accident."

"Then why did the detective take his computer?"

"I only know the police are very thorough in murder cases like this. Lauren had done business with Joseph. The detective is probably just checking to see if there had been any communication between your daughter and your husband that might give them a clue as to why she was killed. It doesn't mean your husband had anything to do with it."

"But he only used it for work."

"They're just being thorough, Mrs. McCoy. They have to see that for themselves. That's all."

Rita sat back in her chair and looked down at the carpet as if trying to work through this story to see if it made sense. Thane could tell it didn't totally ring true to her.

"Did you share your concerns about your husband with the detective?"

She didn't speak for a long moment, looking at Thane as if seeing him for the first time. "I didn't."

Thane didn't say anything but was glad to at least get that one sliver of good news.

"For a long time," Rita said, "I thought anger kept Russell going. Anger toward you, even after you were sent away for Lauren's murder. But after it came out that that Gruber person killed her and he was now dead, I thought Russell would have the chance to grieve properly, but it seemed as though something else weighed on him. Something holding him back."

Thane slid forward until he sat on the edge of the sofa cushion.

"I can't speak to what your husband felt, but I can tell you what it's been like for me." He paused, uncomfortable opening up to anyone, but he almost sensed a kinship with this woman and what she had gone through.

"When I got out of prison, I was angry. Angry that five years had been taken from me. Angry that everyone in the city assumed I only got out on a technicality and that I was still guilty. But then I not only proved my innocence, it also came out who had actually killed your daughter. And that man was now dead. I was therefore exonerated, justice was done, and the city even gave me quite a bit of money for my troubles, but my anger is still there. Of course I'm still going to resent having had that part of my life taken away from me, but I find I still want vengeance even though there is no vengeance left to be delivered. I'm still struggling to get back to the life I used to know, but maybe that's not realistic. All of this is to say that perhaps your husband experienced something similar. Maybe he, too, found it difficult to pick up and move beyond the anger. It doesn't mean he did anything bad. It may just mean that something bad happened to him, and he struggled to work through it."

Rita responded by simply looking at Thane with sympathy and nodding her head. He was glad she didn't start crying, because he didn't want to follow suit.

"Do you go to church, Mr. Banning?"

"No ma'am. Not in a long time."

"Perhaps you will consider giving it a try."

Thane didn't think so. At least not yet. The things he saw in prison caused him to lose any belief he once had in a God, although he also knew the miracle of his daughter's impending birth served as a strong counter point.

"Whether you go to church or not, Mr. Banning, I

will pray you are able to leave the anger behind."

"I'm trying, Mrs. McCoy. I'm trying."

He got up from the sofa, anxious to get away from this conversation. Rita rose and walked him to the door, but before he could open it, she put her hand on his arm.

"I appreciate your words, Mr. Banning. I would like to think everything is as simple as you say. And I'm sure I come across as the distraught housewife who needs to be calmed down and who has no idea what's going on, but Russell and I were married for thirty-six years, and I knew that man better than I know myself. I want to believe he was still only grieving the loss of our daughter, and I was ready to believe that. I decided what would help convince me was whether or not you asked me a certain question."

"What question was that?"

"Whether I had told the detective about my concerns regarding Russell. Why did you want to know that, Mr. Banning?"

Thane felt exposed, and struggled for an answer.

"Well, I guess I just thought..."

Rita squeezed his arm and shook her head.

"That's okay. You don't need to answer. And I don't plan on saying anything to the detective. I'll also continue to keep you in my prayers."

Thane was appreciative of her words, but didn't believe prayers were going to be enough.

23

Kristin neared the end of her tour of the Alpha Gamma sorority at the University of Los Angeles, and not a moment too soon. Feigning interest at the minutiae being covered in the tour exhausted her, as did forcing smiles at the inane humor offered by the sorority's president, Madison Monroe. Kristin wondered if the young woman's role as president was preordained, given her two names.

Kristin had been a member of Alpha Gamma at USC, so she had no problem setting up this time with the ULA chapter. As it turned out, they treated her like a celebrity, with young women along her tour shaking her hand and saying they were excited to meet her.

She found her reception ironic, given she didn't always feel like she fit in at her own sorority. Although a number of her sorority sisters were driven, they said on more than one occasion that Kristin was the alpha, in Alpha Gamma. She focused almost exclusively on her studies, while most of her sisters frequently went to parties.

She was grateful when Madison finally quit identifying the various online streaming services available at the sorority and led her back to the main living room. Kristin thought it sweet that Madison took such pride in the house, but most sorority houses were basically the same. Even so, this was Madison's house, and that made it special in the young woman's eyes.

"So that's the house!" Madison said. Almost every sentence she had said during the tour sounded as though it ended with an exclamation point. She beamed brightly as she directed Kristin to sit on a plush, paisley sofa with her.

"It's beautiful," Kristin replied, trying to match Madison's enthusiasm as much as possible, but she couldn't hit exclamation point levels.

"I hope you weren't uncomfortable with all of the girls coming up to meet you. A lot of us have followed your success in those trials, and to see an Alpha Gamma sister being interviewed on cable news and still being so young, well, we couldn't be prouder!"

Kristin's smile was more genuine this time. The important role she played in two very public trials so early in her career had exceeded her expectations, further evidence that focus and hard work had paid off.

"I have to confess, though," Madison said with furrowed eyebrows and a quieter voice to suggest confidentiality, "we were all a little disappointed to learn your firm is representing the young woman who killed Coach Dixon. But we also know defense attorneys don't always get to choose their clients. Sometimes you have to represent the guilty as well as the innocent."

Kristin thought it best not to tell Madison that they did, in fact, get to choose who they represented. Instead, she took advantage of the opportunity to pursue this topic.

"Oh, that's right," Kristin said, ready to see how reliable the Alpha Gamma grapevine was. "I understand this chapter of Alpha Gammas are great ambassadors for the football team."

Madison's face lit up like she'd just seen a unicorn eating a cupcake. "Ambassadors! I like that! That's exactly what we are! We cheer on the ULA Mustangs at every game. That's why the coach's murder shocked all of us." Madison looked down at the carpet as her lips quivered and tears began to form.

"I understand some of you were asked to escort top recruits around the campus," Kristin said, immediately regretting her choice of words. "I mean you helped them feel wanted and showed them some of the popular spots for students. I didn't mean 'escort' in the negative connotation. Poor choice of words on my part."

Whatever tears had been making their way to Madison's eyes were immediately turned off. She looked at Kristin with skepticism, as if trying to figure out if this sorority sister was friend or foe. Kristin sensed the young woman shouldn't come across quite as offended as she did, unless there was something that bothered her.

"A poor choice of words, indeed." She continued studying Kristin with frosty eyes. "We're sometimes asked to show recruits around, sure. We want them to see everything ULA has to offer, and to help get them to commit to our football team."

"Which is very important. I'm sure Coach Dixon greatly appreciated your help. And did he encourage any of you to do more than show these young men around?"

Madison sat up straighter in an attempt to be able to look down at Kristin.

"Coach Dixon was a good man, and committed to the team and to this school, as are many of us here at the house. We feel we play an important part in the team's success, and we take pride in that."

"I understand that, but did Coach Dixon ever…"

"Coach Dixon is dead! Killed by your client! I'm not going to judge what she did to make money. If she chose to have sex, then that was her choice, but if she decided she didn't want to have sex, she could have said no."

"Is that how things work here with the recruits?"

Kristin could see Madison trying to maintain her composure, but Kristen sensed that any affinity she had tried to develop with the house president was now in tatters.

"Coach didn't ask us to do anything with recruits we didn't want to do. He only wanted us to show them a good time."

"Was it understood what he meant by a good time, even if he didn't say it out loud?"

"Ms. Peterson, we are not whores like your client."

"Sounds to me like you are judging her after all."

"If I'm judging her, it's for the murder of Coach Dixon. We loved that man, and we love our team. But it sounds to me like you are judging us, and I resent that. I don't know what you've heard, but we are simply, as you said, ambassadors to our school. If any of the girls end up hitting it off with a recruit, then sure, things happen, but this is college. The same could happen with someone we meet at a bar."

"I'm sorry. I didn't mean to…"

"Oh, please. Of course you did. You totally meant to imply we prostitute ourselves to football recruits. You know, I talked to my counterpart at the USC chapter. She told me you had a reputation in their house for being too serious. For being too driven at the expense of making friends, which is an important part of being in a sorority. I should have known you weren't interested in touring a sister chapter. You're just here trying to help your whore client."

"Again," Kristin repeated softly in an attempt to lower the temperature of their conversation, "I'm sorry. I feel like my questions weren't worded as carefully as they could have been."

Madison looked at her watch, then stood. "I would think a lawyer would be better at how she worded questions, but regardless, I'm afraid I have a class to get to."

On the plus side, Kristin knew she now wouldn't have to suffer through a giddy hug goodbye. She grabbed her bag and walked to the front door. She turned to apologize one last time, but Madison was already stomping her way up the stairs.

Kristin walked out of the sorority and toward the campus parking garage. She knew she could have handled that better, but trying to giggle and fawn over Madison to get her to believe they were besties wasn't her style. She had to deal with young women like Madison for four years during college, and that was tiring enough. Still, she knew she should have been more willing to play the game if it would help Boo.

She reached the parking garage a couple of blocks from the sorority house when she heard someone call out to her.

"Ms. Peterson! Wait up!"

She turned to see a slender young woman wearing ripped jeans and carrying a backpack. She looked like a freshman, or a sophomore at most, and Kristin recognized her from the sorority.

As she neared, the woman looked back over her shoulder as if making sure no one was watching. She took deep breaths from apparently having run to catch up with Kristin.

"Can I talk with you for a minute?" she said between breaths.

"Of course. What's on your mind?"

The young woman looked around again. "Do you mind if we walk over here so that we're not standing next to the street?"

"Lead on."

Kristin followed her to a grassy spot between two lecture halls. They stood in the shade, a welcome respite from the sun. She also noted it was much more private.

"My name is Jules. I heard what you were asking Maddie. I don't know what you've been told by others, but I wanted to tell you it was probably accurate."

"Can you be more specific."

Jules again glanced around, but Kristin saw this as a tactic to buy some time to figure out what to say and what not to say. It looked like she hadn't realized her initial statement wasn't going to be enough for Kristin.

"Just that a number of girls do make themselves available to try to get prize recruits to come to ULA. And some of them also do whatever they can to keep star players happy so they don't even consider entering the transfer portal and going to another school."

"When you say 'whatever they can…'"

"Whatever the player wants. I mean, nobody is told outright they have to do this, and if one of the sisters feels like she doesn't want to do something with a recruit then they say that's her option, but that might end up costing them.”

“Costing them how?”

“The girls who get the best results get things like prize seating at the stadium, and they’re invited to socials with the athletes and other things. And one time one girl was flunking a class and Coach got the professor to adjust her grade. Scholarships are also in play.”

“Do you think Coach Dixon knew what the girls were doing?”

“Aware? My impression is he was the one coordinating it. Maybe not saying outright that the girls needed to have sex, but you can say something without coming out and saying it.”

“Do you know if the coach ever had sex with any of the sorority members?”

Jules blushed and even took a slight step back, as if distancing herself from the question would keep her from having to answer it. “I can’t say for sure, but I’ve heard rumors that a couple of the girls did things for him in his office. But again, no one has said that outright.”

Kristin paused for a moment and pretended to be processing all of this, but the fact of the matter was this was consistent with what she had been hearing through the grapevine. Mostly she paused to give Jules a chance to get a little more comfortable and to not feel pressured.

“You don’t have to answer this, but were you a part of the group who went out with recruits?”

Jules winced and shook her head before saying she had gone out with a five-star recruit several months ago. The guy immediately let it be known he wanted sex. He wasn’t even subtle about it. He said that the other schools he had gone to had made sure he got laid, and he expected that at ULA as well. Jules had turned him down and the player didn't react well. Not well at all.

She told Kristin bits and pieces of what happened afterward, a story that got Kristin's blood racing.

"If need be, would you be willing to testify in court about this?"

Jules glanced quickly side to side, as if getting ready to make a run for it, then exhaled deeply. Kristin could tell she regretted having run up to share her story.

"Would that be necessary?"

"I'm not sure, but I think it could be a big help, and our client needs all the help she can get."

Jules looked down at the grass for a long moment. "Is it true what the papers are reporting? About the things your client says the coach did to her?"

"I believe it's true, yes."

Jules finally nodded almost imperceptibly.

"I guess I'd testify. If it was important."

"Your sorority sisters wouldn't like it."

Jules nodded in agreement. "That's okay. I'm not planning on being there next semester anyway. It's not the sort of people I want to hang out with anymore."

24

Hannah walked out of the small conference room that had previously been a bedroom with only enough space for a double bed and a chest of drawers. That meant the conference table around which she and her team met also had to be small, but that wasn't a problem because administrative staffing at the shelter was sparse, at best.

As she made her way back to her office, she saw one of the shelter's clients sitting alone in the living room, staring vacantly out a nearby window. Hannah had been thinking quite a bit lately about the incident with Boo and the intimidating man who had tried to remove her from the shelter and had been waiting for an opportunity to talk with this woman who now sat alone.

"Hey, Sheila," she said, startling the young woman. "May I talk with you for a minute?"

Sheila looked up as if she wasn't used to being asked if someone could impose on her time. She nodded, appearing uncertain if that was the right answer.

"A couple of weeks ago, a man showed up and tried taking one of our guests out of the shelter."

As soon as she said this, Sheila looked down toward the floor, and Hannah knew her hunch was right.

"I remember you looked terrified at what was going

down, and me telling you to go back to your room, but as I look back on that afternoon, I get the feeling you knew that man."

Hannah paused, giving Sheila an opportunity to respond, but she said nothing, which to Hannah was the same as responding.

"Did you know the man who came to the shelter that day?"

Sheila still wouldn't lift her eyes from the floor, but eventually she nodded her head ever-so-slightly.

"Did you call him and tell him that that young woman was here?"

Sheila trembled like she was about to be struck.

"I'm sorry. I'm really sorry."

Hannah's heart sank. "You know the importance of keeping the location of our shelter a secret. It's the first rule we tell everyone when they come to stay here."

Sheila nodded, which shook loose some tears. "You gonna kick me out?"

Hannah usually made the judgement call as to whether or not a client was asked to leave the shelter. Often the decision was easy. Repeated drug use, breaking of curfew, stealing from other clients at the shelter. Revealing the shelter's location was another important rule, and Hannah couldn't recall a situation where one guest exposed another guest. That struck her as being an almost unforgiveable breach of trust, yet she tried keeping an open mind.

"I take it you knew the woman who had arrived that day?"

Again, Sheila nodded. "She and I were being pimped out by the same man. I've been trying to get out of that life, and I'd heard he was looking hard for Boo, so I figured if I told him where she was, he might let me go. You know, like he'd owe me a favor. But his idea of a favor is he won't kill you. And now he knows where I am, so he's keeping an eye on the place, waiting for me to leave. I ain't got no choice but to go back to him."

Suddenly the decision as to whether or not to kick Sheila out of the shelter became easier.

"Did you know what Boo had done?"

"You mean to that asshole football creep? I didn't know it at the time, but I heard about it later. I knew Stick wanted to find her. But Ms. Banning, I'm sick about what I done. I liked Boo. She never did nothing to me, and here I go and sell her out. I wish I'd never made that call. Even if I'd been allowed to walk away, I shouldn't have done what I done."

"Did you know about Coach Dixon? What he was like?"

Sheila all but shuddered. "All the girls knew. Boo wasn't the only girl who got sent to him. He just liked her the best. But nobody wanted to be sent to his house. That man was sick."

Hannah paused, not wanting to press things too quickly, but she also didn't know any other way to ease into what she wanted to ask.

"My husband is a lawyer, and he's going to try to help Boo. Would you be willing to talk with him?"

Sheila's eyes grew wide as if she saw her abuser standing in front of her.

"I'm not asking you to testify," Hannah quickly added. "And nobody would need to know you spoke with him. You could just provide him with some background information. Totally off the record."

Sheila appeared to consider, which was more than Hannah expected. She knew it was a big ask.

"Okay, I guess I can talk to him, but I can't go to court or even be seen talking to him. If I do, I'm dead. I mean that literally. As bad of a man as Dixon was, he was Mr. Rogers compared to my pimp."

"I appreciate it. I promise you won't be asked to do anything that will get you into trouble."

"I'm already in trouble. I can't hide out here much longer."

"I know of another shelter outside of L.A. that I can get you into if you want to go, but you have to promise me you'll never tell anyone where that shelter is located. I'm serious."

"I promise, Ms. Banning. I'm all torn up about what I done. I really am."

"I know. And I appreciate your willingness to talk with my husband. You're helping make things right."

Sheila nodded hopefully, but unconvincingly.

"But he don't know what he's up against with Stick," Sheila said in a low voice. "There ain't never been nobody like Stick. Well, 'cept maybe the Devil."

<h1 style="text-align:center">25</h1>

Gideon stood in what used to be the living room of an apartment that was probably on its fortieth generation of rats. The only pieces of furniture in the room were a couple of wooden folding chairs and a worn, plaid sofa that Gideon wouldn't have sat on for anything less than five hundred dollars. It looked like something even bed bugs would have avoided. The whole place smelled like a neglected gym bag.

A wiry man in his early twenties stood next to one of the wooden chairs that had several index cards and pens laying on it. He wore baggy shorts and a sleeveless t-shirt that might have been white when new, but was now the color of moldy bread. The man picked up a card and pen and handed it to Gideon.

"Here's how it works, my brother," the young man said as if he fancied himself a sales entrepreneur. "You write down what you lookin' for, and I write down the price."

Gideon looked at the guy like he was crazy.

"You worried about me being wired?" Gideon asked. "Do I look like a cop to you?"

"No you don't, my brother, but that's how they told me to do it here, so that's how I do it. Plus, it's good record keeping. I use these cards to track each girl's earnings."

The man loudly clapped his hands twice, as if summoning a genie. "Yo! We got us a customer. Let's move it!"

"Let me guess," Gideon said, "you then enter the information into one of them X-L spreadsheets and you do quarterly Power Point reports at corporate."

The man shrugged. "They tell me to do it this way, so I do it this way."

Down the hallway from the back of the apartment came five young women ranging between seventeen and forty, with an enthusiasm level ranging from 0 to 0.1. All of them wore flimsy nighties, and none of them made even the slightest effort to look alluring. One of them didn't even make an effort to look conscious. Only two of them made eye contact with Gideon, but they only seemed to be curious as to what the next piece-of-shit customer looked like. One of them took a slight step back, as if she saw Gideon as the kind of man who could get a little rough, which was true, but he never got rough with a woman. He saved that for men who got on his nerves.

The young man tried handing one of the index cards to Gideon, but he ignored the guy.

"I know it seems stupid, my brother, but it's how we do it."

Gideon turned to the guy, his patience running even thinner than it usually ran. "You got a mother named Mary?" he asked.

The guy looked at him, confused.

"It's a simple question. You got a mother named Mary?"

The guy shook his head no.

"How about your daddy? Was your daddy a drunken, no-good waste of breath asshole named Norval?"

"No."

"Then I don't see how we could be brothers, so quit calling me that."

The man eyed Gideon before again handing him the card.

"You want a girl or not? If not, then get your ass on out of here."

Gideon turned to the young women, one of whom unsuccessfully tried holding back a smile at Gideon standing up to their pimp. Gideon assumed she didn't get to smile often in that hellhole.

"What I want is information, and I'm willing to pay for it. I understand y'all are being run by a mongrel named Stick, and that sometimes he rents you out to men outside this apartment. I'm interested in finding out whether or not any of you ever did any business with that coach over at ULA."

"Hey, hey, hey!" The wiry man threw the index card and pen back on the chair and puffed out his chest in an effort to be at least half as big as Gideon. "Time to go, dude. Nobody answering none of your damn questions. Get the hell out of here."

Gideon ignored the man and continued focusing on the women. "Not looking to get any of you in trouble, and you wouldn't have to talk to no police. I'm just wanting…"

The young man held up his hand like a traffic cop and told the women to get on back to their room. They paused for a moment, then turned and headed down the hall.

Gideon wheeled back around toward the man, putting

one hand on the scrawny shoulder and another hand around the man's wrist, turning the wrist and squeezing the shoulder, immediately dropping the man to the floor.

"I wasn't done talking with them. Call 'em back."

"Let me go, you motherfu…"

"Call 'em back," Gideon said, twisting the arm a little further, causing the man to scream at an impressively high decibel.

"Come back! Come back!"

But the women were already returning to the living room, if for no other reason than to watch the show.

Gideon shoved the guy to the floor and pointed at him like he was a very bad dog.

"Stay," Gideon said, then he turned his attention back to the women. "Again, I want to know if any of you had any dealings with that Coach Dixon asshole. That's all I'm looking for."

The women looked down, with a couple of them glancing at the man still kneeling on the floor. He had shifted his glare from Gideon and now directed it solely at the women.

Gideon understood. He strode over to the guy, who shuffled backwards as if about to be kicked, but instead Gideon grabbed him by the scruff of his neck, pulled the man's phone from his pocket and tossed it onto the ratty sofa, then drug him over to a coat closet next to the front door. He opened the door and shoved the guy inside, once again pointing his finger at him.

"You come out of this closet, I'm going to break you in about a thousand places. Understand, my brother?" But it was a rhetorical question.

Gideon slammed the closet door, thinking Thane

would be proud of him for not actually having hurt the guy. He was learning how to be a responsible member of society and not immediately resorting to violence to solve everything. As long as the closet door didn't open, he would handle this like any other civilized man.

"Okay, so does any of you know anything about girls being rented out to the coach who got himself killed? I'm trying to help the woman who killed him, and all I'm wanting to know is if Stick sent other women over there, or if she was the only one."

The women still didn't say anything. Gideon wondered if any of them ever spoke, but then he saw a couple of them glancing at the others.

"Lookit, I don't have time to talk with y'all individually, but I'm guessing you don't trust that one of you won't rat out the others."

Despite his effort to not have anger be his default, Gideon's patience continued to wane. He then looked down at the notecards and grabbed a card and pen for each of the women and handed them out.

"Here's the deal: I want each of you to write something on your card. If you know don't nothin', write down 'I don't know nothin' three times on your card. But if you do know anything that might help, I'd appreciate it if you wrote it down. You don't need to include your name. I'm just trying to get a sense of whether Stick was a steady supplier of women to this guy or not. And since everyone will be writing something on the card, no one will know if you helped me out or not. Got it?"

Three of the women put a little space between them and the other women and began writing on their cards.

A fourth woman quickly joined in, with the fifth only joining them after seeing Gideon scowl at her.

When the women were done, Gideon took the cards and scanned them quickly. Two of the cards had the words 'I don't know nothing' written on them, and another card asked Gideon to please, please, please beat the shit out of the guy in the closet. Two other cards each said they had been sent to service the football team's strength coach, with each card giving a similar spelling of the guy's name.

Gideon nodded. "Thank you, ladies. Pleasure doing business with you." He moved toward the door, then turned back to the women.

"Any of you want to get the hell out of this place? I get it that Stick's a bad man, but I'm also a bad man willing to help you. If any of you got family you can go to, or I also know of a shelter that could help you, now's your chance."

None of the women moved, which didn't surprise Gideon. Repercussions could be fierce in this business. But as he turned once again to leave, he heard one of the women speak in a quiet voice.

"I'll come."

Gideon turned and saw that the youngest woman had half-raised her hand. One of the older women glared at her and shook her head.

"Stick's gonna hurt you bad."

The girl put down her hand and looked at Gideon to hear his response.

"I'll drive you someplace safe if you want to get out of here."

The young woman thought about it, nodded, and stepped toward Gideon. When they reached the door,

Gideon walked back to the chair and grabbed a jacket whose owner, he assumed, remained in the closet. He put the jacket over the young woman in the nightie, then wedged the chair against the closet door before exiting the apartment.

Gideon pulled the young woman quickly into the stairwell rather than wait for the elevator. He assumed the guy in the apartment had a gun stashed somewhere, and while he hoped the women wouldn't run over to let him out right away, he didn't want to hang out in the apartment building hallway.

As they quickly made their way down the stairs, Gideon asked, "You one of the women who wrote a name on your card?"

She shook her head. "I would have if I'd known anything. Will you still help me, though?"

"Course I'm going to help you. If you don't have somewhere safe to go, I can drive you to that shelter I was talking about up there. A nice woman runs it and she'll do right by you."

They continued down the stairs until exiting out the side of the apartment building. He looked down at the young woman and patted her on the shoulder.

"You made the right decision, my sister."

She looked up at Gideon and gave him her biggest smile yet.

26

As soon as Thane and Gideon slid into a booth near the back of the diner, Gideon brought out his small collection of notecards and handed them to Thane, who read the first one aloud.

"I don't know nothing. I don't know nothing. I don't know nothing." Thane nodded slowly, as if absorbing this new evidence. "I see now why you wanted to meet. I do believe you've cracked the case."

Before Gideon could emit a solid growl, Alice appeared at the booth with her order pad out. Gideon looked up at her and offered a small smile.

"What can I get you boys tonight?"

"Just coffee for me, thanks," Thane said.

"Same," Gideon said. "Thanks, Alice."

"Just coffee? Aw, come on, Shep, how about I bring you a piece of pie? On the house."

Gideon glanced over at Thane whose eyebrows were raised, then looked back up at Alice. "Appreciate it, but I think I'm sticking with just coffee for now."

"You change your mind, you let me know." She turned and walked back to the front counter.

"Shep?" Thane asked.

Gideon shook his head and pointed at the notecards,

but again Thane asked, "Shep?"

Gideon sighed. "She said I remind her of an old German Shepherd she used to have. She said it was all bark and no bite."

"She's obviously never seen you bite anyone."

Gideon again pointed at the cards. "Now, regarding these…"

"Okay, Sh…"

"And if you even think of calling me Shep again, that's the point at which your life will end. Got it?"

"Of course. No need to bite my head off. Or do you bite?"

"I don't care if we're friends or not, I swear to god I'll break off your arm and use it to unclog my toilet."

"That was strangely specific," Thane said, smiling. "You really do have a strong bark, don't you?" He knew he was living on the edge but couldn't resist.

Gideon's mouth clenched. "I'm telling ya, I'm gonna…"

Alice appeared and set the coffees in front of them. She smiled at Gideon before walking away. Thane looked wistfully as she left. "I wouldn't have minded a free piece of pie."

"Yeah, well you don't deserve one because you can be a jerk. Now, back to the cards. Ignore the ones that say I don't know anything."

"You sure? They seem relevant."

Gideon glared at Thane until he returned his attention back to the cards. Thane flipped through the other cards until he came across the two that had a name written on them.

"Morris Westlake. Who's that?"

"Finally," Gideon said. "Two of them girls at the

apartment wrote down the same name. Like one of them cards says, the guy paid for their services."

Thane looked at one of the cards again. "What's a 'string coach'?"

"It's strength coach. Her penmanship is worse than mine."

"No need to insult the young woman."

"I looked him up on the computer. He's the strength coach for the ULA football team, so apparently the head coach wasn't the only one taking advantage of Stick's 'dick door dash' service."

Thane looked at the two cards again. This was, in fact, a good find. And if there were now two men from the team who paid for sex, there were likely others. And even if there weren't, having one of them still alive could be helpful. If nothing else, it might provide further pressure on the University to offer an even better plea deal. He understood technically it would be the D.A.'s office who offered it, but he had no doubt the University was the one calling the shots.

"This is good," Thane said. "You didn't break anything or hurt anyone while getting this, did you?"

"Only thing got hurt was the pimp's pride."

"Look at you, being all diplomatic." Thane was happy to hear Gideon didn't cause any damage. He knew Stick had to already be on high alert and looking for any provocation to strike back. Odds are this would make him angry, but at least it wasn't as sure of a bet as if blood had been drawn."

As Gideon took a sip of coffee, his peripheral vision took in something.

"Don't want to ruin your coffee, but it's possible we got company outside."

Prior to his time in prison, Thane would have immediately turned and looked outside, but instead he now barely moved his head until he could see four large college-age men hanging around his car, with a steroid-filled man in his 40's standing next to them. They were obviously waiting for them.

"Looks like it's meet-the-team night." Thane said.

"Goodie. Maybe I can get me a couple autographs."

Thane nodded, calmly. "Would you pass the sugar, please?"

Gideon passed him a few packets of sugar.

As they walked out of the diner and toward Thane's car, the five men straightened up and threw their shoulders back, trying to make themselves look as intimidating as possible which didn't seem necessary since the smallest one looked 6'4" and had to weigh at least 260 pounds. The others probably nicknamed him Tiny. It looked as though the older guy had brought ULA's offensive linemen with him.

Thane and Gideon, unimpressed, stopped in front of the puffed-up young men.

"Don't you guys have a curfew?" Thane asked jovially.

The supposed adult of the group spoke while the players continued trying to come across as threatening to Thane and Gideon with their glares, which may have concerned normal people, but meant absolutely nothing to ex-cons.

"We're here to deliver a message, and to make sure it's received loud and clear, got it? Quit asking questions about Coach Dixon. He was a good man and doesn't deserve having scum like you trying to dig up dirt about him."

Thane looked at the man and nodded. "Okay."

He moved toward his car, but one of the young men stepped in front of him. Thane sighed.

"What, you need me to sign some sort of notarized statement saying I received your message loud and clear? I got it." He turned to Gideon. "Did you get it?"

"Loud and clear," Gideon said.

"So there you go. Job well done on your part. Feel free to take the rest of the night off."

A couple of the players glanced over at the man who had been doing the talking, as if they had expected a confrontation.

"No," the man said, "I'm saying it's up to you as to how strongly we deliver the message, because trust me, we can deliver it extra strong."

"No need," Thane said. "You are telling us to quit asking questions about Coach Dixon. Message received. Thank you very much."

Again, Thane tried stepping around the slab of beef standing between him and his car, but again, the slab moved to keep in front of him. Thane could hear Gideon start to emit a soft growl. He resisted the temptation to say 'down, Shep.'

"Listen, guys, it's getting late, and I'm tired. I'm willing to do a pinkie promise if that will help you believe me when I say I got your message."

"That mean you're going to back off on Coach?"

"Oh hell, no," Gideon said, as if he couldn't believe anyone could ask such a stupid question.

"Yeah," Thane concurred. "I just meant we got the message. But no, beyond that, we're going to do what we need to do."

"Then I guess we need to do what we need to do," the man said.

"Thank God," Gideon said, "because to be honest, all this yapping is starting to bore the living shit out of me."

"But before you start showing us how tough you are," Thane said, standing with his hands in his pants front pockets, "I want to state for the record that at least a couple of you will be sidelined for the rest of the season if you see this through, so don't be whining about that when it's all said and done."

The young man standing in front of Thane stepped even closer to him, blocking the streetlight like an eclipse. In prison, you'd never step that close to someone you were trying to hurt unless you were already in mid-punch.

"I'm assuming you use your arms a lot in your position?" Thane asked.

The sasquatch glanced at his arms, then back at Thane.

"Whaddya mean?"

"What do you mean, 'whaddya mean?' Do you use your arms a lot when you're playing football? Would you be sidelined if your arm was broken at your shoulder?"

The kid actually seemed to be giving this some thought when Thane brought his hands out of his pocket and threw a handful of sugar into the kid's eyes, then grabbed one of the kid's large wrists with one hand and twisted the arm so the player had no leverage, then Thane grabbed hold of the upper arm with his free hand and bent it backward until he found strong resistance.

The kid screamed, in part because of his burning eyes, but also because Thane was half a twist away from dislocating his arm.

The player standing closest to them started to move, but Gideon dropped him with a couple of solid punches in the gut. The other players advanced forward, but Thane put more pressure on the arm, making the kid scream louder.

"You guys come any closer and I'll break his arm."

"Stay back," the kid cried. "Let me go, man."

"You threw something in his eyes. That's not fair," one of the players hollered.

"Aw," Gideon said, "you want to throw a penalty flag for unnecessary roughness? We ain't even begun to get rough."

Thane turned toward the man who had delivered the message. "You want to explain to the new head coach why he lost two or three players for the season in one night? If not, consider your message delivered, and consider your message ignored. Now I'm going to let this kid go, but if you all don't say nighty-night and walk away, there will be no more talking."

Thane pushed the player he was holding to the ground. Gideon stepped closer to Thane and showed the rest of the team what true intimidation looked like.

"You're Morris Westlake, ain't you?" Gideon said. "I seen your picture on your football website." A couple of the players looked over at Westlake, surprised. Gideon turned to the players. "Your strength coach is watching out for himself here, given that he's also been taking advantage of the same pool of hookers as your coach was."

Westlake looked like he wanted to see this through, but a couple of the players stepped back after looking at Gideon and Thane.

The kid on the ground continued yelling and rubbing

his eyes. "Give me something to wash this shit out!"

One of the players brought out a flask and poured some liquid into the kid's eyes, which only made him scream louder. He began pawing his eyes desperately as Westlake ran over to him and took out a handkerchief and started rubbing the sugar out of the kid's eyes.

"What the hell you got in there?" Westlake asked the player with the flask.

"Whiskey," the kid said, sheepishly.

The players finally helped their teammate up and made their way down the sidewalk. Westlake looked back over his shoulder and tried sending one more message to them, a glare as impotent as his first.

As they watched the defeated team leave the field, Alice appeared next to Gideon and handed him a small Styrofoam container. "You're getting some pie whether you want it or not. That was impressive." She smiled at Gideon, then turned and went back into the diner.

"Why'd you get the pie?" Thane asked. "I was the one with the cool move."

"She probably thought you cheated, using the sugar."

"You're the one taught me there's no such thing as cheating in a brawl."

"Yeah, but she never did time with me, so she didn't know that."

"You didn't even want pie. I'm the one who wanted some pie."

Gideon opened the container and inhaled about half of the piece of pie with one bite. He smacked his lips and nodded enthusiastically.

"This is one damn good piece of pie."

Thane shook his head. "That is so not fair."

27

Assistant District Attorney Arthur Barnes poured Thane a glass of water from a non-descript pitcher that sat in the middle of the conference table in Barnes' office.

"I'm afraid you'll have to settle for tap water, given our city budget. I'm assuming at your private practice—also funded by our taxpayers—you use Perrier water even when making coffee."

"Actually, we use champagne," Thane said as he accepted the glass. "Gives the coffee a bit of a kick."

Barnes didn't smile. A rotund man in his mid-50's, Barnes was the prosecuting attorney for the Cash Dixon murder trial. Even though he had to have been making a good salary, his suit and tie looked like they came from the bargain rack at JCPenney, and several years ago at that. He had a formal air about him, sitting up straight at the table, his shoulders thrown back and his chin slightly raised as if ready to take on an inevitable insult. Thane couldn't imagine the man sitting around his backyard having a beer with neighbors.

"I realize the last two men from this office who went up against you are no longer here," Barnes said. "Stone, for obvious reasons, barely had the chance to clean out his office. And Barry Warlick retired after the two of you tangled. I believe he had planned to retire anyway, although I'm sure it came about a lot quicker than he had expected."

"I'm hopeful any animosity you may have about the past won't impact our dealings with the Dixon case."

"Actually I don't hold any animosity at all. I wasn't part of Stone's inner circle and didn't have a great deal of respect for him. I believed he played a little too loose with the rules from time to time, as you know better than most, although please believe me when I say I didn't realize how loose he played with them. Totally unforgiveable. Plus, I'm a devout Christian, and for whatever reason, that seemed to make Stone and some of his lackeys uncomfortable. Maybe they thought my morals might be a problem for them, but apparently those morals worked out just fine for me. As for Warlick, well, he was another Stone sycophant who got sloppy. So no, I don't harbor any hard feelings toward you. In a lot of ways, you did me a favor. When I referenced those two men, my point is that you're dealing with someone different now."

"How so?" Thane asked.

"Honest."

Thane nodded. That was his goal as well this time around. And hopefully not having to fight corruption with corruption would help him get back to practicing law the right way.

"I'm also a straight shooter," Barnes said, "which is why I wanted to talk with you this afternoon. "If this goes to court, I'll be seeking the maximum penalty—which, for all practical purposes, is life." If I was doing this solely for the publicity, I'd ask for the death penalty, but you and I both know it's been almost twenty years since California executed anyone. Plus, as a Christian man, I don't believe in killing another human being, so your client is looking at spending the rest of her life in prison."

"You don't see extenuating circumstances?"

"You mean going to his house and taking money for having sex, then being paid for said sex? It's not rape when the woman takes money for it upfront, that's consensual. If things did get out of control and she killed him to stop him, then we could talk, but it was over, and she had the ability to leave."

"Take the money and run," Thane said.

"No, take the money and report the crime. If Coach Dixon did cross any lines—and I'm skeptical he did—your client should have called the police. I have absolutely no tolerance for the vigilante justice that seems to be sweeping this country. Shooting another human being because they came onto someone's property or knocked on the wrong door. People shooting other people because they didn't look like they belonged there. All these 'stand your ground' laws that make people act like they have the right to kill someone else makes me want to puke. If you're truly at risk of being seriously hurt, then of course you can defend yourself. But if a person is no longer being threatened, shooting the other person isn't justice, it's vengeance. Just call the police. How hard is that?"

"When you're being pimped out by someone known to kill the women he sells for the slightest infraction, I can see where that might be hard. But let me guess: your answer is to call the police on the pimp, too."

Barnes sighed and shook his head. "I'm not saying it's all black and white. I'm simply saying killing another person is not the answer, although if she had killed her pimp instead, we'd have far more to talk about in terms of length of sentence."

"So taking someone's life is bad, but there are degrees of badness," Thane observed.

"You know as well as I do there are. Coach Dixon shaped more young men's lives in a positive way during his lifetime than your client could in a thousand years. You peddle in sin, you have a lot more to worry about than our justice system."

"That would be a good slogan for your campaign. Or at least the word on the street is you're going to be announcing your candidacy for District Attorney soon."

"I have not made a decision either way."

"That sounds like a textbook response from a politician."

"Any future plans that I may or may not have will not impact this trial. If I decide to put away your client for the rest of her life, it won't be because you think I'm running for District Attorney."

"Then it sounds like a plea deal is off the table. That's what I wanted to know."

Thane slid his chair back when Barnes held up his hand.

"On the contrary. If your client pleads guilty, I will ask for a sentence of no longer than twelve years. Anything less than that is simply not viable, given the Coach's popularity."

The offer stunned Thane. He would have been surprised by anything under twenty-five years, but twelve? If taken, Boo would be out of prison in her mid-thirties, a far cry from spending the next 50 – 60 years behind bars.

"Given your disdain for my client's alleged action, I'd like to better understand this surprising plea deal. Are there any other conditions to this offer?"

"To be honest, I'm surprised you'd want to understand anything other than how quickly you could get something signed. But there is one stipulation. Your client will need to sign an NDA to not talk to anyone about the case or anything she claims was done to her. If she does, the offer will be rescinded immediately."

It now made more sense to Thane. If Barnes ran for District Attorney, offering such a light sentence for the murder of a beloved public figure wasn't the way to do it. But if he had the backing of the University, fundraising and public support could get a whole lot easier. ULA was clearly playing a major role in these negotiations. Men like Sterling Silver wanted nothing more than to keep the tawdry details out of the press.

"I'll talk to my client about your offer."

"You know as well as I do that this is an exceptionally generous plea deal. I can't believe you wouldn't agree to it in principle right now."

"And you know as well as I do that my client is the one who needs to agree to it."

"I also know she will likely do what you recommend. So fine, you obviously can't commit to the deal right now, but I'd like to know if it will be your recommendation that your client take it. If I were you, I wouldn't look a gift horse in the mouth."

"If the Trojans had looked their gift horse in the mouth, there would have been more Trojans running around. But if it helps you feel better, I agree that it's a very favorable offer."

Thane left his meeting with Barnes feeling encouraged. Never would he have imagined he would be able to get his client a plea deal as low as that. The judge would also have to agree to it, but he assumed the University's influence extended that far as well.

And if twelve years was the initial offer, maybe Thane could get an even lighter sentence, although he didn't want to get greedy. Given the popularity of Coach Dixon, Barnes could only go so low in his offer before it became politically damaging. Still, if Thane could get his hands on evidence that further exposed Dixon, perhaps the University would be even more motivated to avoid a trial.

As Thane left the office building, he saw District Attorney Day walking toward him.

"Good afternoon," Thane said. "I just got done talking to one of your colleagues."

"Arthur, I'm assuming."

"You assume correctly. The Dixon case."

"Is there any other?" she said, laughing. Thane knew that a case of this magnitude had to be taking up the majority of the oxygen in her department.

"I'm sure you're aware of the plea deal being offered."

"Of course. I am, you know, the District Attorney. That's kind of part of my job description."

"Given the generous nature of the deal being offered, I appreciate the recognition of the heinous extenuating circumstances surrounding Dixon's murder."

"I'm not sure we're acknowledging that, but it does seem to be a good deal for your client."

"But personally, you have to be disgusted by Dixon's actions, and the ability of men in power like that being able to get away with that sort of behavior."

"Well, given that he's dead, I'd hardly say he got away with it."

"But we have no problem going after the women who…"

Day raised her hand to stop him. "I've assigned this case to Arthur, and I'm going to let him try it his way. As with most things in life, there are politics involved, and I feel it's best to let him run with this."

"I understand he may be running for your job. How about you? I'm hopeful I'll soon be reading you're running as well so we can get the term 'interim' removed from your title."

"I have not made…"

"…a decision either way," Thane finished her sentence for her. "Yes, I understand. But for whatever it's worth, I hope you do. You're exactly what this department needs."

Day didn't acknowledge his words of support, but he guessed they meant something to her. In the District Attorney's office, being a black woman made her a double minority. After Richard Stone resigned once Thane had exposed his tactics in court, the mayor appointed Angela Day as the interim District Attorney. He shored up support from the progressive side of his base by appointing a black woman, but once he was re-elected, he called for a special election scheduled to take place in five months.

"I'm hopeful you and Arthur will have a better working relationship than your last two previous encounters with this office," Day said.

"It couldn't be any worse, could it?

28

"Seriously?" Kristin exclaimed. "Out in twelve? That's unbelievable!"

Neither Gideon nor Letitia said anything, but Thane could tell everyone was surprised, if not suspicious, that this was a trick.

"That's desperation," Thane said. "ULA is raising a ton of money off Dixon's death, and a lot of that will dry up if people start hearing more about the man."

"She'll take it, won't she?" Kristin closed her iPad as if there wasn't anything else to talk about regarding the case now that there was such a good plea agreement.

"I'm speaking with her in an hour. I'd be surprised if she doesn't jump on this, but it's hard to say for sure. It's easier to decide for someone else that they should agree to go to prison for twelve years. Harder when it's you."

"Yeah, but if you're not even claiming you're innocent, twelve is a hell of a lot shorter than twenty-five or thirty."

"I still want us to keep working on this until it's over. The more we learn about Dixon, perhaps the sweeter the plea offer will be. So, on that note, does anyone have any updates?"

Letitia opened a manila folder and placed six pieces of paper in the center of the table.

"Police reports for six different traffic stops involving Dixon. No charges were filed on any of these. They're only the initial stops and conversations the cops had with Dixon. None of them went anywhere, though."

Thane read one report about a car being pulled over for suspicion of drunk driving, but the driver was determined to be under the limit.

"I don't see Dixon's name anywhere on this."

"No," Letitia said, "but it's his license plate and his driver's license number. It's not a given it's him, but the odds are about 99%."

"Good work getting these."

Letitia looked at Thane, surprised. "I didn't do anything. They were under the door this morning when I opened up. I figured that public defender woman you worked with on my brother's case left them for you. Did she not say anything about it?"

Thane studied a couple of the other documents. They didn't look like the sort of thing Sheri could have gotten her hands on, since charges weren't brought. They looked more like the fruits of a successful hacking effort by a fifth-grade computer prodigy.

Thane adjourned the meeting. He needed to get to the jail and give Boo what he hoped would be an easy sell.

Following their team meeting, Kristin waited until Gideon returned to his office. She gave him a minute to do whatever he did following a team meeting—she guessed it wasn't much—before knocking on his door, realizing as she knocked that she hadn't ever gone into his office before. She had certainly smelled it on numerous occasions as she walked past, but had never ventured in. Fortunately, he almost always kept his door closed, whether he was in there or not.

"Yeah?" Gideon said from inside the office.

Kristin opened the door partway and leaned in. "Mind if I come in?"

Gideon appeared to be puzzled by this question, as if it may be some sort of trick, then he waved her in. His office sported a collection of fast-food bags, wrappers and humungous Styrofoam cups stuffed with what appeared to be empty french fry boxes.

Even though it was only 9:00 a.m., the smell of fast food was so heavy she felt she could have tasted it had she stuck her tongue out. It smelled like he used a french-fry scented air freshener.

Gideon rose and took his jacket off the only other chair in the office, using his jacket to dust off the seat cushion before returning to his own seat. Kristin glanced carefully at the seat cushion before sitting.

"It's sort of like sitting next to a fast-food grease fryer," Kristin observed, but Gideon didn't respond. "I might have to get my cholesterol checked after we talk."

"I spent twenty-two years locked up. I gotta be honest with you, cholesterol ain't a big concern of mine."

While Kristin didn't totally agree with that philosophy, she had to admit she wasn't in a position to judge.

"But I'm guessing you didn't stop by to comment on my eating habits, although with you, who knows?"

Kristin rarely was uncomfortable speaking her mind, but she found herself struggling to find the right words.

She decided to quit trying to say it exactly right and just put something out there. She figured Gideon would appreciate her being direct.

"I wanted to know if you could teach me self-defense," she finally said. "Just a few things. I took a couple self-defense classes in college, but that was a while ago. Plus, I'm sure you know some things the instructor didn't."

Gideon didn't laugh or give her a hard time, which she greatly appreciated. In fact, he appeared to be sizing her up as if he understood exactly what she needed.

"I just figured it never hurts to keep up-to-date on..."

"This about Stick?"

She paused, but of course they both knew it was about Stick. So many things lately seemed to be about Stick. She nodded.

Gideon continued studying her, then leaned forward on his chair.

"Don't take this the wrong way," he finally said, "because I know you're a force of nature in a lot of areas in your life, but the idea of someone like you being able to put someone like Stick down with a karate move or a well-placed kick is a fantasy. I'm sure those self-defense classes can teach you something, but when you're talking about someone like Stick, they ain't going to do shit for you."

Kristin wanted to get angry at Gideon, but she knew he was speaking the truth.

"I taught Thane a few things when he got to Forsman, but it took him two or three years before he could handle himself against most anyone in there. I'll be honest, he surprised the hell out of me, but he had the advantage of being driven by anger."

"I'm angry," Kristin said softly. "I'm really angry."

That appeared to stop Gideon for a moment. His voice also turned softer.

"I know you are. I can see it, and it bugs the living shit out of me because I want to be able to help you, but I'm sort of at a loss." He leaned back in his chair and looked down at the carpet before looking back up at her. "Listen, if you find yourself in a scrape with someone again, best advice I can tell you is go for the eyes. Sometimes people don't do that because they think that's not fighting fair, but if someone is coming at you, then you gotta turn into an animal, and I don't mean like a dog; I mean like a damn rabid bear. And I'm not talking about poking someone in the eyes like you're one of them Three Stooges. You get your fingernails into the eye sockets, dig as deep as you can, but once you blind him, you jump away, cause his hands will still be working. And of course there's always the well-placed foot between the legs, but that's not always as easy as it looks in the movies. A lot easier, though, if they can't see anything."

Kristin pictured trying to claw out Stick's eyes and was confident she'd have no problem going in deep. Whatever it took to incapacitate him, she would do it.

As if reading her mind, Gideon continued. "Want my real advice? Get a gun. Get a gun and keep it with you at all times where you can easily get to it and if you see Stick even looking at you wrong, you shoot him dead right there on the spot."

Kristin offered up a small laugh and smiled at Gideon.

"You think I'm kidding, but I ain't. I'm sure you're one of them anti-gun people, but in this case, you oughta make an exception. You see Stick leaning against your car, or walking down the street toward you, or knocking on your apartment door, you take your gun out and shoot him. Aim for the chest and fire at least three shots. Don't wait for him to do nothing. Shoot him dead. Tell the police he was attacking you and there ain't a single cop going to charge a young, professional, white, blonde woman, not when it comes to someone like Stick. Hell, they'd probably give you a medal."

Kristin thought Gideon was right. Well, not about the medal, but someone who looked like her could shoot someone with Stick's reputation and the odds were there would be no charges. Sort of ironic, given Boo's arrest for doing that exact same thing.

Gideon also guessed correctly about her position on guns. A couple of months ago, she couldn't imagine owning a gun, let alone being willing to shoot someone with it, but she had bought herself a Glock G19 a couple of weeks ago and had already spent a couple days on the shooting range. She had also applied for a concealed weapons permit, but she wasn't waiting for the permit to come through before carrying it in her purse.

"I appreciate the advice," she said. "And if you think of anything else, please let me know."

She started to stand, but then paused and sat back down. Again, the words weren't coming easily to her.

"What's on your mind?" Gideon asked. "You wondering if you should also put a couple of shots in the back of Stick's head? Probably not a bad idea."

What was on her mind was something she'd been struggling with ever since Stick had walked out of her apartment building.

"How does someone like that exist?" she asked, truly

wondering. "I mean, is he just wired differently, or is he missing something most humans have? Where does that sort of evil come from?"

Kristin figured Gideon would simply offer up a shrug of his shoulders or say something glib, but to his credit he seemed to at least try to answer.

"There are lots of people out there like that. Not many as bad as Stick, but he ain't alone. People who live in the kind of world you do usually aren't exposed to too many of them except through the news, but they're out there. Hell, lot of people likely think I'm one of them."

"You aren't anything like Stick."

"Yeah, but you don't know me all that well."

"I feel like I've got a pretty good understanding of you."

"Sorry, kid, but I'm guessing your assessment of me is going to have a lot of stereotypes in it."

Kristin looked at him and tried to truly take him in. She knew studying him made Gideon a little uncomfortable.

"Okay, here's my assessment of you. You're someone with an anger problem. You've had bad things happen to you when you were younger, and you never learned how to deal with them. You can be violent, and you can be dangerous, and I'm betting the stereotype you're talking about is that of a big, gruff man who actually has a heart of gold, but I believe some of that is true, even if you don't believe it yourself. You helped Thane when he was in prison. I saw how you were around your sister Pearl and when we were helping Gus, and when you went to confront Stick after he threatened me. You don't like bullies, and you don't like to bully anyone, especially anyone weaker than you. I think the biggest difference between you and Stick is you want to be good, whereas someone like Stick has no interest in that. You aren't quite sure how to fit into regular society, but you're starting to suspect there are other tools for fixing problems besides your fists. But you're not ever going to convince me that you're not a kind person. You just need to work on your anger." She glanced around the room and inhaled a deep breath. "And cut down on your cholesterol."

She expected Gideon to wave off her assessment, or to make a cynical comment about her description of him, but instead he looked at her with a surprised expression on his face.

"Thanks again for your suggestions," Kristin said as she once again stood and headed for the door.

"Hey, hold up." Now it appeared to be his turn to struggle for the right words.

"Since you asked for my advice on something, let me ask you something, and I'd appreciate it if you didn't laugh." He paused, and Kristin guessed he was about to change his mind, but he didn't.

"How do I talk to a woman?"

The question surprised Kristin. "What do you mean? Like what to say, or how to approach someone you like?" There was no way in the world she was going to give him a hard time. She wasn't sure she'd ever seen Gideon open up like this to her.

"I mean, I haven't spent a lot of time around women, what with my years in prison. I'm not exactly a good catch, what with me being out on parole and all. What do men and women talk about? I feel like anything I say is going to come out wrong. And don't tell me I need to talk about my feelings. I ain't talking about my feelings."

"Don't worry, I'd never ask a guy to do something that crazy. You'd pull a muscle or something. I guess my main advice, which should be easy for you, is to listen more than you talk. Hear what she talks about, and show an interest in it, even if you aren't interested. I don't mean be fake about it, but at least ask her questions. And if she talks to you about a problem, don't start by trying to fix it for her. Sometimes a person just wants to vent. And if she asks you a question about yourself, try to answer honestly. Don't say what you think she wants to hear. Be honest, because that will come out eventually anyway. But most of all, be yourself."

Gideon looked at her as if waiting for her to take a shot at him, but it didn't come.

"Be yourself," she repeated, "and if it's someone you're interested in and it doesn't work out, then it doesn't work out, but when it's a good fit, it will be magic."

Gideon appeared to be trying to take all this in, but she sensed she had led off with advice from an advanced class and he needed something a little more specific. Something from an introductory class.

"Or compliment her shoes," Kristin said. "That can also work."

Gideon nodded and jotted down the word 'shoes' on a sticky note and looked at it before stuffing it in his pocket.

"I can do that," he said with a hint of optimism.

29

Letitia heard the door from the law firm open and looked up from her position at the front desk. She expected it to be yet another wearisome reporter, but if the tall, immaculately dressed black woman entering was a reporter, she would have been an anchor for a network news station. She appeared to be in her mid-50's and exuded a regal air that made her look like she'd just stepped off a Fortune 500 magazine cover. Letitia always appreciated seeing another black woman putting forth such an impression.

"Hello, how can I help you?"

"My name is Iris Robinson, and I wondered if there was any chance I could speak with Mr. Banning. I don't have an appointment, so I apologize for just dropping in."

"I'm afraid Mr. Banning is out of the office right now. Can I take your contact information and ask him to give you a call when he gets back?"

Iris paused, as if weighing the pros and cons of leaving her number was far more involved than Letitia would have expected, then decided against it.

"I can reach out another time."

"Can I at least tell him what it's about?"

When she finally explained who she was, Letitia wished that Kristin—or even Gideon—weren't both out on some sort of business, so instead she brought out her cell phone.

"Hold on. Let me text Thane and see if he's free to talk."

"That's okay. I'd rather talk with him in person, if it's all the same."

"I'm sure he'd want to talk with you. Are you sure you won't leave me your number?"

"Thank you, but just let him know I'll reach out again soon."

"I'll at least text him and let him know you stopped by."

She brought the phone up to her face and pretended to be texting Thane, but instead opened her camera app and took a couple of photos of Iris as she turned and walked back out of the office. As soon as the woman was gone, Letitia immediately called Thane at the Twin Towers jail.

"You'll never guess who I just met," Letitia said when Thane answered, still amazed.

Thane sat across from Boo in one of the claustrophobic interview rooms created for lawyers to talk with their clients. He thought she continued to appear composed, and not overwhelmed by having been in jail for several days. People reacted differently to their first days in jail, although most reacted by withdrawing, or displaying fear or anger, or all of the above. But while Boo was petite in stature, she gave off the impression of being able to take care of herself unless, perhaps, confronted by a man well over twice her weight. Cash Dixon, for example.

He told her about the plea deal now on the table, prefacing his presentation by saying how surprised he was at how low the Assistant District Attorney was willing to go in terms of sentencing, but he also said the odds were good this came at the request of the University.

He watched her nod along as he went through the details. He thought for sure she was going to jump at the opportunity, not expressing excitement, but at least conveying a sense of relief that her sentence would not be longer. His confidence, however, became shaky when he told her about the non-disclosure agreement and her inability to say anything about Dixon or the things he had done to her. When he outlined that expectation, her face tightened. Apparently, the decision had become harder.

"I wouldn't be able to talk about all the things that asshole did to me?" Boo confirmed.

"I'm afraid not."

"Or how I believe the University was at least somewhat aware of the rumors?"

"Again, no."

Thane wished he could see inside her head as she went through whatever calculations were important to her.

"I'll do whatever it is you want to do," Thane said, "but I have to say, it's a good offer. More than good, actually."

Boo didn't respond. He recognized she might have a different definition of a good offer, but a plea deal of twelve years for what could have been considered capital murder of a highly prominent person was virtually unheard of.

"But if you decide to fight the charges, we'll fight the charges."

"You don't believe we'd win, though, do you?"

"It would be an uphill battle at best. A very steep uphill battle. You've said you shot him because of what he did to you, but that happened after he had done those things, so you basically are saying you shot him to prevent them from happening again in the future. In the best of circumstances, that would be a tough sell."

"But for a black, female sex worker and former drug addict…" Boo's voice trailed off.

"…who killed a very popular, very successful white man, so no, these aren't the best of circumstances."

"Do you feel I was justified doing what I did?"

Thane wasn't sure how to answer that, so he fell back to the predictable answer.

"My job is to represent you to the best of my ability, not to say whether or not you were justified." He paused, feeling like she deserved better than that. "But I understand why you did what you did. I do understand."

"Yeah, I had a feeling you did."

"If the judge lets us get into specifics of what Dixon did to you, that will help us. And there's a young woman at the shelter where you went who has agreed to testify about women being provided to Dixon and others in the athletic department."

Boo looked at Thane and shook her head. "Don't count on that testimony."

"You know the woman?"

"No, but she'll either get scared and change her mind, or Stick will get to her and make her disappear." She paused and thought more about her situation "I gotta be honest, I don't like our chances."

"Then that brings us back to the plea deal."

Boo again leaned back in her chair and fell silent for a long moment before finally speaking again. "Twelve years, huh? And if I don't take it and am found guilty?"

"Best guess would be thirty years, although you might be eligible for parole after twenty, but 'eligible for' isn't the same as it being granted."

Boo barely nodded in understanding. It looked like she was having a debate with herself.

"Twelve years may go faster than it seems," Thane offered.

She looked at him skeptically. "Did your five years go fast?"

"No. It felt like twenty."

"I appreciate your honesty more than you know. I don't want to feel like I'm being sold on this."

"So, what are you thinking? Are you trying to figure out the odds of being found innocent, or being found guilty but getting a lesser sentence, or..."

"I'm thinking about the NDA. Not being able to share my story. I believe the university knew bad things were going on, but they let it happen. I want the world to know what sort of man Dixon was. I want justice."

"You want justice, or you want vengeance?"

"I already got vengeance, but can't they sometimes be the same thing? Is it always an either/or choice?"

Thane understood what Boo meant. She had been wronged terribly. She had been taken advantage of and used in a way that left nothing but anger and bitterness, and she now looked for a way to remove it, or at least to lower its intensity. He understood it very well.

Finally Boo leaned forward and looked him in the eye with an expression that conveyed resolution.

"I want to see this through. Even if I end up spending the rest of my life locked up, I want everyone to know what Dixon did to me, and how other women have been taken advantage of by university bigwigs, and the way they offer up young women to football recruits like they're part of a swag bag. People might not believe me, but I can at least try to shine a light on those cockroaches. I can't point to a lot of great achievements in my life, but this is something I can do."

Thane wasn't totally surprised by her response, although he wondered if he could have presented the plea deal in a way that would have helped her better see the rare opportunity being offered.

"As I said before, I'll proceed with this however you want…"

"But?"

"But you might find that noble intentions start to mean less and less the longer you're locked up. And…" he paused as he tried to figure out how to express what he was feeling, "…and if you're successful in exposing what has been going on at ULA, you might find you're still angry and you're still bitter, and that nothing has changed as far as how the University operates, except now you'll also be in prison."

"Understood," Boo said, and Thane thought she honestly did understand.

Boo slid her chair back, now that the decision on the plea deal had been decided, but Thane held up his hand.

"One more thing. My assistant called me a few

minutes ago and told me a woman stopped by my office wanting to talk with me. She claimed to be your mother."

Boo didn't show any sort of reaction other than shaking her head. "My mother is a drug addict and likely dead. There's no way my mother stopped by your office."

Thane pulled his phone from his pocket and brought up the picture Letitia had texted him and showed it to Boo. She looked at it and immediately scoffed at it.

"That's not my mother." She looked at the photo a moment longer, then looked up at Thane. "Any idea why she would be saying she is?"

Thane turned the phone around and looked at the picture again himself.

"That's a damn good question."

30

As Judge William Miller slowly lowered himself into his desk chair, Thane did a quick survey of the man's office. He wasn't sure he'd ever been in an office so devoid of personal items. No photographs, no mementos, no knick-knacks that reflected an individual's personal interest, not even an ornately framed diploma to tout the judge's credentials. The office almost looked like a rental space, except the judge's name on the door said otherwise.

Judge Miller had called both Thane and Assistant D.A. Arthur Barnes to his office to offer up the legal equivalent of a boxing referee's pre-fight instructions, although Thane had the feeling he would be the main recipient of these instructions.

In his late 60's, Miller had a reputation as being a prosecutor's judge. He wasn't seen as being blatantly unfair or hostile to the defense, it's just that more often than not, his sympathies seemed to lie with the District Attorney's office.

"Gentlemen," Miller began, "I appreciate you both taking the time to join me today."

Thane knew the judge wasn't appreciative at all. He had requested a meeting with the two lawyers, and they damn well better show up as requested. But it was nice of him to act like they had done him a courtesy by showing up.

"I suppose it goes without saying that since Mr. Banning is the defense attorney, this case should quietly fly under the radar." Miller looked at Thane and all but shook his head. "Seriously, Mr. Banning, how is it you never seem to have cases that deal with things like forged checks or alimony disputes?"

Thane wasn't sure if the judge was kidding or not, but when Miller appeared to be awaiting an answer, Thane felt obliged to offer up something.

"I'm trying to keep a low profile, Your Honor. Ask my team."

"And how's that been working out for you?"

"I'm still trying."

Miller nodded as though he believed him, which Thane knew wasn't likely. The judge then turned to the prosecutor. "Mr. Barnes, we are here mostly as the result of a conversation you and I had the other day on the phone. You raised some good points and, therefore, I thought it made sense for us to establish a few things up front. Would you care to summarize your request for Mr. Banning?"

Barnes sat up a little straighter, as if he'd just been called on in class.

"Happy to, Your Honor. I am confident Mr. Banning will be trying his best to attack the character of Coach Dixon, and will do whatever he can to tear down the reputation of this man."

"If you'd also like me to introduce into evidence his winning record while at ULA, I'm happy to do so," Thane said.

"Mr. Banning," Judge Miller said, "if you could find a way to temper your sarcasm, that would be greatly appreciated."

"I'll do my best, Your Honor," although Thane wasn't sure he was being sarcastic.

"As I was saying, I am requesting that evidence pertaining to Coach Dixon's alleged inappropriate behavior be limited to what took place the night of the murder."

"Inappropriate behavior?" Thane said. "Inappropriate behavior is having too much to drink then telling someone you've never liked their spouse. Inappropriate behavior is using your hands to grab croutons at a restaurant salad bar. What Cash Dixon did was far beyond 'inappropriate'."

"Mr. Barnes' choice of words aside," Judge Miller said, "I understand his request."

"Your Honor, we have reason to believe my client isn't the only woman Dixon was 'inappropriate' with, which will go to show a pattern of behavior. I'm not looking to attack his character. I'm simply looking to reveal his character by introducing facts and testimony. I also plan to show he created a culture amongst some of his staff that resulted in them doing the same thing, and that this behavior was at least suspected—if not outright known— by University of Los Angeles administration."

"And if the University or Coach Dixon's staff were the defendants on trial," Barnes said, "then that might be more relevant, but right now your client is the one on trial, and it's for the killing of Coach Dixon."

"Maybe the University should be on trial."

"But they're not," the judge said, inserting himself back into the conversation. "I understand the point Mr.

Barnes is making here. And…" Miller raised his hand when it was obvious Thane wanted to say something, "…I also understand your position, Mr. Banning."

"I'm not sure you do, Your Honor."

"I don't care. I believe I do. Regardless, during this trial, Mr. Banning, you may offer evidence that directly ties the deceased's behavior to his interactions with your client. That's reasonable. But I will not allow you to sling mud at the Coach's reputation with accusations outside his behavior with the defendant."

Thane noticed that there were people who referred to the murder victim as 'Mr. Dixon' or 'Coach Dixon,' and there were people who simply called him 'Coach.' The latter group, which now included the Judge, used the term in a more personal way, as if Dixon was a buddy of theirs. 'Coach' was shorthand for 'he's our guy.'

"Your Honor, there is a pattern of abuse within the athletic department that is relevant to this case. I know of at least one other coach who I can show also dealt with women who were being sexually trafficked, and I also believe I can show where young women are being used to entice star players to come to ULA to play football there."

Thane saw Barnes give the judge a look that appeared to be saying 'see? What did I tell you?'

"I'm not looking to sling mud, Your Honor," Thane continued. "But behavior and patterns of what is accepted are relevant to this case. I'm assuming the prosecution is going to argue the defendant shouldn't have taken the law into her own hands but, instead, should have worked within the system. I intend to show that 'the system' wasn't there to watch out for her."

Judge Miller paused for longer than Thane thought

he would to consider his point. Finally, he responded.

"I understand what you're trying to do, Mr. Banning, and it's a fine line to walk." Miller paused again, and Thane knew better than to interrupt whatever the judge was considering. "I also know that a young woman's future is at stake here, so here's what I'm going to do. You may talk about behavior between the victim and your client. And, if you want, you can try to show system failures, but if I feel like you're simply slinging mud in order to enter salacious details to gin up media reactions, I will shut you down right quick. I run a courtroom, not a circus, and based on past trials you seem to do best performing in a circus atmosphere. I'm not going to let you try to tear down someone in a desperate attempt to win a challenging case, but if, as you say, the facts point to a certain type of behavior, I'm open to having the facts speak for themselves. But they damn well better be facts, because Coach deserves better than hearsay. Perhaps he had some moral flaws, but overall, I believe he was a good man."

"I get the feeling you and I have different definitions of 'good man'," Thane said. When he noticed the judge's lips tighten, he quickly added, "And that isn't sarcasm."

"Why do I get the feeling you're not going to be successful walking that fine line?"

Thane left the courthouse, frustrated but hopeful. The latitude Judge Miller gave him exceeded his expectations, even though the judge correctly assumed he planned to pursue a tear-it-down approach to the institutions he believed helped enable the behavior of a broken man like Dixon. He also thought showing such relationships would help make Dixon's heinous behavior more believable to the jury.

At the same time, perhaps the judge's parameters would help Thane focus on the case at hand and not confuse the jury by trying to expose all of the wrongdoing that Thane believed took place in other parts of the university. He recognized that, ever since being released from Forsman, he often went out of his way to try to expose corruption and the ways in which powerful systems were taking advantage of the individual, but that wouldn't always be in the best interest of his client. He told himself he needed to keep the focus on the person he represented instead of using them as a vehicle to bring down corrupt systems.

But he so much wanted to bring those systems down.

Thane hoped that feeling came from a desire for justice, but he recognized the strong possibility that it came from a place of anger.

He noticed a couple of police officers heading into a family cafe a block or so from the courthouse, a place often filled at lunch by cops, lawyers, and courthouse employees. Thane had eaten there on more than one occasion, and the thought of their menu brought about hunger pains.

He headed across the street to grab a bite, but as he approached the diner he paused when he noticed the profile of Detective Struthers sitting at a small table. Suddenly, Thane's hunger quickly became replaced with curiosity at the attractive woman sitting across from the detective. Struthers and the woman appeared to be having a quiet conversation.

The woman looked familiar, and Thane wondered if he had seen her around the courthouse. As much time as Struthers spent testifying in court, it wouldn't have surprised Thane to learn the detective had met someone there. Still, he never thought of the detective as having a personal life.

Thane quickly stepped away from the window so that he wouldn't be caught staring at them. When he made it partway down the block, starting to feel nauseous, he stopped abruptly, as if he had run into an invisible wall. He recognized the woman.

He brought out his phone and checked the photo Letitia had sent him of the woman pretending to be Boo's mother. She was the same woman talking with Struthers.

It made sense now, or at least more sense than it had. Thane originally guessed the woman to be a journalist lying in an attempt to speak with him, but he realized she was working with Struthers. Thane also knew, beyond a doubt that he was the focus of their attention.

What he couldn't figure out was how Struthers could make Thane's current case work in the detective's favor.

31

Thane once again sat on the floor of the baby's room, next to the crib which was—at least theoretically—finished. Theoretically because, even though it looked ready for use, there were still five small parts on the floor next to him.

He shook the crib, and it didn't fall apart, so that had to be a good sign. He also leaned over and used his weight to push down on the bedding in the crib; nothing appeared to be at risk of breaking. Normally he wouldn't be overly concerned about a couple of extra parts—it certainly wasn't the first time this sort of thing happened when he assembled something—but this was for his daughter who would be a tiny bundle, defenseless against her father's incompetence.

Thane had been feeling defenseless ever since seeing Detective Struthers talking to the woman trying to pass herself off as Boo's mother. He knew there was a plan in place to take him down, but he couldn't figure out what it was. He supposed that was the sign of a good plan. The sort of plan someone like Struthers would have put together.

It surprised him a little that Struthers would resort to tactics like that, but maybe he didn't know the detective as well as he thought he did. Struthers had one of the highest clearance rates in the L.A. police department, and getting creative in setting up a suspect might have been part of his success.

Whatever Struther's strategy, Thane clearly saw himself as the detective's main suspect. He had thought this was possible—even likely—but still he hoped he was overreacting. Now that he found himself in the detective's sights, the fear of going back to prison hung over him like a blade. He had to figure out a way to make sure that never happened again.

He looked at the questionable crib and imagined his baby daughter sound asleep in it, wrapped in a tiny blanket, unaware of what it meant to have a father locked away.

Hannah entered the room and watched him sitting on the floor, his attention now back to the extra pieces. She lowered herself down next to him and picked up a spare washer.

"Doesn't look important," she said.

Thane smiled but didn't say anything. He was usually better at hiding his concerns, or at least he hoped that was the case but he knew Hannah could pick up on his angst.

"What's up?" she asked.

Thane wished he could answer that question honestly. He decided he could at least try to share part of the truth.

"I'm a little scared. You know, the whole 'going to be a parent' bit."

Hannah took his arm in hers and leaned into him.

"You're going to be great. Well, maybe not if she gets a bike that needs to be assembled…" she said, looking at the extra pieces on the floor, "but for the most part, you'll be a great father."

Thane nodded even though he wanted to shake his head.

"I worry I'm not going to be there for her."

"We'll always be there for her, even when we screw up. She'll know that."

"But I mean that literally. What if I'm not here? What if I'm taken away again?"

This wasn't a conversation Thane meant to have again. There was nothing Hannah could say to make it better, nor could he say anything to help her understand why it was a real possibility. Well, actually there was something he could say to make it understandable. He could tell her the truth, but that wasn't something he was ready to do. She had enough on her mind getting ready to give birth.

"What is it that's happened, Thane? There's something going on that's been bothering you for quite some time, and I can't help but believe it would help if you talked to me about it. I think it would help you. I know it would help us."

Thane knew what she said was likely true, but 'likely' wasn't the same as 'definitely.'

"I don't know. I'm probably just stressed thinking about tomorrow's trial," he finally said, doubtful she would believe that. "Being back in a courtroom always brings back bad memories. There is next to no chance Boo will be found innocent, but she's also still adamant about rejecting the plea deal."

"And you don't think she'll change her mind?" she said, apparently willing to let Thane dodge his real concern one more time.

"I'm hoping she will. But I doubt it."

In a way, Thane admired Boo's willingness to put into public view what she did, and why she did it. But even though she thought she did the right thing, that didn't mean the law would agree. And even if the court of public opinion ended up supporting her, a different court would be handing down her sentence.

Boo had been wronged and she wanted to make things right. She wanted to expose the cancer within the athletic department, and she took ownership of trying to do just that. She was angry, she wanted justice, and she took it upon herself to administer it. Same as Thane had, except he wasn't admitting it. Did that make him more of a coward or more of a realist? Maybe he was both.

"I know you'll do the best you can," Hannah said. "I have to be honest, I'm torn on this one. It angers me the things that were done to that young woman, and it's obvious the University wants to cover it up so it doesn't impact their fundraising, which pisses me off."

"But?"

"But murder wasn't the way to get out of that situation. I understand there are a lot of factors here, and that she lived a life exponentially different than me, but I can't believe there wasn't another option besides killing the man. If you want to tell me she snapped and had an emotional breakdown and that's what led to the murder, I might understand it. But if this was a conscious decision she made after the fact, then I wish she had taken another path."

"Maybe she believed the system wasn't set up to help her get justice."

"Or maybe she preferred revenge," Hannah said quickly.

Yet another example where both things could be true.

32

The air in the packed courtroom felt electric, par for the course for a trial in which Thane starred. So far, he was batting three for three in terms of filling a room. For the majority of the first case, he played the part of the villain, at least until the true bad guys were exposed. The next case found people wanting to learn more about him, and suddenly everyone appeared to be on his side, despite their prior animosity toward him.

But every seat in the courtroom would have been filled for this particular trial even if Thane hadn't been involved. For many of those in attendance, Thane was just the cherry on top. Many of the people who showed up were demanding justice for the murder of their beloved coach. Thane was now starting to be cast in the role of just another crooked defense attorney trying to free a brutal killer.

Most of the wannabe spectators who showed up were relegated to a roped-off area outside the courthouse, due to limited space inside the courtroom itself. The majority of those ended up leaving soon after learning they wouldn't actually get to watch the proceedings, although many stuck around with signs supporting Coach Dixon. When Thane entered the courthouse an hour earlier, he saw a large group of bulked-up young men who had come out to support their fallen leader. He recognized a couple of the players from the night outside the diner, but only one of them made eye contact, glaring at Thane as menacingly as he could from the safety of his friends.

A smaller group of people were located on the other side of the courthouse, distanced from the larger group. Many of these individuals held signs protesting against sexual assault and the trafficking of young women.

But now the jury had been seated and the judge settled in, at which point the bailiff called the court into session. Boo dressed in a simple black pantsuit and her face showed no emotion. Thane feared the jury might get a message through her body language that she didn't care, but he also couldn't tell her to fake more sympathetic expressions. Jurors had a knack for being able to tell when a defendant was acting, and that usually made things worse.

Thane looked over at Kristin, who was sitting on the other side of Boo. Kristin looked back at him and nodded, a quiet acknowledgement that their roller coaster ride was about to begin and that they were ready, even if neither of them truly felt totally ready. She then glanced at Boo, looking as though she wished she could figure out what was going on inside their client's head.

Gideon sat in the gallery directly behind the defense table. There wasn't really anything for Thane to say to him, as his friend and colleague never participated in the actual trial, but Thane always felt more comfortable having the big man nearby. If nothing else, Gideon's presence was a reminder that Thane could get through difficult challenges.

After reading aloud his list of expectations for the spectators sitting in the gallery, Judge Miller nodded to Arthur Barnes. Thane found it ironic that the whole thing had the feel of an opening kickoff to a monumental football game.

Barnes returned the judge's nod and slowly stood, glancing down one more time at his notes written on a legal pad before slowly making his way to the front of the jury box, looking almost resentful at having to waste his valuable time on a case so obviously clearcut.

"Ladies and gentlemen, over the next several days we are going to hear a number of sad and upsetting stories about the defendant, Bonnie Cruise. Stories about hardships she has faced, and examples of how she has been mistreated. And I don't say this facetiously. I truly mean it. This young woman has been dealt a bad hand."

Barnes looked over at Boo as if wanting her to know he truly felt for her, but Boo didn't acknowledge his gesture of pity. Barnes turned back to the jury.

"But there are a lot of people who have been dealt a bad hand in life. Probably some of you have experienced hardships and traumas. The question comes down to how one handles these hardships. How one plays their hand."

Barnes pointed back toward Thane without turning around to look at him. "I have no doubt the defense is going to try to make this case seem far less straightforward than it really is. They're going to try to complicate the story in order to hide the true heart of this case: a young woman killed a man after having had sex with him for money. She had been to his house before, so it's not as though she didn't know him. She knew what he was like, and she knew what he wanted. And she didn't shoot him because she feared for her safety, or because he wouldn't stop doing something when she asked him to: she shot him after getting dressed and ready to leave and the victim was in his kitchen by himself."

Thane wondered whether or not Barnes would be forthcoming about Dixon's behavior and the fact that the coach had paid for sex, but the Assistant D.A. had to know this would come out anyway so it was best to deal with it in his own words.

"The question at the heart of this case is whether or not the defendant had to kill Coach Dixon, or if she could have taken a different course of action, to which I reply, of course she could have taken a different course. She could have gone to the police. Defense will try to say she couldn't go to the police, but that's ridiculous. We are a land of laws, not vigilantism. If someone mistreats us, we don't get to shoot them. If someone does us wrong, we do not get to murder them. That's not how it works, and we need to send that message now. You need to send that message."

Barnes paused, as if ready to add more, then turned and retook his seat.

"Mr. Banning," Judge Miller said.

Thane looked at Boo for a moment, then stood and walked to the center of the courtroom.

"Despite what the prosecution says," Thane began, "I'm not looking to try to complicate what I agree is a straight-forward case. A young woman was repeatedly sexually assaulted by a man who treated women like a piece of property, like a perk that came with being a coach for a big-time football program. And after repeatedly saying no—not to the act of sex itself, but to things he forced upon her while they were having sex—and after repeatedly being ignored, my client did not believe there was going to be an end to this abuse. She got to the point where she believed the only way out of this cycle was to kill herself, but she knew that would only result in some new woman being sent in her place, because there is always another woman available to be sent."

"And yes, I like the idea of her being able to go the police. What a wonderful world where a 22-year-old black sex worker can go to the police and say she was mistreated by an exceptionally popular white football coach at a major university and then sit back and watch justice be delivered. Or perhaps she could have gone to the University and asked for their help. Or talked to the man who kept sending her there and asked him to stop working with Mr. Dixon."

"I like that dream, but I'm assuming many of you know as well as I do that the system is not set up to protect people like Bonnie Cruise. Instead, the system protects men like Cash Dixon. You will even see part of that system in place during this trial. The things I will be able to say, and the evidence I'm allowed to present, will all have to be tempered by rules that say we need to focus more on protecting Mr. Dixon's reputation than finding justice for Ms. Cruise."

Thane paused, almost surprised Barnes didn't object—even though objections were a rarity during opening statements. Or maybe even the judge would admonish him for questioning the fairness of his courtroom, but that would be even rarer during opening statements. But then again, an attorney rarely claimed upfront that a trial was set up against his client.

Judge Miller didn't appear ready to intervene,

although he also didn't seem too amused by Thane's implication.

"But does any of that give Ms. Cruise the right to shoot Mr. Dixon?" Thane had decided to try his best to refer to Dixon as Mr., rather than as 'Coach.'

"Perhaps not if you feel, as the prosecution apparently feels, that the abuse at the hands of Mr. Dixon was over and, therefore, Ms. Cruise was no longer in danger. But it wasn't over. It hadn't been over for quite some time because there was always a next time. A never-ending cycle of violence and abuse, despite my client's pleas to Mr. Dixon to stop. If you would feel better if she had shot him while he was abusing her, then go ahead and criticize her sense of timing, but keep in mind, based on her experience, this abuse was never going to end unless she ended it herself. Was that taking the law into her own hands? I suppose it was, but someone needed to take it, and I intend to show that Ms. Cruise saw no other option to make the abuse stop."

Thane looked at the jury and noted a wide range of expressions. He thought several of the jurors were hearing his words as a desperate attempt to find some sort of excuse for Boo's actions, which wasn't far from the truth. There were, however, a couple of other jurors who he sensed were at least considering what he had to say. It only took one juror to determine a case.

He returned to his seat. He wanted to explain to the jury, based on his own personal experience, how he believed there was sometimes a difference between what was legal and what was right, and how he knew that firsthand. But he knew that wouldn't do anyone any good. Especially him.

33

Deputy Assistant D.A. Barnes opened the prosecution's case by playing a 911 call received at 12:50 a.m. from a nearby neighbor of Coach Dixon reporting a gunshot in the area. There were scores of neighborhoods in L.A. where the sound of a gun would not be a reason to call the police, but Dixon's neighborhood was not one of them. One didn't pay that much for a house to live in an area where guns could be heard. As such, the police arrived quickly.

After setting the stage with some basic background information, Barnes called Detective David Hawkins to the stand. Hawkins said he had been on the force for twelve years and had solved 91% of the murder cases assigned to him, considerably higher than the 74% clearance rate in the city as a whole.

Thane guessed the jury perceived Hawkins on the stand the same way he did: professional, confident, and very capable, but also a little arrogant.

"Detective Hawkins," Barnes said, "can you give us your best sense of the timeline from the night of the murder?"

Hawkins brought out a small spiral notebook from his sportscoat pocket and flipped it open to the relevant page.

"The defendant—Ms. Cruise—called a cellphone

number at 12:11 a.m. the night of the murder."

"And were you able to track down the owner of that number?"

"No, sir. We believe it was a burner phone. Women in Ms. Cruise's line of work often call to let their pimp know they have arrived at a customer's home, and most pimps now use burner phones."

"I see. Go ahead, please."

"As you previously noted, a 911 call was received at 12:50 a.m. reporting a shot fired, although the caller wasn't able to say where the shot came from. Dispatch sent a patrol car to the neighborhood in question, but the officers did not see or hear any other disturbance, so they resumed their normal patrol."

"When did you discover Coach Dixon had been shot and killed?"

"We received a call at 7:48 the following morning from his housekeeper who found him lying dead in the kitchen."

"At which point you were called in to investigate?"

Hawkins told the jury he had arrived at 8:35 a.m., followed shortly by forensics and other support staff. Dixon's body was lying on the kitchen floor on his back with a hole in his chest. Forensics had since estimated the time of death between 12:00 a.m. – 1:00 a.m., consistent with the time of the 911 call.

The conversation then shifted to Thane's client.

"And how did you come to identify Ms. Cruise as a suspect in the murder?"

"Coach Dixon had a Ring doorbell, which enabled us to get a clear image of Ms. Cruise arriving at the house at 12:15 a.m."

"Four minutes after the call to the burner phone, which supports your assumption that the defendant had called to confirm her arrival at her destination."

"That's correct," Hawkins said.

"At this point, I would like to play the video footage received from Coach Dixon's doorbell."

Barnes turned on a large monitor near the jury box, and a video image appeared of Boo walking up to the door and standing for a moment before stepping into the house. The image was clear and indisputable.

"So now we had an image of the suspect," Hawkins continued. "We also found fingerprints and a few drops of blood that weren't a match to the coach's."

Thane thought he saw Hawkins's lips tighten for a quick moment, as if he read that last note off the page without meaning to do so. The detective quickly returned to the photo and the fingerprints.

"The photo enabled us to track down the suspect. In addition, we also have footage of the suspect breaking the doorbell."

Barnes directed the jury's attention back to the monitor which this time played a video scene of Boo stepping out the front door and glancing down the long driveway before swinging a hammer at the doorbell, at which point the image went dark. The time on the video displayed 12:52 a.m.

"And what was your take on this action by Ms. Cruise, Detective?"

"She stated she thought that by breaking the doorbell, she would in turn make previous video footage inoperable, but that's not how those devices work. The video is stored in the cloud for this very reason. The only thing the defendant did was to further confirm her role in the events that took place that evening. Approximately three minutes after breaking the doorbell, the suspect then made one more call."

"The same burner number as before?"

"No, a different number. We are still trying to track down the identification of that number as well, but I suspect it will also be a burner phone."

"And how did you finally identify Ms. Cruise?"

"We showed her photo to a number of people, including various sex workers who sometimes provide us with information. We eventually got an anonymous tip from a caller who provided us with Ms. Cruise's name, most likely from someone who saw her picture but didn't want to directly involve themselves with the police. Again, that's not uncommon. At that point, we were able to track the location of her cell phone, which showed Ms. Cruise hiding out at a local women's shelter. We took her into custody and were able to match her fingerprints and…" Hawkins caught himself this time, "…and other forensic evidence found at the scene of the crime."

"Thank you, detective. No further questions at this time."

Thane thought the best he could do was get an improved plea deal that hopefully Boo would accept. He knew in most cases a plea deal would either be off the table or at least not as generous by this time, but he hoped the University's desire to keep the sordid details of the case out of the public eye might actually cause Barnes to come down even further in his offer.

Thane rose and approached the witness stand. Hawkins turned in his chair to face Thane. The detective almost had a smile on his face, as if interested in seeing firsthand how Thane operated in court.

"Detective Hawkins, you mentioned showing Ms. Cruise's photo to various sex workers in the area, and later getting an anonymous call giving you the name to go with the photo. Why did you ask area sex workers? Was there something that made you think a sex worker had been involved?"

"I wasn't sure, but the image of the defendant and the time of evening when she showed up at his house made it seem at least a possibility."

"And did you show her picture to other individuals as well?"

Hawkins paused, which Thane felt he passed off as trying to appear thorough in his thoughts, even though Thane had no doubt the man knew the details forward and backwards.

"I also reached out to a couple of assistant coaches from the ULA football team."

"And why did you do that?"

"I always strive to be thorough."

"Had you heard rumors of sex workers sometimes being used by members of the football team, for example, in the area of recruitment?"

"I don't put much stock in rumors."

"I didn't ask if you put much stock in them. I asked if you had heard them."

"Objection, Your Honor," Barnes called out. "Asked and answered."

"Asked, but dodged," Thane replied.

"Sustained," the judge said. "Move along, Mr. Banning."

"Do you remember what time you showed the photo to some of the coaches on Mr. Dixon's staff?"

"I believe it was around 1:50 p.m. the day after the murder."

"And when did the anonymous call come in providing Ms. Cruise's name?"

"The call came in at 2:45 p.m. that same day."

"And were you able to trace the number from which the call was made?"

Again, Hawkins checked his notes. "The number traced back to a vacant office in ULA's English department."

"I'm afraid I'm not familiar with the layout of the ULA campus, detective. Can you tell me if the English department building is relatively close to the offices of the Athletic department?"

"It's about three blocks away, give or take."

"You said the caller was anonymous, but I don't believe you mentioned whether it was a male or female voice leaving the message."

"It sounded like a male."

"Ah, thank you for that additional information. When you said you talked to some sex workers and then got an anonymous call identifying the person in the photo, it made it sound like it came from one of them."

"I don't know who it came from. That's sort of the whole meaning of the term anonymous."

"Fair enough," Thane said. "But you showed the photo to members of Mr. Dixon's coaching staff, and less than an hour later a male voice called from a phone approximately three blocks from the coach's offices with Ms. Cruise's name. That provides a clearer context. But maybe I'm the only one who thought you were implying it was another sex worker who called."

Thane looked over at the jury as if to say he knew each and every one of them thought the same thing.

"Good thing I asked," Thane added. "Always good to have as much information as possible."

Thane walked back to his table and acted as though he was looking at his notepad, to give time for the jury to think about whether they, too, had made the same assumption as Thane said he had made. He always liked reminding the jury to not take everything they were told at face value. If Hawkins could pretend he had to look at something to refresh his memory, so could Thane.

"You mentioned blood at the scene of the murder that didn't match Mr. Dixon's. Did the blood match that of the defendant?"

"It did," Hawkins answered, looking a little surprised that Thane asked a question that could hurt his client, although Hawkins had to realize other evidence already proved she was there.

"And where did you find this blood? On the kitchen floor? Near the body?"

Again, Hawkins hesitated before finally answering. "It was on a small kitchen utensil."

"A whisk, if I'm not mistaken, is that correct?"

"That's correct."

"The sort of kitchen tool used to stir things like eggs when cooking," Thane added.

"One of the smaller sizes," Hawkins added. "Not the large type."

"In addition to the blood, was there also fecal matter on the whisk that could be matched to the defendant?"

"Yes."

"I'm surprised you didn't mention that earlier. It seems as though every bit of evidence tying the defendant to the scene of the crime would be brought forth. And did Ms. Cruise tell you that Mr. Dixon had taken that whisk and had inserted it in…"

"Objection, Your Honor," Barnes said as he rose. "Any evidence on that item matched back to the defendant. That's all that's relevant."

"Sustained."

"Your Honor," Thane said, "it's also relevant that…"

"The objection has been sustained, Mr. Banning. Move along."

Thane looked over at the jury as if they were all in on an unspoken secret. "I understand. In this case, it's not relevant." Thane returned his attention to the witness. "Detective, the police report said that Ms. Cruise's fingerprints were also on the doorknob of the door leading from the garage to the kitchen. Do you happen to know why she was in the garage?"

"No, sir, I don't."

"Did you also check tools out in the garage for Ms. Cruise's blood? Perhaps a screwdriver…"

"Objection, Your Honor."

"…Or a wrench, or even a drill bit. One of the smaller ones, of course…"

"Your Honor!"

Judge Miller banged his gavel to silence Thane. "Objection is sustained. Mr. Banning, do not continue down this path. I'm warning you right now."

Thane glanced over at the jury, then turned back to the judge.

"My apologies," Thane said, unapologetically.

"Mr. Banning, do you have any additional questions for the witness?"

"Not at this time, although I want to reserve the right to recall Detective Hawkins at a later date. I also want to thank the detective for pointing out that the whisk was one of the smaller ones. I'm sure Ms. Cruise appreciated Mr. Dixon's consideration in that regard."

"Your Honor!" Barnes bellowed.

"No further questions, your Honor."

34

Thane and Gideon sat in Thane's office, both of them leaning back in their chairs, neither of them talking. It reminded Thane of their time in prison, where the two men could sit together, not saying a word, in part because there often wasn't much to say. At least in his office, they didn't have to keep their guard up for possible assaults like they had to do in prison, not counting the ever-present threat of Stick.

When they got back from day one of Boo's trial, the two men and Kristin had gotten together to discuss how the day went. Kristin vented about the judge muzzling them to protect the reputation of Dixon, as well as the good name of the University. After complaining about that, she left the meeting to follow-up with the young woman from the sorority whom she'd asked to testify.

Gideon hung around after Kristin left. He agreed with everyone else that Boo should take the plea deal. He had served enough time behind bars to know that taking a moral stand because it was the right thing to do could also be a stupid thing to do, especially if that moral stand made you spend more time behind bars.

Gideon also struck Thane as being angry on Boo's behalf in light of everything she had gone through. Thane knew Gideon didn't deal well with bullies. He suspected there had been something in Gideon's past that made him so quick to defend the weak. He suspected it had something to do with his sisters—and the father Gideon rarely spoke of—although on those few occasions when he did speak of him, the words weren't kind.

"Any chance Boo is rethinking her boneheaded decision to turn down the plea?" Gideon asked, finally breaking the silence.

"I don't know. I told her it will be tough to get the sort of details out into the public record that she wants out there, so maybe having seen it today will change her mind, but today when we left, she was still all in."

"God, I hate people who believe they can change the system by taking a stand. This shit will keep happening regardless of what Boo does."

"I understand how she feels, though. She's angry, and she wants to lash out at the system."

"The system won't even feel it," Gideon said. "Is the deal still on the table?"

Letitia leaned into Thane's office.

"A Mr. Silver from the University is here to see you. He says he doesn't have an appointment and will understand if you can't see him."

"That's fine. Send him on in."

Thane turned back to Gideon. "Silver is the head fundraiser at ULA. My guess is he's the University's point person, or he simply has the most at stake."

Letitia escorted Silver into Thane's office.

"I'm sorry to drop in unannounced," Silver said, extending his hand, "but I thought I'd take a chance on catching you."

"No problem. This is my associate, Gideon Spence."

Gideon gave Silver a half-raise of his hand, displaying no interest in rising or a handshake. "Hi ho," Gideon said.

"I haven't heard that since I was a kid," Silver said with a pretend smile. "Never gets old, though." Silver turned back to Thane. "Do you have a minute to talk?"

Gideon slowly raised himself off the chair and headed toward the door. "I'm sure this ain't a public relations dream come true, but you better do right by our client. There's a lot of ways bad shit can come out in the wash."

"Mr. Spence, is that a threat?" Silver said in an amused tone.

"No," Thane quickly answered for Gideon, "it wasn't a threat."

"You sure?" Gideon asked Thane. "If it wasn't, then that's on me because I meant for it to be one."

Gideon walked out and shut the door behind him.

"I do like men who are direct," Silver said. "That's often difficult to find in academia, and especially rare in the world of fundraising."

"Maybe you need to hire more felons." Thane motioned for Silver to take a chair. "What can I do for you, Sterling?"

Silver leaned back in his chair and studied Thane for a long moment. "I suppose I should try to be more direct like your associate."

"Well, I'm not sure Gideon is the best role model, but I do usually respond better to directness."

"I'll bet you do." Silver nodded, as if Thane had said something quite profound. "Then direct I shall be. It's my understanding you were offered an exceptionally generous plea deal by the District Attorney's office, but you turned it down."

"Actually, my client was offered a plea deal and she turned it down. And just out of curiosity, should I assume Barnes will be running all offers by you first?"

Silver shrugged. "Arthur doesn't share much with me in the way of the facts of the case, but obviously ULA is a major player in this city, and if we were going to be angry at a plea deal, that would not be good politics for the D.A.'s office."

"Especially not for Barnes. Is it safe to assume ULA's support of his run for D.A. might seriously be impacted depending on the outcome of this case?"

"The election is several months away. It's not something I'd want to talk about just now. But what I came here today to find out is what it would it take to get your client to settle."

"I can't speak to that with certainty, but I believe she would like it acknowledged that your coach was a sick, sadistic son-of-a-bitch who hurt women, and that others at the University knew about it. Or at least other members of the athletic department knew some things about it."

Silver blanched at the description of Dixon, although Thane would have been surprised if he tried arguing against his sentiments. Silver took in those words and thought before speaking.

"I see you share your colleague's comfort with being direct."

"It's one of the things you learn in prison. Best to be upfront and get things on the table."

"In that case, the whole purpose of the plea deal is to prevent that exact thing from happening. I'm sure you already knew that, since you're not a stupid man. I fear, though, you may have a stupid client."

Thane bristled at Silver's words but kept his cool. "My client is not stupid. She's angry. You know what they say about a woman scorned? Imagine a woman abused with a whisk."

Silver held up his hand, looking as though he wished he could rewind their conversation and start again. "I'm sorry. You're right. It's not fair to call her stupid. It's just that her intention is the reason for the generous plea agreement. But I'm here to offer a better deal."

"I thought plea deals came from the D.A.'s office."

"And officially they do, but I talked to Arthur, and I believe he can be made to see reason, but if I know the offer is going to be rejected, I don't want to put him in the position of having made a spurned offer. In other words, obviously this is not an official offer, but if your client would be receptive to it, I believe I can make it happen."

"So what is this new and improved unofficial offer?"

"Eight years, with possible parole after five. Trust me, that's as low as anyone would be able to go and still keep their jobs. Arthur is in a difficult position, and less than eight years for the murder of a man like Dixon would be seen as a complete failure on his part."

"I believe even eight years would be met with anger."

"No doubt, but it's a level of anger I believe we can manage. If we could do less and survive the fallout, I would support that as well."

Thane thought Silver might actually do well in prison, at least for a while. Clear-eyed about this situation, he wasn't letting sentimentality get in the way of his goals.

"In addition—and this is something that would have

to be an unwritten understanding—once Ms. Cruise gets out of prison, I can make arrangements for her to get a degree at no cost to her, should she decide to try to turn her life around. It wouldn't be at ULA, for obvious reasons, but I can make it happen elsewhere. You have to admit, all in all, that's one hell of a plea deal."

"Your need for justice for Dixon's death appears to be flexible."

"Dixon is dead. Nothing in your client's sentencing will bring him back. Plus, as the father of three daughters, I'm not looking to defend him as I learn more about his actions, should they be true."

"The new stadium, on the other hand…"

"I'm sure you've read stories in the Times about the significant increase in donations that have come in the name of Coach Dixon. It's been stunning, but I'll be honest, after today's testimony, I expect to see donations drop by at least twenty percent tomorrow. I can't continue letting that sort of hit continue, so if your client won't accept eight years, there will be no offer left on the table, and Barnes will absolutely annihilate her. He'll show that you can't believe anything she says. I recognize it's up to her to accept the deal, however, I also believe you could have a significant impact on her decision. And if you are able to talk her into accepting this deal, I believe there could be great opportunities for you and your firm to help ULA with a healthy portion of our legal work."

Thane couldn't help but smile. He could see why Silver was successful in his job. For a man like Silver, the bottom line was the bottom line. Everything led to how much money he could raise.

"Let's say you are able to get a large amount of money

as a result of Dixon's murder. Do you have plans to announce that the new stadium will be named in honor of him? I mean, that seems like the smart move for someone literally trying to raise hundreds of millions of dollars."

Silver broke eye contact with Thane for the first time since they began talking, then eventually looked back up at him. "That's not something we've done."

"But it could be. Perhaps part of the plea deal could be that nothing will be named after Mr. Dixon, other than perhaps a port-a-potty."

Silver thought about it, but remained non-committal "I'll tell you what, you get your client to agree to eight years and an all-expense paid college education, and we can talk. If she agrees in concept, I can do a cost-benefit analysis on the naming rights."

Thane stood, and Silver reluctantly did the same, looking as though he had hoped he could get more of a commitment on this new offer.

"You have to admit, this deal far exceeds anything you could have imagined was possible."

"It's a fair offer."

"Fair offer? Who are you kidding? Fair would be your client spending the rest of her life in prison, but fair isn't always something we can take into consideration in my job."

"Fair would also be people like Dixon being exposed as the dirt they are, but like you said, 'fair' isn't always something we can count on."

"I know you can't speak for your client, but what does your gut tell you? Think she'll take the deal?"

"I honestly don't know," Thane said. "Did I mention she's angry?"

35

As Silver walked past the reception desk and out the main entrance, Letitia waved Thane over. She held up a piece of paper and handed it to him.

"That woman who claims to be Boo's mother called for you again. I didn't know whether or not I should interrupt your meeting with the fancy guy, so I took a message. At least she left her number this time."

"Thanks. I'd rather connect with her on my schedule anyway." Thane still wasn't sure how to play this. He knew Struthers was pulling the strings, but to what end, he couldn't figure. He would rather approach her when she wasn't expecting him, rather than let her—or Struthers—dictate the time and place.

As he headed back toward his office, Kristin blew out of hers like a sudden storm. She looked like she would have kicked something had there been anything to kick that wouldn't hurt her foot.

"Jules, my ULA sorority witness, says she's no longer willing to testify about the athletic department hiring them to entertain football recruits."

"Is she nervous about the publicity?"

"The president of the sorority called a house meeting and said they needed to rally around the university and that that's where their loyalties lied."

"And that's all your witness needed to flip?"

"No, it was when little Miss Queen Bee said scholarships could be taken away just as easily as they were given out, and Jules would have to drop out without it. She said a number of young women at that sorority have been given generous scholarships, which is a far larger percentage than is the case with other sororities."

"It makes sense the University would work closely with one sorority where they can keep more of an eye on everyone."

"This pisses me off," Kristin said. "I don't blame Jules for backing out, but ULA is obviously more interested in protecting their brand than they are in fixing the problem. This is what it looks like when a pimp goes corporate."

Hannah walked down the shelter's hallway before stopping and lightly rapping on one of the doors. After a moment, she knocked a little harder, but still no answer. She tried the door and found it unlocked, so she opened it a few inches.

"Sheila? You there? It's Hannah."

When she didn't hear anything, she walked into the room. Occupants at the shelter got their own bedroom. Some of the larger rooms accommodated women who were there with children, but most of the rooms were smaller, barely large enough to accommodate a single bed, a chest of drawers, a stuffed chair, and a small writing desk with a wooden chair. There were a couple of shared living spaces elsewhere in the shelter if one wanted to watch TV or stretch out on a couch.

Hannah looked around and could immediately tell it was deserted, not just of its occupant, but of anyone's possessions. She checked a couple of the dresser drawers and the narrow closet and found both of them to be empty.

She walked back downstairs to the main admission office. "Betty, can you tell me if Sheila checked out?"

The older woman called up a page on her computer and scanned it.

"If she's gone, she didn't tell us she was leaving."

This wasn't unheard of, although it didn't happen a lot. Sometimes if a woman decided to go back to an abusive relationship, she might be embarrassed to tell anyone at the shelter, so instead she would simply slip out with the intent of making things work this time around. But Hannah didn't think that was the case here, given that Sheila had earlier agreed to talk to her lawyer husband. That could be more than enough to make anyone run away.

As Hannah turned to go back to her office, Betty checked something out on the computer and called out to her.

"She had a visitor yesterday."

"Visitor?" This puzzled Hannah because they didn't allow visitors at the shelter. If a client wanted to meet with a loved one or friend, they had to make arrangements to meet them off-site.

"How did she have a visitor? Did she actually tell them how to get here?"

Betty looked up at her, concerned. "These people

already knew."

Hannah looked at the name on the log and immediately knew she needed to tell Thane when she saw him after work.

She walked out the main entrance and noticed a large, menacing man leaning against her car, staring at her with dead eyes. Yet another uninvited visitor. The man looked like someone who easily could have been in an abusive relationship, not solely from his appearance but from an aura of violence that seemed to radiate from him.

Hannah stopped and texted Betty "Code 2," which simply meant there was an unknown person hanging around the parking lot. Not a sure sign of danger, but reason to be extra vigilant before unlocking the door or letting any of their clients go outside for a while. She also knew someone would now be watching through the window in case the police needed to be called.

Hannah took a photo of the man still leaning against her car, then continued walking toward him. She figured it could have been a coincidence that he was leaning against her car, but she was certain he was waiting for her.

When she reached her car, she stood about six feet from the man who had yet to move.

"Saw you taking my picture. You profiling me?"

"I'd take a picture of anyone not staying at the shelter leaning against my car, so don't take offense."

"I don't take offense. I've always found cutting someone up into little pieces is more effective than taking offense."

"What can I do for you, Mr…"

"Mister. That's rich. How very civilized of you. Name's Stick. I'm a friend of your husband."

Hannah's immediate thought was that Thane knew this hulking, menacing man from prison, although she would be surprised to find out they had been friends. The bigger question remained: why was he waiting for her, and how he knew how to find her?

"You're a friend of Thane's?"

"That surprise you?"

"A little, yes."

"Then maybe you don't know your husband as well as you think you do."

That was a thought bothering Hannah more and more over the past several months.

"But you're right, we ain't friends. I don't want friends. I'm more like a business associate. I did a big favor for him not long ago, and it's now time to pay back the favor, but he doesn't seem to want to pay me back, and that's not a wise decision."

"Shouldn't you talk to him?"

"I tried talking to him, but I'm not sure he heard me."

"Try again."

Stick pushed himself off her car and loomed over her. Hannah hoped she put forth an air of strength and confidence, but she felt a chill at the way this man looked down at her.

"It's best you don't tell me what to do. Ain't nobody tells me what to do. I'm telling you that because when someone pisses me off, sometimes loved ones around that person get hurt, so it only seemed fair to let you know since you have a vested interest in getting your husband to work with me. I'm guessing you can better convey the importance because if you can't, then I will hurt you, and I will hurt your child. Hurt you both real bad."

Hannah didn't know how to respond to this sudden threat. She had no doubt the man meant what he said, and while she didn't want to feel intimidated, that's exactly how he made her feel.

"I'll tell him we talked," Hannah said as soon as she was fairly confident her voice wouldn't break.

"You do that, because next time, there won't be any talking."

Stick remained standing in front of her car door, staring at her. Hannah stared back at him, not ready to ask him to step aside, but also not willing to step back, either. Finally, the man gave what appeared to be his best impersonation of a smile.

"I can see where the two of you make a good couple. I actually like your husband. He's got a backbone, which I respect, and I get the feeling you do, too. The problem with backbones, though, is they can be snapped in two." Stick then looked at Hannah's pregnant stomach. "And a baby's backbone? Shit, they can be broke with just a couple of fingers. I know that from experience."

Stick turned and walked away, whistling 'Hush Little Baby' as he went.

Hannah waited a moment, so it didn't appear like she was scrambling to get in the safety of her car, but she didn't wait long. She got inside, locked the door, and started the car. She watched Stick walk away, then took a deep breath before she started driving.

36

Thane heard Hannah open the sliding glass door leading onto their deck, most likely holding two drinks in her hands. He often sat in one of their Adirondack chairs after a long day, looking at the trees separating his backyard from their neighbor's.

Thane still was most at peace sitting outside, his backyard providing a special respite, but he was comfortable most anywhere not closed off by walls. During his five years at Forsman, at most he was granted one hour a day in the courtyard, barring bad weather or lockdown situations, which happened more frequently than he would have expected. And standing outside in the prison courtyard wasn't the same as being outside somewhere else. Guards with guns and fellow inmates with bad intentions, for example, tended to put a crimp in the general ambiance.

Hannah appeared and handed him an old fashioned before lowering herself into the chair next to his. Getting up and down wasn't quite as easy for her as she closed in on her ninth month of pregnancy. She took a long drink of her seltzer water.

"How was your day?" Thane said as he took a sip of his drink.

"The kind of day that makes me wish I could switch drinks with you instead of having to wait for what's-her-name to make an appearance."

"Sorry to hear that. What happened?"

"I have some bad news for you, and then possibly some badder news. Which would you like first?"

"I thought this sort of conversation usually also included an option of good news."

"That's what kind of day it was. You should have been able to tell by me using a word like badder."

Thane could identify with a day that didn't include much good news. His five years in prison rarely came with a 'good day' option, unless one's definition of 'good' was the lack of anything bad happening.

"In that case, let's start with the bad news."

"The young woman at the shelter who said she'd be willing to talk with you about Dixon went AWOL. Disappeared. She's apparently changed her mind about helping you."

"That's the second person today."

"The thing that might interest you is a Detective Hawkins came by the shelter and apparently met with her yesterday. They're supposed to call and set up a time as a courtesy, but my sense is he's not very courteous."

"Do you know how he knew she was there? Or even who she is? I hadn't included her yet on our list of witnesses."

"No idea. He's the same detective who came to the shelter and arrested Boo, but I don't know how that fits together, or if it's even connected."

"Then I guess that brings us to the 'badder' news," Thane said.

"Maybe it's not actually bad. It's just I spoke with someone who claimed to have worked with you in the past, but he was a bad dude."

"Did he give you a name?"

Hannah took a long drink from her glass, as if wanting to cleanse her mouth in advance of saying the man's name.

"I may have misheard, but I'm pretty sure he said his name was Stick."

Thane somehow managed to keep himself from whipping around and peppering Hannah with questions. His muscles tightened so quickly, he was surprised the glass in his hand didn't shatter.

"What did he want?"

"He said he had done you a favor in the past, and now he was expecting you to do the same. Is he someone you knew in prison?"

"A reasonable guess, but no. You need to stay away from him."

"Happy to, but he was leaning against my car, waiting for me."

Now Thane couldn't help but turn toward his wife, even though he knew his expression would only worry her more.

"He went to the shelter?"

Hannah took another long drink. Thane could tell she would rather be able to never mention Stick again.

"He did, and it was uncomfortable, to say the least."

"Did he threaten you?" Thane could hear the edge in his voice coming to the surface, despite his effort to remain calm.

Hannah could only nod. Thane saw she had feelings

of anger and fear of her own, with each emotion fighting to take priority.

"What did he say?"

Hannah finished her drink with one long last gulp, then only shook her head.

"Hannah..."

"It's enough to know he threatened me. And—our baby."

Thane moved to rise, but Hannah grabbed his arm, causing him to sit back down.

"Who is this man?"

Thane didn't know how much he could tell her. He obviously couldn't tell her he had asked Stick to help intimidate a witness from his previous case. He had known at the time that asking a man like Stick for something would come back to bite him, but at the time he couldn't figure out any other way to free his client.

"Stick is the man who's been pimping out Boo and a lot of other young women. He wants to make sure I'm not going to involve him in the case."

"If I'd known he was the sex trafficker, I might have tried kicking him in the balls."

"No," Thane said sternly. He knew she was joking, but he needed her to understand the danger this man posed.

"He's a sick animal and more than dangerous. If you see him, you need to walk away. Call 911 immediately, even if he's not doing anything threatening. He has killed people and will most likely kill again if he doesn't get his way."

"Then you need to stay away from him, too. He seems to be angry with you."

"I'll be careful, but I can take care of myself. That sort of psycho isn't new to me. I had to deal with men like that in prison."

"But you're not in prison anymore. You can call the police."

"I know. And I will."

He turned back to once again face the trees, but there was no tranquility left for him at that point.

"No, you won't," Hannah said. "I can tell by that look in your eye. Thane, you need to call the police. Don't do anything that will get you hurt. I'll be fine. I work at a secure facility, and I'll be extra vigilant. Just promise me two things."

Thane had expected her to make him promise something, but had assumed it would only be one thing.

"First stay away from him. That man has no soul. I don't want you anywhere near him."

"And what's the second thing?" he asked, not promising to do the first.

"Do what you need to do to help Boo. I work with women every day who are bullied and threatened. I can't let myself fall victim to that same type of behavior."

"I promise," he said, without clarifying he was only referring to her second request. As for staying away from Stick, well, that wasn't going to happen.

37

Thane had to force himself not to speed toward the bar where Stick hung out. He left his house a couple of hours after his conversation with Hannah. He would have gone immediately, but he figured Stick wasn't there that early.

He tried to come up with an excuse for leaving so Hannah wouldn't know what he was going to do, but he knew she wouldn't fall for anything but the truth. He told her he was going to talk with Stick and would be doing so in a public place. He only wanted to make sure Stick knew they would go to the police if they saw him again. He said everything would be nice and friendly, although he figured she might be skeptical of that last promise.

She told him she didn't want him to go. One didn't have to spend more than ten seconds with Stick to recognize his capacity for violence. But Hannah most likely thought of Thane as he used to be, prior to going to prison, and not what he could be like after five years on death row. He, too, had the capacity for violence, despite trying his damndest to move away from that. But right now, if violence was needed to keep Hannah and their child safe, so be it.

He pulled up outside the decrepit bar where Stick and his crew hung out. He sat in his car for a few moments trying to calm himself with deep breaths, but once he realized that wasn't going to help, he got out and entered the bar.

As was the case the last time he had met Stick there, the place looked mostly deserted. A couple of derelicts who looked like they had been embalmed sat at the bar, and a wiry old man with a rat-colored ponytail acted as bartender.

At the far end of the place, Stick and two of his minions were hanging around the pool table, as though Stick hadn't moved since the last time Thane confronted him there, although the two young guys accompanying Stick were different this time around. Both appeared to be in their late teens, and neither appeared to be in the running for any school scholarships.

Stick sat on a high barstool watching his two underlings play pool. Thane wondered if Stick ever played, or if he simply watched it all from above. It didn't matter. Thane wasn't there to play.

The pool players stopped and watched Thane approach the table. One of them made a move to intercept him but Stick subtly signaled the kid to let him approach.

"Oh, good," Stick said. "You got my message."

"You need to stay away from my wife." In prison, a person was quick to say what they wanted. You simply put it out there and then saw where things went from there.

"And you need to keep me out of Boo's problems."

"I don't recollect your name coming up so far."

"And I don't recollect anything happening to your wife and baby child so far. I didn't do nothing but explain to her the facts of life. Or the facts of death, depending how this plays out."

Thane wanted nothing more than to break a pool cue and shove the jagged edge into Stick's eye and through whatever insect-sized brain he had, but he had also learned in prison to control his temper. It wasn't easy, though.

"If she even so much as sees you again, you're the one who's going to be dead."

This was apparently too much of a threat for the two young men to let go unacknowledged. One of them stepped toward Thane, but once again, Stick shook his head.

"Step back, Hawk. This clown ain't gonna do nothing. He knows I got him on tape asking me to help him lie in a trial."

The young man paused before stepping back to the table as the other kid spoke up.

"But he shouldn't be disrespecting you like that, Stick."

Thane turned and looked at the kid, who appeared to weigh 120 pounds at most.

"What's your name?" Thane asked. He continued staring at the kid until he finally answered.

"Bob," the wannabe tough guy answered.

"Well, listen up, Bob, I'm going to…" Thane paused for a moment. "Hold up. Your name is Bob? Shouldn't it be something like Razor, or Mad Dog? I thought all you punks went by tough names."

"My name's Bob. What the hell's it matter to you?"

"I'm just saying, that's not exactly a gang name."

"It's my name. You asked me my name, I told you my name, so shut the hell up."

"You think your friend's real name is Hawk?" Thane

asked. "How about you go by Robber, or something like that. I'm assuming Bob is short for Robert."

"It ain't short for nothing. It's already short enough. Who the hell is Robert? I don't know no Robert."

Thane looked back at Stick. "I take it your criteria for gang membership doesn't require any sort of test." He looked back at Bob. "Okay then, Bob, listen up. I'm giving your boss-man more respect than he deserves by not wiping the bottom of my shoe on his face."

"Careful, counselor," Stick said, tension coloring his words.

Thane knew Stick couldn't care less what Thane said to him directly—Stick went by actions, not words—but he wouldn't want to be mocked in front of his crew. Thane turned back to him.

"I need you to understand you're not playing with some civilian who is going to call the authorities and file a complaint against you. If you come around my wife again, I will take you out, so stay away from her. I don't think that's too much to ask."

"Not too much at all, long as you leave me and my business out of your mouth during your trial. Listen, I'm not looking to cause you sorrow. It's like walking out in the woods. Person goes into the woods, they not in there to try to kill mosquitos. That's not why they're walking in the woods, they're just looking for a little peace and quiet. But if the little fuckers start biting a person, they're going to be slapped down hard. So all's I'm wanting is for you to understand repercussions can be a son-of-a-bitch if you start to irritate me."

"Look at you, tossing around four-syllable words like you read a book or something. You sure you can even define the word repercussions?

"Yeah, repercussions: the death of a loved one and a soon-to-be loved one because someone didn't listen to me."

Thane slowly walked up to within a foot of Stick.

"If you threaten my wife again, I will take you out."

"Okay, sounds like now we're starting to repeat ourselves, so go on home knowing you delivered your message. But the ball is in your court, lawyer-boy. You want 'em to be safe, then keep 'em safe. I don't know why you keep acting like you don't have a choice in the matter."

Thane knew he wasn't going to get any further with their conversation. If he wasn't willing to kill Stick right then and there, he would only be wasting his time hanging around any longer. That didn't keep him from staring at Stick a moment longer in the hope the thug could tell that Thane wasn't afraid of him.

Thane left the bar and sat in his car for a couple of minutes, deciding it was best to try to lower his temperature before getting on the road.

The idea of Stick threatening Hannah and their baby kept forcing itself into the front of his thoughts. He wanted nothing more than to get back to being the man he was before going to prison—law-abiding, honest, peaceful. Someone with a moral compass that actually had a true north on it.

But there always seemed to be something pulling him back toward his prison self. A reason, an excuse. He knew, though, that just because something pulled him, that didn't mean he needed to allow himself to be pulled.

On the other hand, Hannah's life was possibly at stake here, as well as that of his unborn daughter. He was committed to no longer taking illegal short cuts in the courtroom, but that was different from protecting his family. Was there anything he wouldn't do for them? He knew there wasn't.

And if he didn't take action and something did befall Hannah, would he ever be able to find his way back to the light again? He knew the answer to that was a hard no.

He pulled out his phone, stared at it for a long moment, then dialed a number.

"It's Thane," he said, before pausing. "Any chance of me hiring you to do a job for me?"

Gideon watched uncomfortably when he saw Alice walking toward him with his coffee. He had stopped by almost an hour ago with the intention of just getting a cup of coffee and asking the waitress out, but instead he got coffee, and then a full dinner, then a piece of pie, and now a fresh cup of coffee. He knew he was stalling, but his time would run out soon.

He couldn't remember the last time he asked out a woman, or even if he ever had, at least not on a real date. His days in prison began as a teenager, and his stints of freedom between incarcerations were usually brief. Definitely not enough time for courtship.

He didn't believe his nephew or Thane when they told him Alice was interested in him, but then again, what did he know about women? He would see if Gus and Thane were right, and if he ended up embarrassing himself, well, he'd get even by pounding the shit out of them. Well, not his nephew, but he'd come up with something.

"Here you go, sweetie." Alice leaned on the stool next to Gideon and looked around the diner. Other than Gideon, there was only one elderly couple in a booth in the corner who looked like they had no place else to go. "Been a long day. Glad it's winding down."

"Oh," Gideon said, looking around, not having noticed he was one of the last people there. "You can put this in a to-go cup, if you want, and I can get out of your hair."

Alice laughed. "You don't have to do that. That wasn't me trying to hint anything. On the contrary, it's nice to have a few minutes of downtime to chat with you."

"Oh," Gideon said once again, finding that his range of conversational skills were on full display. He looked at Alice and saw her smiling at his awkwardness. He immediately shifted his attention to the coffee, downing it like he was in a chugging contest.

Once he guzzled down the coffee, he decided he couldn't keep stalling, but nerves once again got the better of him. He looked down at her feet.

"I like your shoes."

They were boxy black shoes that were functional for someone on their feet for long hours. Gideon thought they looked solid, the sort of industrial strength shoes that would last a long time.

Alice looked down at her shoes and smiled. "You do, huh?"

"Yeah, I got a pair of shoes a lot like those. They been good shoes."

"Well then, there you go," Alice said. Gideon thought she would laugh at him, but her smile didn't end up extending to the point of mockery. "What else is on your mind tonight?" she asked, as if she were reading him like a book. The kind of book used to teach first graders.

"I don't know," Gideon managed to say. "I guess since you brought it up—and I'll totally understand if you don't want to—in fact I'd be a little surprised if you did—cause you know…"

"Sweetie, we'll be closing in a few minutes. What's your question?"

Gideon reminded himself of some of his more memorable fights in prison. One time he took on four inmates at once, and while he ended up in the infirmary, he had been able to take three of the four out before getting hit over the head with an iron pipe. He wasn't sure how he could do that but now be acting like some sort of coward. He needed to man up and get this over with.

"I was wondering if you might have any interest in doing something some night. I mean, doing something with me, not on your own, although I'd understand if you'd rather do that."

"What'd you have in mind?" Alice asked, lowering herself onto the stool next to him and spinning herself so she faced him directly.

Her question caught Gideon off-guard. "I ain't got no idea," he confessed. "To be honest, it never occurred to me the conversation would go any further than asking you."

"Why'd you think that?"

"Because, well, because of who I am."

"But that's one of the reasons people go out. To find out who each other really are."

Gideon nodded as if this made sense, although little made sense to him at that moment.

"One of the first things you'd learn about me is that I'm out on parole. I been in prison a whole lot of years, which is reason enough for you to not want to do something together."

"Were you innocent?"

If Gideon had taken a drink of coffee when she asked that, he would have sprayed it across the counter like in an old comedy.

"Nah. I don't know that I've ever been innocent."

Alice stood up and straightened her apron. "Good to hear. I wouldn't have gone out with you if you'd said you were innocent. Too many liars out there. Give me an honest man any day of the week, even if he's done time."

Gideon thought about that and again nodded in agreement, even though he didn't usually equate someone doing time with someone honest, but maybe he was wrong about that. Her words then made him think of another question.

"Wait a minute. Is that a yes?"

38

As he drove down the 105, Thane got a call from Letitia, letting him know she had finally tracked down an address for the elusive Iris Robinson. While it was usually simple to track down someone's information from their phone number, Iris had apparently taken steps to make it more difficult. In fact, a friend of Letitia's who worked in Silicon Valley was impressed with how Iris had hidden her identity, but he had nevertheless been able to help Letitia overcome the roadblocks that had been set up, under the condition she never reveal who gave her the information.

Thane told Letitia he'd be coming into the office after stopping by Iris's home unannounced. He wasn't sure this was the best move right now, but it would certainly be unexpected, and sometimes unexpected revealed all sorts of helpful information. He just hoped that was the case with this situation.

He pulled up to an attractive, two-story home in Baldwin Hills, close to Culver City. The front yard and shrubs were immaculate, and the house itself looked well-kept. Thane wasn't expecting Iris to be living somewhere so nice, but he realized he had been looking at her as some sort of informant willing to help out Detective Struthers, whereas she could have been an undercover detective. In fact, that made more sense anyway.

A dark blue Ford Taurus sat in the driveway, and a light burned in what Thane guessed was the kitchen window. He waited a couple of minutes, telling himself he wanted to see if Iris would appear in the window, but mostly he gave himself time to make sure this still felt like the right way to go. He finally decided that letting it play out on its own only made it more likely that Struther's plan would be successful.

Thane got out of his car and walked quickly across the street toward the front door. He thought if Iris saw him approaching, she might not answer, and he wanted to see her reaction when facing him. He expected it to be one of surprise.

He rang the doorbell and waited for a moment until the door finally opened, and Thane found himself standing face-to-face with Detective Struthers. They both had a reaction of surprise, but it was Struthers who managed to speak first.

"What are you doing at my house?"

This wasn't something Thane had considered. No wonder it was difficult for Letitia to track down Iris's cell phone number: cops knew tricks to hide personal information. Also, since he believed Struthers was orchestrating this whole thing, it made sense the calls were made by a phone he provided. If he had thought it through more, he wouldn't have been so surprised with this development.

Thane started to explain he thought he was there to see a woman who had been trying to contact him, which was true, but before he could offer up that explanation, a larger surprise came from around the corner.

"I'm assuming he's here to talk with me," a woman said as she walked toward the door. Thane looked over and saw the woman from Letitia's photo walking toward them.

"I called and left a message, although I didn't realize you'd be coming by in person," she said when she reached the door. Struthers, looking totally thrown off his game, stepped to the side as the woman extended her hand.

"I'm Iris Robinson. It's nice to meet you." She glanced over at Struthers, then back at Thane. "I'm Vince's wife."

It was the first time Thane had seen Struthers appear rattled. He could tell the detective didn't like this at all, and yet he also didn't seem to be in a position to stop it. He reached behind the door and grabbed his sport coat off a hook, all but glaring at his wife as he moved past Thane.

"I gotta go to work."

"Goodbye, sweetheart."

Thane and Iris watched Struthers get in his car and start it up. He looked at the two of them for a long moment, as if trying to decide if he could do anything about this, then put the car in gear and pulled out of the driveway and down the street.

"Please, Mr. Banning, do come in."

Thane entered and followed her into a modest but brightly colored kitchen. The thought of being in the detective's house seemed surreal. Iris nodded for him to take a seat at their kitchen table and offered him a cup of coffee, which he accepted, if for no other reason than to get a few more seconds to try to figure out what was going on.

Iris sat a cup of coffee in front of him before leaving

the room for a moment. When she returned, she held a framed photograph. She took a seat across the table from him.

"I appreciate you stopping by. I naturally assumed you would call, but this is even better."

Thane took a long sip of coffee, having no idea how to play this other than to ask what he wanted to know.

"You said you're married to Detective Struthers."

"To Vince, yes. He doesn't make me call him detective, although sometimes he can make it feel like he's more comfortable with that name. He and I have been married for almost twenty-six years now. Bonnie is our daughter."

"She told me her mother was gone."

"I'm sure she did, but I can assure you she's my daughter." She handed Thane the photo of Struthers, Iris, and a younger Bonnie Cruise.

"She tells people she was abandoned when younger," Iris said, "but she knows that she's the one who did the abandoning."

Iris took the photo back from Thane and looked at it for a long moment, as if wishing she could go back to that point in time.

"My daughter has led a troubled life. She's headstrong like my husband and if I'm being totally honest, like me as well. But having a cop for a father was difficult for her. Vince is a good man, but in his job he sees a lot of darkness and a lot of pain, and that caused him to be over-protective of his only child, which in turn caused her to rebel."

"So Boo—I mean Bonnie—lied to me. Why do you think she didn't want me to talk with you?"

"I'm sure it's more a case of her not wanting to involve

us. She's not proud of what she has become, and while we have been estranged for several years, I do believe she doesn't want to embarrass us or put her father in a difficult position. She uses my mother's maiden name as her last name, and I continue to use my maiden name, so in a family of three, we all use a different name, but that doesn't make us any less of a family. She will always be my daughter, and I'll always want the best for her. That's why I wanted you to represent her."

"My wife is the one who introduced her to me."

"But I'm the one who told Bonnie to go to that shelter and to find a way to talk with your wife. I've read about you in the newspapers and knew she was the director there. I hoped you would take on Bonnie's case."

Thane now wanted something stronger than coffee, but it wasn't even 9:30 in the morning. Still…

"And your husband was okay with that?"

"Oh God no!" Iris said, laughing. "Although deep down, I think he's actually glad to have someone like you helping our daughter. He may come across as all business, but I am confident he puts family first. However, this was all my doing."

"And why did you want me to represent her?"

Iris leaned back in her chair and brought her coffee cup to her mouth, but she only smelled the coffee before setting the cup back down.

"I know Vince would absolutely hate what I'm about to tell you, and I'll try to respect his confidence during our talk, but my daughter has been charged with murder and absolutely nothing else comes close to being more important to me than that. My husband suspects you did things in your last two trials which may not have been ethical. His sense is you have been willing to do whatever it takes to exact justice, whether legal or not, which runs counter to everything he stands for. And yet, at the same time, he also seems to believe you are a good man. You have no idea how rare that is for my husband. So that's who I want representing my daughter. A good man willing to paint outside the lines in order to help his client, even if the shade of paint is morally gray."

Thane tried imagining Struther's reaction to his wife telling him this. It was also a gut punch to Thane to hear confirmation from the detective's wife of Struther's suspicions of him.

"I'm not sure why your husband believes what he believes, but while I'm open to pushing the envelope for my clients, I don't look to paint outside the lines. The lines are there for a good reason."

"I understand, and I wouldn't expect you to say anything different. And I admit I'm only going based on things Vince has said about you, but he's also an incredibly good judge of character. Either way, your success in your cases has been impressive, and that's the sort of lawyer I want representing Bonnie. But now that you know everything, I do have one question."

"And what is that?" Thane said, finding it hard to believe he truly knew everything at that point.

"Knowing who Bonnie is and, more importantly, who her father is, do you still think you can represent her with your best effort?"

"That doesn't change anything. I wouldn't have taken the case if I didn't believe I would give it my best effort. I actually have a lot of respect for your husband. I have no doubt he's honest and moral, and while I don't like to hear he thinks I may have done something inappropriate, I'm confident he'll be fair and will come to see he's mistaken."

"I'm sure he'll be fair, although he's rarely mistaken."

"So, what is it specifically you have been wanting to talk with me about? Or is this it?"

Iris sighed and her expression turned more serious. "The police have asked to question me about a gun I owned, which they believe to be the murder weapon. I had a feeling this would happen eventually, which is why I was reaching out to you, but apparently last night they connected the second call Bonnie made the night of the shooting to my cell phone, so they were able to make the connection between the two of us."

"And also, I'm assuming, your husband's connection."

"Needless to say, it's awkward for the police department, but Vince is in no way involved in the investigation, and so far, the press hasn't made the connection, but if they do, then they do."

Thane thought back to his conversation with Struthers in his office when the detective told him if he had any questions about the case, to let him know. Thane had wondered why the usually intractable man was suddenly offering to help. He now realized this was one way of helping his daughter.

"I understand it could seem like a conflict of interest for you to help me with my being questioned by the police, but I would nevertheless appreciate it if you would."

"It would most certainly be a conflict of interest."

"I know," Iris said, "but once you hear me out, you'll understand why I'm convinced it will help her."

39

The minute Boo walked into the small room to meet with him, Thane sensed she knew what he was there to talk about. Iris told him she wasn't in communication with her daughter, so Boo didn't know the ruse was up because of a phone call from her mother. She simply had to have known the truth would come out sooner rather than later.

Boo sat in the chair across the table from Thane, and his suspicions were confirmed.

"I'm guessing you want to talk more about my mother," she said.

"I had a couple of other questions first, if you don't mind. To begin with, did you realize you've been charged with capital murder?"

Boo obviously knew there was no real reason to answer that question. Of course she knew what she had been charged with.

"And did you know if we're going to have any chance at all in reaching the best result possible, I'm going to need you to be honest with me?"

Again, Boo didn't respond, but instead stared at him as if waiting for him to make his point.

"I'm serious," Thane said. "Did you know those things?"

Boo sighed and slumped back in her chair.

"I did know those things, but since it's question and answer time, let me ask you a couple. Do you know how much pain and embarrassment I've caused my mother? My father, too, but the hell with him. He was always a cop before being a father. But my mom? She deserves far, far better than me, so when I told you she wasn't a part of my life, that was me trying to keep her out of it."

Thane started to respond, but Boo put up her hand.

"I know. It was a stupid thing to do, especially when she had already reached out to you. I knew it was only a matter of time, but I didn't want it to come from me. She deserves better than this. She deserves better than me."

"But what she wants is for me to do everything I can to help you, so how about we respect her wishes in that regard? But I can't do my best to help if I don't know the truth."

"And nothing but the truth."

"Or at least anything that might help."

They sat in silence for a long moment. Thane finally decided the best way to see how truthful she would be was to compare her story to what Iris had told him earlier that morning.

"Tell me again about the night of the murder, but this time focus solely on any communication you might have had with your mother, if any."

Boo sighed. "After I shot Dixon, I called my mom and told her what I'd done."

"And what did she say?"

"She said she would come pick me up. My dad was on duty that night, so she could meet me there without having to explain anything to him."

"And she picked you up?"

Boo's eyes became moist, and she quickly flicked aside the one lone tear that made a break for it down her cheek.

"She wanted to help me. She told me to give her the gun, and she would get rid of it for me." A few more tears formed, but this time she let them fall. "She said she would do anything she could to help me."

Thane watched as Boo's tough facade cracked. She showed more concern and emotion for her mother than she had shown at any point for herself. Thane figured she didn't view herself as deserving any sympathy.

"Is she going to get in trouble?" Boo said. "For getting rid of the gun?"

"I don't know. The police have determined she owns the same model gun used to kill Dixon, so they already want to question her about that. If there is a connection with the murder weapon, I'm pretty sure they'll try to pressure her to tell them what she did, and that would include helping you."

"Dammit."

"I highly doubt the D.A. will charge her with anything if she cooperates. They're primarily going to be interested in getting her testimony. In fact, her lawyer will likely be able to get her a plea deal where they don't charge her with anything if she tells them what happened."

"What do you mean 'her lawyer?' You need to be her lawyer!"

"That's not a great idea. There's a serious risk of there being a conflict of interest."

"I don't care. I've already told the cops I shot Dixon, so what does it matter if they know my mom threw away the gun? That doesn't hurt my case any. They know I shot him."

"Boo, you're my client. I can't help a witness provide evidence against—".

"What does that evidence do to my case? I've already said I killed him. Who cares if they know what happened to the gun? Look, if you don't help her, then I'm going to plead guilty. I won't even take the deal they're offering. I'll plead without an agreement, and they can put me away for life."

"Good idea," Thane said, starting to get angry. "That will sure teach me a lesson. Listen, I can help her find a great lawyer. It won't help her to have me represent her. I'm not even sure the court would allow it."

"I don't care. I want you to help her on this. I trust you."

Thane could tell Boo wasn't going to budge on this. He also appreciated her support of her mother. But that didn't mean he thought this was a good idea.

Hannah left the shelter around 1:00 p.m., hoping to grab a late lunch at a nearby salad bar. It was only a few blocks away—totally walkable—but the past couple of days she'd driven. She didn't think she had anything to worry about with Stick, at least not unless Thane told her otherwise, but she was still unsettled enough that she continued to drive.

She was also much more cautious whenever she crossed the parking lot toward her car, which is why she noticed yet another large, rough-looking man sitting low in his car, facing the shelter's entrance, looking as though he didn't want to be noticed. She couldn't help but shake her head.

She walked over to the beat-up Impala and saw the man offer up an embarrassed smile and a half-wave. He rolled down his window.

"Well, what a surprise seeing you here," he said.

"Hey, Kyle. Yeah, I'm guessing you didn't know I worked here, did you?"

Thane had represented Kyle in his last big case. The man, who had once been an adversary of Thane's while they were in prison, had been charged with the murder of Thane's former boss and friend, Joseph Crowell. But as they worked together, Thane and Kyle grew closer, to the point where Thane finally started calling Kyle by his real name and not his nickname, Kilo.

Kyle shrugged, still red in the cheeks. "Thane didn't mention whether this was an undercover job or not. Hope I didn't get him in trouble."

"It's okay. Thane has trouble keeping secrets from me anyway," although as she said that, Hannah knew it wasn't true. She knew he was hiding something, but she didn't know what it was or why he was so reluctant to be open with her.

"You notice anything out of the ordinary?" Kyle asked.

"No, it's all quiet. If you're going to be hanging around, would you rather wait inside where it's more comfortable?"

"No, it's best I stay out here. I don't expect any trouble, but I'd rather see it coming than be surprised."

"If you need anything, let me know. Good seeing you again, Kyle."

"Yes ma'am."

As Hannah turned and continued on toward her car, Kyle called out to her.

"Actually, could I use your restroom? It's not something I can do in a bottle."

"Thanks for the explanation, Kyle," she said, smiling. "Come with me."

40

Thane sat on one of the wingback chairs that D.A. Angela Day had positioned in her office, while Assistant D.A. Arthur Barnes sat across from him. Day had rolled her desk chair so she could be part of the discussion if needed, but she remained a little bit removed from the two men.

"You can't be representing Iris Robinson," Barnes said.

"I agree I shouldn't be representing her. No argument from me on that. But as I said earlier, I'm afraid I am representing her, so maybe we can save the ethical debate for later. Ms. Robinson and her daughter both understand the potential conflict, but each still wants to go forward with this."

Barnes shook his head to make sure he had conveyed his disgust, although he had already made that clear to Thane. "So, what will it take to get Ms. Robinson to testify?"

"Blanket immunity. She's willing to tell you everything she knows in exchange for not being charged with a crime."

"No conflict of interest there." Barnes muttered.

"Again, I agree with you, but the reality of the situation is my client has already admitted to shooting

Mr. Dixon, so if it turns out that the gun used in the shooting is the one owned by Ms. Robinson, that seems to be irrelevant to the case. I'm not even sure why you're so determined to find it."

"Because I am thorough," Barnes barked. "And Detective Hawkins is thorough. And neither of us trust you, so I'm going to dot every i and cross every t, and the gun is one of those missing pieces. I want to know where it is and get it to forensics."

"My client is willing to tell you everything she knows."

"Including where the gun is?"

"She hasn't shared much with me, but I'm confident she can tell you the location of the gun."

Barnes sat back and chewed on the tip of his pen, as if trying to figure out any possible way he was being set up. Given Thane's reputation, that was a reasonable thing to do.

Finally, Barnes looked over at his boss. "Angela, what do you think?"

"Your case, your call, Arthur. I only wanted to be present to make sure Mr. Banning understood how inappropriate it is for him to be representing Ms. Robinson. I totally agree with what you said, Arthur."

"Then we're three for three on that question," Thane said.

Barnes turned back to Thane. "If your client is caught in any lie, no matter how small, the deal is off the table."

"She understands."

"And she can't pick and choose which questions she wants to answer. She might be providing information extremely damaging to her daughter's case."

"She's prepared to be totally forthright. She's willing to cooperate with your office, so long as she isn't charged with a crime. She realizes her daughter has already confessed to the shooting, so there doesn't seem to be any need to not be truthful with you."

Barnes glanced over again at Day, but apparently she wasn't going to get involved in this decision. Thane wondered if that's because she gave her team the autonomy they needed to try their own cases, or because she thought Thane was setting up Barnes and would end up making him look bad. He assumed the former, since he always thought the D.A. was a good leader.

On the other hand, it was an election year.

"Alright," Barnes said. "You have a deal."

41

Thane sat next to Iris and across from Arthur Barnes at a long, rectangular table in a non-descript room in the D.A.'s office area. A young woman, looking like an intern from a local law school, sat next to Barnes with her MacBook open, ready to take notes.

Iris dressed professionally, looking like one of the attorneys working in a nearby office. She also appeared nervous. Not that being interviewed at the District Attorney's office wouldn't be cause for some anxiety, but she had been so insistent on doing this that Thane assumed she wouldn't look so uncomfortable.

Barnes took out his phone and reminded Iris that their interview would be recorded and then, after they had concluded, her statement would be transcribed into a sworn statement to be signed by her. After turning on his recording app and setting the stage with the date, time, names of those present, and where the interview was being conducted, Barnes confirmed Iris's relationship to the defendant. He stated for the record that anything she said could not be used against her in a court of law, contingent upon every question being answered honestly. However, anything she told them could be used against her daughter in her trial. If the D.A.'s office could identify any false statement on Iris's part, the entire deal would be rescinded, and Iris could be prosecuted for hindering a legal proceeding. Barnes asked if Iris understood the parameters of their immunity deal, and she said she did. With that, Barnes began his questioning.

"Ms. Robinson, do you own a SIG Sauer P938?"

"I owned such a gun, which I bought and registered in 2015."

"You say you owned the gun. Do you no longer have it?" Barnes asked.

"No, it is no longer in my possession." Iris took a drink of water as Barnes glanced at his notepad.

"And where is it now?"

"Somewhere in the Pacific Ocean. I can't say where, exactly. I took a ferry to Catalina Island and dropped it over the railing about halfway there. I'm afraid that's about as specific as I can be."

"And when was this?"

"The morning after Mr. Dixon was shot. Sometime between 9:00 – 10:00 a.m."

"And why did you throw the gun into the ocean?"

"I wanted to dispose of it. It was used in the shooting of Mr. Dixon."

Although Iris had seemed nervous to Thane, she answered all of Barnes' questions calmly and directly, without hesitation. But then again, the questions hadn't directly involved her daughter yet, although that was about to change.

"Before you disposed of your gun, did you always keep it in the same place?"

"Yes. I have a small gun safe underneath my nightstand. I always kept it there."

"And did your daughter Bonnie know about the gun and where you kept it?"

"She did."

"And did she know the combination of the safe?"

"Yes, she did. We had it for home protection, so I wanted her to have access to it if needed. Back when she lived with us."

Barnes scribbled something on his notepad, even though the intern was typing steadily along.

"And on the night of the murder, did you receive a call from your daughter?"

"I did. She called me from Mr. Dixon's house."

"From inside the house?"

"I can't say for sure that she was in the house, but I'm certain she was at least on his property. She could have been standing outside."

"Did you leave your house after getting that call and meet your daughter that night at Coach Dixon's home?"

"I did."

Barnes paused, as if wanting to give Iris a moment before he dove into questions directly implicating her daughter.

"And did she at that point give you the gun and ask you to dispose of it?"

"No, she did not."

"She didn't ask you to dispose of it? Is that something you decided to do on your own?"

Iris nodded. "It was my idea to dispose of the gun."

Thane listened as intently to her story as Barnes and the intern did. She had shared next to nothing of what happened the night of Dixon's murder. Thane had tried to get her to understand it would help him tremendously to know the details before she spoke, but she would not oblige him. Her reluctance to be open frustrated him and made him think twice about letting her talk with Barnes, but he did not doubt her desire to help her daughter.

"When you met your daughter, at what point did she give you the gun?"

"She never gave me the gun."

Even the intern looked up from her keyboard at this, then quickly returned her focus to her laptop. Barnes paused and glanced at Thane, as if trying to figure out where this was heading.

"She never gave you the gun? Did you take it from her, or find it in her belongings? How did you come to once again get possession of your gun?"

"It never left my possession. At no point that night did Bonnie touch the gun."

Barnes once again looked at Thane, but Thane hoped he looked as confused as everyone else. It sounded like a desperate strategy to try to help her daughter.

"Ms. Robinson," Barnes said, "again I want to stress to you that this immunity deal is null and void should you lie at any point during this questioning."

Iris nodded, her confident facade starting to crack.

"You disposed of a gun you said was used in a murder, but you claim your daughter was never in possession of the gun. Can you explain this to me?"

"She was never in possession of the gun because she didn't kill Mr. Dixon. I did."

Barnes threw his pen on the table and looked as though he wanted to punch Thane for orchestrating this con job, but Thane was as surprised as Barnes had been. He also knew, though, that Barnes would be able to tear apart her story with little to no effort.

"Ms. Robinson, please. The call reporting the shot

came in at 12:50. Your daughter called you at 12:55, and your home is at least fifteen minutes away. You said you left home after getting the call, therefore, you couldn't have been the person who killed Mr. Dixon."

As easy as that, Barnes brought Iris to tears. She tried speaking a couple of times, perhaps in an attempt to say how it could be possible, but she obviously couldn't come up with an explanation that would hold water. She looked at Thane for his help, but he couldn't do or say anything that might help her.

"Mr. Barnes, my daughter is a good person. She has had a tough life, and the things that man did to her, well, she didn't deserve that. Nobody deserves that. You have to understand, she has a good heart. She has simply made some bad choices in her life, but she's trying to atone for those. Please. This is all my fault. My husband and me, we let her down. We're the ones who should be punished."

Barnes fumed as he asked Iris to wait in an adjoining office and ordered the wide-eyed intern to return to her cubicle. When it was just Thane and him, Barnes directed his anger at Thane.

"She's obviously lying to protect her daughter. Who the hell did she think she was going to fool? Given the phone records, and no other evidence to the contrary, there's no use continuing this interview."

Thane wanted to respond, but he couldn't act as though he disagreed with Barnes' assessment. He also felt that agreeing with Barnes could only hurt his client so instead he said nothing.

"As pissed off as I am to have wasted my time, I'll be honest and say I think you were as surprised as I was." Thane nodded strongly at that assessment.

"So I'm sure it goes without saying that the immunity deal is off," Barnes said gruffly. "And I can't say right now whether I'll be charging her for getting rid of the gun and being an accessory to the cover-up, but I'm guessing I won't. As a father, I understand a parent's desire to do anything to help their child. If Ms. Robinson can be made to understand that spreading this story won't be to anyone's advantage, I'll likely be willing to let it drop. But if she tries selling this load of crap to a newspaper or anywhere else, I'll hit her with whatever charges are available to me."

"That's more than fair," Thane said. "I appreciate your understanding."

At least Thane now understood why Iris wouldn't share the details of her story with him. She knew he would try to talk her out of it. But he also would have been able to show her that her story wouldn't hold up.

Thane and Iris didn't speak as they walked to his car. He wasn't even sure what to say, in part because Iris already looked completely defeated. He wondered if she thought there was a chance her strategy would have worked, but in retrospect now saw how delusional she had been. When they were in the car and pulling out of the parking garage, Iris turned to him.

"I'm sorry I didn't share this with you. I knew what you'd say."

"I understand why you're doing this. You love your daughter and want to help her, and Barnes also knows this. But you had to know your story wouldn't hold up under scrutiny."

Iris nodded and looked out the passenger side car window.

"I believe you did whatever you needed to do in your last two trials to find justice," she said after a quiet moment, "because you didn't think you'd find it any other way. My daughter has been trafficked and sexually abused by a number of men in power, and now that that abuse has been exposed, everyone is more concerned about protecting the name of her abuser than trying to find justice for Bonnie. So I'm willing to do whatever I can to help my daughter find justice."

"But I don't believe you helped your daughter," Thane said, totally understanding how she felt. "Instead, you came real close to getting yourself in trouble alongside your daughter."

Iris once again nodded. "When you have a child, you'll understand."

42

Thane sat with Gideon at the nearby sports bar they went to once a week. Thane tried to eat healthy but from time to time he needed a greasy burger and fries. He thought of it as a special treat. Gideon thought of it as Tuesday. "You ready for tomorrow?" Gideon asked.

"Do you mean do I have any sort of coherent defense to offer the jury tomorrow? Or am I ready to flounder in court for a few hours? If the latter, then the answer is hell yes."

The prosecution had rested their case after Barnes brought updated information to the attention of the jury. The second phone number Boo had made was to her mother, who was at home when her daughter called. He also showed through Iris's gun registration that the defendant's mother owned the same make and model as the gun used to kill Dixon.

Barnes decided not to call Iris to the stand. Even though he could tear apart the story she had told during her interview, he obviously didn't think it was worth establishing the general location of the gun if it meant her possibly going off-script.

The prosecution had a rock-solid case. The question of who shot Dixon wasn't up for debate. Thane saw his primary goal as trying to get a reduced charge, or at least a more lenient sentence from the jury. He knew he wouldn't get as good of an outcome as the one Silver had offered, but Boo had turned that offer down as well. Thane made a half-hearted effort to get Boo to see what a gift this latest offer was. Half-hearted because Boo already recognized how generous the offer was. She just didn't care.

Thane wasn't sure how well Barnes' argument against vigilantism would play with the jury. Intellectually, it made perfect sense, but Thane knew the U.S. had been moving more and more toward violence as a reasonable response against supposed threats, although he wasn't sure that applied to someone who looked like Boo. Self-defense played better when a rich white person had dealt with someone on their property, especially if that someone wasn't white.

"You don't think Barnes bought the mother's story?" Gideon asked.

"Would you?"

"Nah, but I like to think I'm smarter than most prosecutors."

"That might explain the number of years you've spent locked up."

"It could. Yeah, I suppose it could."

The bartender placed a can of Coke in front of Gideon and a beer in front of Thane. When Thane took a long drink, he saw Gideon side-eyeing him. Thane rarely drank during the day, and while just a beer, it was still something outside his usual pattern. They both learned to watch for behavior that didn't match past patterns when they were in prison.

"Boo's mother said she'd do anything to help her daughter. She said I'd understand once I had a child."

"That don't surprise me none, although I'm guessing you already knew that."

Thane nodded but didn't reply. He took another long drink and stared at the beer bottle's label.

"What's you conjucating on?" Gideon said. "Something on your mind?"

Thane didn't answer at first, then finally put his beer bottle down and focused his attention on his fries.

"I'm going to tell you something, but you have to promise not to take matters into your own hands."

"Would you believe me if I did promise that?"

Thane thought about it for the briefest of moments. "No, probably not."

"Then why go through the motions? What's going on?"

Thane needed to talk to someone about what he was wrestling with. His main concern was that Gideon would end up getting into trouble, and it wasn't Gideon's fight. Still, Gideon was the only person he could talk to about something like this.

"Stick threatened Hannah the other day."

Even though Gideon didn't visibly react, Thane could see his friend's body tightening up, ready for a fight.

"When?"

"Couple days ago. He waited for her in the parking lot where she works. Threatened her, and our baby."

Thane was grateful Gideon hadn't already grabbed a steak knife and stomped out the door right then and there.

"What are you thinking of doing?" Gideon asked.

"Usually, I find myself thinking about killing him, but I can't keep doing that."

Gideon glanced at Thane. It was the first time Thane had directly referenced having killed someone in the past. He had no doubt Gideon knew Thane had in some way been involved in what happened with Joseph and the detective who had committed the murder for which Thane had done his time. He probably assumed Thane had killed the men himself, although maybe he had also figured out that Thane had simply set things up so that the murdered woman's father could get his own justice.

"I've been thinking about what Iris said about doing whatever it took to help her daughter," Thane said. What do I do with a guy like Stick? I can't wait until he hurts Hannah or the baby to hit back at him. I need to leave him out of this case, but what if that hurts Boo? Do I sacrifice her to keep my family safe?"

"Nobody could fault you for that."

"Or do I do something that gets rid of Stick once and for all? I feel like those are my only options. I did threaten him, but threats aren't going to do anything."

"Threats would just make him laugh."

"I'm serious about you not getting involved with this," Thane said.

"I know you are, and while that's my first reaction, believe it or not I'm trying to do better this time around."

Thane looked at Gideon, hoping his surprise wasn't too obvious. Gideon shrugged.

"What?" Gideon said. "You're trying to do better; I'm trying to do better. I want to give this a real shot this time around. Hell, it's already been over a year and I'm still out here doing great shit like eating lunch at a bar." He took a grizzly bear-size bite of his burger, but couldn't hold back a smile. "You gotta admit, it's a little bit funny that you're more likely to kill someone than I am, although I wouldn't blame you if you did. I'd also help you if you asked."

"Stick says all I have to do is leave him out of this trial, and he's probably right about that, but knowing him, he'll be wanting something else down the road, and then something else. Plus, when I think of him talking to Hannah, I want to break something."

"I'm guessing his neck," Gideon said.

"That's where I'd start."

43

Thane, Kristin, and Boo sat at the defense table. Boo was motionless, staring at the floor as if it had hypnotized her. Court was scheduled to resume in a few minutes and Thane was mentally rehearsing how he would present his case.

Although Thane had received a lot of publicity from having won his previous two cases, this one was different. In his first two cases, he had had absolutely no doubt as to his clients' innocence because they were both charged with a murder Thane had put into motion. With this case, it seemed pretty clear that Boo had committed murder. He now had to get the jury to see there were extenuating circumstances. If she had killed her pimp, the jury most likely would be more lenient. Thane certainly would be, although for different reasons.

And if Thane wasn't able to get a reduced sentence for Boo, at least he could honor her desire to expose the people and institutions that enabled Dixon's heinous behavior. If she was going to go down as a martyr, he wanted her to feel like she had at least been able to make her point. It wouldn't be easy, though. And, as Gideon had said, it wouldn't change anything. But at least they could try.

Thane called Sterling Silver to the stand as his first witness. He noticed a couple of people smile upon hearing the name as Silver approached the stand. After establishing Silver's position and general responsibilities, Thane began the heart of his questioning.

"Mr. Silver, you've been in your position for almost twenty years now. For the first seventeen years, your office helped raise an average of one hundred five million dollars a year for the University of Los Angeles. But in the last three years, the university has seen annual donations increase to close to two hundred million. It was also in the last three years that the university's football team ranked in the top 20, and this year they were ranked as high as number eight in the nation. Do you attribute some of your success in fundraising to the success of the football team?"

"There are always a number of reasons for the success of fundraising campaigns," Silver said, sounding like a consummate professional, "but yes, having a successful sports program almost always has an impact on a school's fundraising effort, regardless of the school."

"And you currently have a special campaign underway focusing on the construction of a new stadium which, I'm assuming, will help continue the growth of the football team's success. Is that right?"

"That has been the experience of other schools, yes."

"Have your donations increased significantly since the death of Mr. Cash Dixon?"

"People have responded wonderfully to the tragic death of our coach. Believe me, it's not how I want to raise money, but I believe Coach Dixon would be happy to see people responding to his dream of building a new stadium for our wonderful university."

It didn't surprise Thane that Silver could turn even testimony at a murder trial into a fundraising message.

"I guess you have to make the best of a bad situation," Thane said.

"Objection," Barnes said without rising. "I don't see what any of this has to do with the death of Coach Dixon. Is the defense counsel implying the chief fundraiser is responsible for the man's death in an effort to increase donations? If not, can we get back to the matter at hand?"

"Actually, I believe Mr. Dixon was already the primary cash cow for ULA," Thane said.

"And that is relevant to this case how?" Judge Miller asked.

"Your Honor, the prosecution has on more than one occasion suggested that the defendant should have asked for help rather than taken the action she took. I'm simply trying to show that that would have been a lot harder than it sounds. For example, should this young, black, female sex worker have gone to the University and asked that Mr. Dixon be fired? How do you suppose that conversation would have gone?"

Judge Miller thought about Thane's argument for longer than Thane had expected. The judge further surprised Thane by ruling in his favor.

"Overruled."

"The University of Los Angeles has a no tolerance stance toward sexual harassment of any kind," Silver said.

"The witness will only answer questions asked of him," the judge said kindly.

"That's okay," Thane said. "Let's talk about that. I believe what you just said is in the university's code of conduct, correct?"

"That's correct."

"Then I guess if it's in your code of conduct, it must be true."

"Your Honor," Barnes said again, this time louder.

"Mr. Banning," the judge said, "I understand the argument you're trying to make, and I'm comfortable giving you a small bit of road to pursue it, but don't try turning that road into an interstate. And once again, I'm not sure sarcasm is going to be your best approach."

"Understood, Your Honor." Thane returned his attention to Silver.

"The only other thing I want to ask about has to do with scholarships. I understand the vast majority of scholarships go through the financial aid department, but your development office does hold the purse strings to some scholarships as well?"

"Yes. We have some donors who give money to my department, and they have specific requests for how the money is to be allocated. A successful journalist might request that their money be used for scholarships in our communications school. Alumni from small towns may want scholarships given to someone from a rural area. Those sorts of donations are not uncommon."

"But aren't those funds usually given to the financial aid department and earmarked accordingly?"

"Yes, but sometimes a donor prefers to work directly with us."

"Is Luther Fournier such a donor?"

Silver hesitated for the first time during his testimony. Up to that point his delivery had been smooth and reassuring as befitted a man in his position, but Luther didn't appear to be a topic he wanted to discuss.

"Mr. Fournier is one of several such donors, yes."

"He has donated a lot of money for athletic scholarships and has also been a major donor for the new stadium." Thane walked back to his table and picked up a notepad, even though he already had the information memorized. He had found in the past that jury members tended to focus more when a lawyer walked back to his table, as if what he was about to say was extra important.

"Besides the new stadium, the only other area that his donations have gone is to young women who belong to the Alpha Gamma sorority. Fifteen full scholarships have gone to members of that sorority, with none going to any other sorority or fraternity. Do you know what his connection is to this sorority?"

"I'm afraid I don't," Silver said, looking disappointed that he wasn't able to help. "It's possible his wife or daughter at one time were part of that sorority."

"Mr. Fournier has never married, nor does he have children."

"Then maybe a niece. I'll be honest, when a donor is willing to give us money that will help students get a strong education, I don't usually pry too much into their motivation. I usually just say thank you."

"As long as it doesn't violate the university's code of ethics."

"That goes without saying."

"But I wanted you to say it anyway. No further questions, Your Honor."

After Barnes said he had no questions for the witness—making sure the jury understood he believed this whole thing had been a waste of their valuable time—

Thane told the judge that his associate, Kristin Peterson, would be questioning their next witness, at which point the bailiff called Jules Carson to the stand.

The young woman who approached Kristin after her visit at the sorority had once again changed her mind regarding testifying. She didn't stand immediately upon being called, but instead remained seated for a long moment, looking as though she was trying to decide whether or not to reverse course yet again. She finally took a deep breath and stood, apparently realizing that the time for deciding about testifying or not had long since passed.

She walked to the front of the courtroom and took her seat in the witness box after being sworn in. She appeared to scan the other faces in the courtroom gallery as if concerned that others from her sorority had come to intimidate her.

Kristin immediately walked up to the witness box and offered Jules a small smile, which seemed to calm the young woman somewhat. Kristin established the sorority that Jules belonged to and reminded the jury that the Alpha Gamma house had received a disproportionate number of scholarships funded by Luther Fournier.

"Ms. Carson, when you first joined the Alpha Gamma sorority, you didn't have a scholarship to ULA, did you?"

"No, I didn't quality for financial assistance, nor were my grades in high school strong enough to merit any sort of academic scholarship."

"When you pledged Alpha Gamma last year as a freshman and moved into their house, how were you paying for school?"

"A combination of financial support from my family and some loans, although my dad recently lost his job, so I wasn't sure I'd be able to stay in school any longer."

"But then two months into your freshman year, you were awarded a partial scholarship, funded by Mr. Fournier."

"Yes."

"Do you know why you were given that scholarship?"

Jules looked down at her lap, as if ashamed to answer the question. Kristin didn't press her or ask the question again, but instead waited for her to be ready to answer. Finally, she spoke in a voice a little softer than had been used when answering the previous questions."

"I was told it was a 'Babe' scholarship."

"Because you were attractive?"

"That's what I was told."

"And what was the expectation of recipients of these scholarships?"

"There is a group of sorority sisters who work with the Athletic Department to help show potential recruits around the campus and to hang out with them during their visits."

"And you agreed to do this?"

"They assured me I didn't have to do anything I didn't want to do, but it was also made clear that the more available I made myself to the recruits, the better the scholarship would be."

"And who made that clear to you?"

"The president of our sorority. Madison Monroe."

"And did you interpret making yourself available meaning your willingness to have sex with recruits?"

"Objection," Barnes called out. "Calls for speculation."

"Sustained," Judge Miller said. "Move along, counsel."

Kristin turned back to Jules. "Can you please tell the court what happened near the end of your freshman year?"

Jules stared straight ahead but didn't appear to be seeing anything in particular. Her eyes teared up, but she didn't wipe them. She finally focused back on Kristin.

"I went out with a player the team desperately wanted to recruit. Some four-star high school player considering coming to ULA. We had just left a bar, and when we got in my car he said he wanted me to go back to his hotel with him. He'd been drinking, and he kept pawing me. I knew what he was expecting, so I told him I had an early class the next morning and I had to call it a night."

"Then what happened?"

"He said his decision as to whether or not to come to ULA in the fall depended on whether or not I went back to his room with me. I apologized but said that wasn't going to happen."

"And how did he respond?"

Jules tried answering a couple of times, but the words seemed sticky and had trouble coming out of her mouth. She finally was able to say them by speaking quieter.

"He raped me."

Kristin nodded and gave Jules a moment to collect herself.

"Jules, I'm not going to ask you to get into the details of that night. What I want to talk about is what happened afterward."

"I ran back to my sorority. The next morning I had a call. It was Coach Dixon. He yelled at me for chasing away a top recruit. He was furious. I tried to tell him what happened, but he kept talking about how much they needed that player. He didn't hear a single thing I said, or if he did, he didn't care. After I hung up, Madison pulled me aside. She said I shouldn't report the rape, but instead should keep it quiet. She talked about how my family would react and I shouldn't put them through that, and that she would talk to someone and they would make things right by me. Like anyone could make something like that right."

"Did she say who she was going to talk to?"

"A Mr. Silver in the development office. And that afternoon I got a call from someone from his office saying that my scholarship for this year now included full room and board. All expenses paid."

"When Mr. Dixon was murdered and you talked with me about what happened to you, did anyone at your sorority say anything to you about testifying today?"

"They said I should keep it inhouse, but I said I thought I should tell my story. The next day they told me my scholarship was being rescinded. I was losing all financial support, although Madison said she was sure this could be taken care of if I didn't testify."

"You initially told me you weren't going to testify, but later you changed your mind. What made you decide to testify?"

Jules' demeanor shifted from one of hurt to one of anger. She sat up straighter and looked over at the jury.

"Because I didn't want to be a part of a school that would allow something like this to happen to one of their students. I was raped, then I was yelled at by the head coach, and then I was rewarded for staying quiet. All I wanted was to study computer programming. This is supposed to be some of the best years of my life, but instead it's been a nightmare."

Kristin glanced back over at Barnes before turning to Jules again.

"I won't ask you to 'speculate' but I want to confirm the following: you agreed to help entertain football recruits, and soon after you were given a modest scholarship. You were raped by one of those recruits, and when you agreed not to report it, you were given a full scholarship. And when you said you were going to testify today, the scholarship was suddenly taken away, is that correct?"

Jules nodded. "That's correct."

Kristin looked over at the jury. "I'll let you all speculate for yourselves."

"Objection," Barnes again called out.

"No further questions," Kristin said as she returned to her chair.

44

Detective David Hawkins appeared as the final witness for the day, summoned to the witness stand once again, but this time at Thane's request. Hawkins not only leaned back in his chair but also crossed his legs. Thane wondered how that casualness would play with the jury. But Hawkins seemed almost amused to once again be the center of attention.

Thane began his questioning by presenting copies of the police calls that had been dropped off at his office in a manila envelope. Hawkins said they appeared to be real and asked where Thane had gotten them, but Thane said that wasn't relevant to the topic at hand.

Thane said he had confirmed with the police station that there had been seven calls by various police officers who had pulled over the same car for suspicion of drunken driving. At least three of the calls from the officers described dramatic swerving and what appeared to be definite intoxication, but in all seven cases a ticket was not written. Hawkins pointed out that none of the calls named Coach Dixon by name, although all seven were for a car with Dixon's license plate.

"Detective Hawkins, what do you suppose the odds are of different police officers pulling over the same car seven times for suspected intoxication, but all seven times the person was let go?"

"Objection, calls for speculation."

"Sustained."

Thane nodded, unsurprised. "When an officer pulls a car over for suspected drunk driving, what is the usual protocol? I believe the officer usually collects the driver's license and registration, then goes back to the car and gets the station to run the information through the system. Is that correct? And if drunk driving is suspected, is there a breathalyzer test or is the driver asked to step out and walk a straight line or perform other coordination tests?"

"It can vary," Hawkins said. "That's certainly a couple of options, but if an officer decides the person hasn't been drinking too much, they won't go through any of this."

"If they were to conduct a breathalyzer test or a physical coordination test, how long does that sort of thing take?"

"Again, it can vary."

"How about on average? Five minutes? Ten minutes? Longer?"

"I would say five minutes or so. Could be longer."

"And at least another five minutes or so to call in the information on the driver's license."

"That's a reasonable guess."

"In six of these seven calls, the officer informed the station that the driver hadn't been drinking and allowed him to continue on his way within three minutes or less after pulling over the car. That's about the amount of time it would take to walk up to the car, check the suspect's driver's license and establish his identity and, perhaps, to suggest the driver be a little more attentive on the rest of his way home."

"Objection. Once again, Your Honor, counsel is making some broad assumptions."

"I'm not saying that's what happened, Your Honor. I'm not saying the officers realized who they had pulled over and quickly sent the driver on his way. I'm simply asking about the amount of time that would take had that been the case."

"Actually, Mr. Banning," Judge Miller said, "you are at least implying that's what happened. Objection is sustained. Move along."

"Detective, on October 28th, did you visit a Sheila Tremaine at the L.A. Women's Shelter for Emergency?"

Thane could tell he had caught Hawkins off-guard by this question, but the detective didn't pause too long before answering.

"Yes, I did."

"And why did you want to talk to this woman?"

"It was my understanding she may have had information about the defendant."

"You went and talked with her early that afternoon. Are you aware that, shortly after you spoke with her, this young woman slipped out of the shelter without telling anyone and hasn't returned since?"

"No, I wasn't aware of it. I simply had some questions to ask."

"We were planning to have her testify for the defense. Did you ask her if she realized how much danger she would be in if she were to testify at this trial?"

"I did not. I simply wanted to know what she knew about the defendant."

"Did you tell her that Coach Dixon was a good man

and didn't deserve to have his reputation dragged through the mud?"

"No, I did not," Hawkins said, his legs now uncrossed. He sat up straighter to convey the firmness of his answers.

"Are you saying it's a coincidence that almost immediately after talking with our witness, she ended up leaving the shelter?"

"That's exactly what I'm saying. And I don't appreciate what you're implying."

Hawkins was right about his intention. Thane had no idea what Hawkins said to the woman at the shelter, although he suspected the officer wasn't interested in helping Thane with his potential witness.

"Have you seen or been aware of incidents where someone powerful or famous got away with something because of who they were, and efforts were made to keep those actions from public knowledge?"

"I did nothing of the sort in this case."

"I didn't ask if you did, I simply asked if you were aware of that sort of thing happening with the police when dealing with influential people."

"I'm sure that has happened."

"Again, I'm not asking if you're assuming it's happened. I'm asking if you're aware of incidents where it has happened?"

"Yes," Hawkins finally said, as if stating the obvious.

"Thank you, detective. No further questions."

Barnes followed up by reiterating the fact that the police calls into the station had not resulted in any tickets being given and, in fact, it wasn't even a certainty that it had been the coach who had been driving. He also made sure the jury knew that it made sense that a detective would talk with a possible witness if he believed that person might know something about the suspect in the case.

Court adjourned once Detective Hawkins stepped down from the witness stand. The detective tried glaring at Thane as he walked past the defense table, but Thane ignored the man.

"We need to put Stick on the stand," Kristin said.

Thane and the rest of his team at the office looked at her. Each seemed to be trying to figure out whether they should be surprised at her statement, or if they should have seen it coming. On the one hand, it made sense from a strategic standpoint, but on the other hand, it was almost certain to invite a whole world of trouble into their lives. Thane in particular understood this, although he couldn't talk about the incriminating recording that Stick held over him, nor did he want to talk about the threat against Hannah.

"Our whole strategy so far has been to show the jury that Boo didn't have anyone to turn to for help," Kristin explained. "We've tried as best we could to show that the University wouldn't have done anything about it had she gone to them. In fact, we've shown they were part of the problem. And we showed that the police had given Dixon free passes in the past and likely would have watched out for him if Boo had gone to them. We all have to admit, though, that while we hopefully scored some points, they were shaky at best.

But if we're lucky enough to have actually shown there

wasn't anyone who would help her," Kristin continued, "the big question that will still be on the jury's mind is, 'Why didn't she just say no? Why did she keep going back to Dixon's if he was so abusive?' And I believe the only real way to do that is to introduce them to Stick."

"Couldn't we have one of his other women testify as to what he's like?" Letitia asked. "Or get a cop familiar with Stick to talk about what a sick asshole he is?"

"Assuming we could even get another one of his women to testify, we'd be setting her up to be hurt, if not killed. And sure, we could get a cop to testify, but it's not the same thing."

"I don't know about that," Letitia said.

"You've heard us talk about Stick and the things he did," Kristin said, focusing on Letitia. "But when he came into the office the other day, are you telling me you didn't sense how dangerous he was on an emotional level? Wasn't it different than hearing us talk about him?"

Letitia didn't break eye contact with Kristin, and Thane thought she would be offering up a counterpoint, but instead she reluctantly nodded. "You're right. I had a strong reaction confronting him face to face."

"It's different," Kristin said, "hearing about him and actually hearing him. We need for the jury to sympathize with Boo, for them to see why she had no way out."

Thane and Gideon made eye contact. They both knew what usually happened when you poked a psychopath. Thane was going to speak, but Gideon beat him to the punch.

"Stick wouldn't take kindly to that. You'd just be bringing on trouble by putting someone like that on the stand. That's not to say I don't understand where you're coming from. I'm just saying that the dominos that could fall afterward might not be worth the possible benefit."

"The risk to us," Kristin said, "versus the possible reward for Boo."

Thane obviously had his own motivation not to put Stick on the stand. The recording would almost certainly come out, but not before Stick hurt someone. If he could be sure Stick would be coming after him personally, he would be more comfortable with the plan, but Hannah and their baby were also in play.

But he also agreed with Kristin's logic. This would be Boo's best chance. Show the jury how everything was stacked against her. Everyone was always quick to say what they would do in a certain situation when they didn't actually have to do it. But put the jury face to face with someone like Stick and maybe they would have a little more empathy for Boo.

Kristen continued, "Look, I'm not saying we should put him on the stand if Boo isn't comfortable going that route. If she isn't, then we'll leave him alone. But if she is, I believe that's what we should do."

Thane stared at the tabletop as he ran the different scenarios through his mind until he noticed everyone looking at him, waiting to hear his thoughts.

"Would Boo agree to this?" Thane asked Kristin.

"I've broached it with her, and she understands the upside to it. She's also tired of being scared of Stick. Besides, she's not the one who would be questioning him on the stand. We'd work it so he would be sure to blame us."

"Oh, he'll definitely blame us," Gideon said. "Men

like Stick are happy to blame anyone who crosses their path."

"Let's figure out the questions," Thane said, "and we can make the final call then. But what you're suggesting is probably the best thing for Boo."

"But not for us," Gideon said, as he turned to Kristin. "But I respect the hell out of you for it. And I know you ain't gonna like this, but you shouldn't be in the courtroom that day. One less reason for him to blame you for any of this."

Kristin shook her head before Gideon even finished speaking.

"I have to be there," Kristin told Gideon.

"How come?"

"Because I should be the one questioning him."

45

Kristin came up with a list of potential questions after the team decided that putting Stick on the stand was Boo's best chance for leniency from the jury. And Thane had finally given in to Kristin's insistence on her being the one to question Stick. He knew she needed to stand up to him and let go of the fear that had paralyzed her, but he also knew that while that sounded all well and good, she'd also find herself worrying about repercussions. And for good reason.

He agreed to let her question Stick because she would be more likely to anger him. Stick likely didn't have as much patience with women challenging him, which meant Kristin might be more effective in bringing out his violent side. Or his more violent side. Thane didn't think Stick had a non-violent side.

Thane wondered who had delivered the subpoena to testify to Stick. He was confident the man or woman who handed Stick the piece of paper didn't stay around for him to read it. They may have even let Stick know they were only the messenger, figuring the phrase 'kill the messenger' might be a real possibility.

A few minutes before Stick was scheduled to testify, Thane pulled the bailiff aside and asked him to stay close by and ready for possible conflict. He didn't think Stick would strike out physically in a courtroom, but he also knew one couldn't always tell what someone like Stick would do. Stick wasn't the sort of person who played by the rules, unless they were his rules.

Thane sat at the end of the defense table in his usual position, except he pushed his chair a little further back and angled it in a way that would allow him to quickly intercept Stick if the sociopath decided to charge at Kristin. Gideon continued to sit in the gallery behind the defense table, but this time he made sure he had a seat on the aisle so that he, too, could quickly join the fray if something was to break out.

Kristin had been quiet on the drive to the courtroom. Thane had asked her a couple of questions, thinking it might help her to talk through her strategy, but he quickly decided to let her approach the day however she saw fit, and she apparently wanted to approach it with limited conversation.

Thane couldn't tell if she was nervous, intimidated, or confident. A combination of all three was most likely, along with a host of other emotions as well, but if that was the case, only her confidence was offered up for public display.

Their plan was straightforward: get the jury to see Stick for what he was. They needed the jury to understand why Boo couldn't simply say no to the man and why going to the police could also be dangerous. They didn't expect Stick to implicate himself in any of this, nor did they believe he would try to defend himself; they simply wanted the jury to better understand who Boo was dealing with, and to do that, they figured they needed to get under Stick's skin. That effort started the moment they called him to the witness stand.

Kristin stood and looked at the judge. "Your Honor, we call LaVern Lawson to the stand."

There was a moment of quiet as no one stepped forward until finally Stick pulled himself up from his seat and made his way to the front of the room at a slow pace, as if trying to show that the only reason he was testifying was because he decided to, and not because anyone made him.

Stick slowed even further as he passed close to Kristin, towering over her and giving her a look unmistakable in its menace. She didn't step back as Stick walked by close enough to almost brush arms with her. While he did this with the obvious intention of trying to intimidate her, he had already played into her hands. She deliberately didn't step away so that the jury would see the difference in size between her and Stick, and Boo was even smaller than Kristin. Thane noticed a couple of the female jurors subconsciously push back a little in their chairs, as if trying to put a little more distance between them and this man.

The bailiff walked up to Stick with an air that said he was used to tough guys in his courtroom, and he wasn't intimidated.

"Raise your right hand and state your name for the court."

Stick stared at the bailiff, who simply stared back at him, repeating the instructions one more time.

"Raise your right hand and state your name."

Stick finally lifted his right hand a small amount so his hand was at a 45-degree angle to the floor.

"Name's Stick."

"Please state your legal name."

"Everybody calls me Stick. That should be good enough for you."

At this point, Judge Miller inserted himself into this dance, having no patience for any sort of delay. He, too, had obviously dealt with men like Stick in his courtroom before.

"Sir, please state your given name so that we may proceed. It's not a trick question, and I'm confident it's something you can provide us."

Stick looked at the judge with no emotion. Thane didn't think Stick was trying to intimidate the judge, rather, he seemed to be letting the judge know he didn't care what the judge did or didn't want.

Finally, Stick turned back to the bailiff.

"LaVern Lawson."

"And do you swear to tell the truth, the whole truth, and nothing but the truth."

"Always," Stick said. He lowered himself into the witness stand before being told to take his seat. Nobody told Stick to sit. The witness then turned his soulless eyes toward Kristin with a burning intensity. He was not amused, and he wanted to make damn sure Kristin knew it. But Kristin didn't falter when moving toward the witness stand.

"LaVern," Kristin said before glancing up at Stick with the slightest hint of a smile on her face. She paused as if she just realized something. "I just remembered, my grandmother's name was Laverne. She was a lovely woman."

"I go by Stick."

"Stick. That's cute. Growing up, did you parents try to teach you how to fetch?"

"Your Honor," Barnes sighed, "is there a relevant question anywhere in the near future?"

"Sorry, Your Honor," Kristin replied, "I've just always been interested in how nicknames come about, but Mr. Barnes is right, it's not relevant to this case." She turned once again to Stick. "So, LaVern…"

"Listen up, Barbie. Three strikes and you're out, though I'm guessing one strike is gonna be enough for you."

"Mr. Lawson," the judge said, "do not even think of threatening any member of this court."

"Actually, Your Honor," Kristin said, "this witness probably doesn't even consider that much of a threat."

"Not a threat at all," Stick said. "Just a fact."

"Mr. Lawson…" Judge Miller.

"Seriously, sir," Kristin again addressed the judge, "compared to what he has said to me in the past, this is friendly banter." Kristin turned her attention back to Stick. "Remember when you forced your way into my apartment a few months ago? You kept calling me Barbie because you said I reminded you of the Barbie dolls your sister used to play with."

"I don't remember none of that."

"Seriously? Remember you told me how you used to take a power drill and drill a hole up its behind and you'd pretend your sister's screams were actually the doll screaming. And then when her screaming started getting on your nerves, you'd tear the head off the doll. Then you said I reminded you of those dolls, and you said you could do the same thing to me."

Several members of the jury, which up until then had been fairly good about keeping a poker face, winced at this story.

"Your Honor," Barnes said, this time standing. "Where is this going?"

Kristin turned toward Barnes. "I just wanted the judge to understand that what LaVern said a minute ago wasn't as harsh as it probably sounded to most people in the courtroom. I've heard his threats before, and believe me, this morning's was mild compared to some of his other threats. But I'll return to the questions I had for the witness."

"You're mighty brave in a room full of other people to protect you," Stick said. "I don't remember you being so brave before."

"And you're not as tough-acting when it's not just you and a woman alone in a room, but thanks for confirming we've spoken before."

"Your Honor," Barnes again said, "counsel is badgering the witness."

"He's my witness," Kristin countered. "But I'm trying to get back to the matter at hand."

"Please try harder, counselor," Judge Miller said.

"Mr. Lawson, do you know the defendant? And remember, you are under oath, and the court does tend to take things like perjury seriously."

Stick appeared to think about it as he looked dead-eyed at Kristin, then apparently came to the conclusion that it would be easy to show he did know Boo.

"Yeah, we crossed paths every now and then."

"Did she work for you?"

"Yeah, time to time she did the odd job for me."

"Do you ever have trouble getting the people who work for you to do what you want them to do?"

"That ain't never a problem."

"Ever have to discipline an 'employee' for not doing what you wanted?"

"Never had to do it more than once," Stick said with certainty.

"Is that because they're not physically able to do it again after you've disciplined them?"

Stick didn't answer, but instead just offered up an unnerving grin.

"Did those jobs involve having sex with men for money."

"Nah," Stick said, grinning. "That shit's illegal. She was just to provide company to men who wanted someone to talk to. Why, she tell you different?" Stick turned his glare toward Boo.

"Actually, I'm the one who gets to ask the questions here."

"Well, actually," Stick said, leaning forward slightly, "I'll ask any question I damn well please."

The jury didn't take their eyes off the witness, as if they were watching a bomb with a lit fuse and they were leery of it exploding.

"That may be the case," Kristin said, her voice now starting to sound unsteady, "but in here you have to answer my questions. You can't make me answer your questions."

"You wanna bet?" Stick's voice was coated with menace. "I'm pretty sure I can make you do pretty much anything I want, whether you want to or not."

"Mr. Lawson," Judge Miller shouted.

"Is that my best chance for getting your forgiveness?" Kristin asked. "By doing whatever it is you want?"

"Barbie, that ship sailed long ago. There ain't going to be any forgiveness. Not for you. Not ever."

Kristin suddenly looked shaken. She paused for a long moment, then turned away from Stick.

"No further questions for this witness," Kristin said.

"Damn right there ain't," Stick said to a murmuring courtroom as he rose. He stepped down from the witness box as Barnes told the judge he had no questions for the witness. Even the judge didn't admonish Stick for getting up before being dismissed, likely figuring the best thing that could happen was getting this man out of his courtroom.

Kristin walked back to the defense table, looking unsteady, and sat down. Even Boo, who up till then had shown little response to things that had taken place in her trial, glanced over at Kristin with at least a hint of sympathy in her eyes.

Thane knew Kristin had achieved her goal of getting the jury to see how difficult, if not impossible, it would have been for Boo to have told Stick she wasn't going to do something he wanted her to do. She was determined to get Stick to show himself, and for her to appear intimidated by him. They couldn't have Kristin stand up to him with confidence, because that might get the jury feeling that Boo could have done the same thing.

But Thane couldn't tell if Kristin was just wanting to make sure the jury saw how intimidating Stick could be and that even this lawyer was frightened of him, or if she had also just now realized she had pushed Stick too far. It was one thing to poke the bear and get the response you wanted; it was another thing to keep poking until the bear was dead set on mauling you.

Thane thought she had been too aggressive taunting Stick into showing himself. There was an old cliché in prison movies where the new prisoner figures the best way to establish themselves with all the other inmates was to go up to the toughest convict and punch him in front of everyone else. The reality was the toughest convict got that way for a reason, and it was far more likely the new prisoner would be dead before the day was up.

Stick directed his stare at Thane as he passed by the defense table. Thane knew what being too aggressive with Stick meant for them. It wasn't going to be good.

46

After their morning with Stick, Thane and his team left the courthouse. Thane was struck by how strong and energized she appeared after taking on the man who had so intimidated her several weeks ago.

Obviously she recognized the danger she had put herself in, but she appeared to be more angry than scared. Gideon rode back to the office with her, and would also likely be accompanying her to her apartment for a while, whether Kristin knew he was there or not. Thane guessed, though, she would welcome his company. She was strong, but she wasn't foolish.

Thane headed in the other direction toward the parking garage. He got on the elevator with three other people who had come from the direction of the courthouse and pressed the button for the 10th level of the garage. He could sense an older couple watching him, and he figured they had either come from the trial, or they simply recognized him from all of his recent publicity. Either way, he was grateful they didn't try to start a conversation with him.

The elevator doors opened and closed on the third level, letting the older couple off the elevator, at which point only Thane and a pumped-up man in his late 20's wearing sweats were left. Thane would have been more comfortable standing behind the guy, rather than in front of him, but at least a couple of feet remained between them, so that would help if things went bad.

His level of alertness had gone up because the guy hadn't pressed a button for a different level of the parking garage, even though he had gotten on the elevator before Thane. If the guy had gotten off with the older couple, that would have made sense, but now it was just the two of them going on up to level ten. Given the number of cars each level held, it was obviously possible the two men had parked on the same level, but that didn't explain why the guy hadn't pushed the button for 10 when he got on the elevator. It only made sense if he was planning to go to the same level as Thane, regardless where that was.

Thane didn't know if the man was there to defend Cash Dixon's reputation, or as a messenger of Stick's. Not that that would have been of upmost importance if violence were to break out, although it would give Thane a better sense of how the man would come at him.

It's when he heard the young man making a sound like he was chewing gum that Thane realized he was likely one of Stick's minions. The man hadn't made the sound while there were others in the elevator, and Thane would have been able to tell if the potential assailant had put something in his mouth after the doors closed.

The soft sound of the man's tongue moving against his cheek was one of the first sounds Gideon taught Thane to listen for when he arrived at Forsman. A sound he had heard on more than one occasion, a sound as distinct—and potentially as deadly—as the cocking of a gun hammer.

Prison wasn't the sort of place where one could walk around displaying a weapon, but a razor blade was quick to cut a man's jugular vein or to simply cause scars to the face, and it was easier to hide in one's mouth than one might imagine by either placing half a blade under the tongue or pressing it against the inside of one's cheek. In prison, Thane had had a conversation with a man for half an hour without noticing the man had a razor blade in his mouth.

The warning sign, however, occurred when someone used their tongue to move the blade in order to have it slide out their mouth like some macabre Pez dispenser. At that point a sort of slurping or smacking sound in the mouth was hard to hide, and that's what Thane heard now. And given that that was a trick almost always learned in prison, Thane figured Stick had sent the man, since a college football player wouldn't know how to pull that off.

As the elevator reached the fifth level, Thane hit the button for the eighth level, speaking as he did so.

"Did Stick ask you to come after me, or are you taking matters into your own hands?" Thane then whipped around and saw the young man frantically trying to get the razor blade from his mouth while at the same time throwing a punch at Thane.

Thane leaned back, listening to the fist whip past his face unimpeded. He burrowed his own fist deep into the man's ribs, causing the attacker to exhale loudly. Thane quickly put his right hand over the man's mouth to keep the razor from being expelled and pressed him against the back of the elevator, holding him firmly in place with his left arm.

Thane then slapped and punched the man's face, alternating between his cheeks until he could tell from the thug's pained reaction where the razor was located, at which point he focused on hitting that side of the man's face. He then took his hand and pressed it hard against the cheek holding the blade, moving his hand around as if giving the man's face an extremely hard facial massage, except he could tell from the man's muffled screams that the razor was not being used as the man had intended.

The man tried calling out, but his tongue had apparently been shredded enough to make it impossible to articulate whatever profanities he wanted to throw Thane's way. Instead, the only thing coming out of his mouth unimpeded was blood.

When Thane believed he had done as much damage as he wanted to do in the man's mouth, he pulled his attacker from the back wall, grabbed the back of his pants with one hand and held his head down with the other and flung him head first against the elevator door, then turned him in the other direction and did the same thing, the mirror on the back wall cracking under the force. Thane knew the same was likely true about the young man's head.

When the elevator stopped on level eight and the doors opened, Thane again turned the man around and tossed him out onto the parking deck. The man moaned softly as he laid face first on the pavement. The only movement from the man was the pool of blood growing ever larger around his face.

The elevator door closed and proceeded to the top level. When Thane stepped out, he immediately pulled out his cell phone and called Kyle, letting him know what happened and asking him to be extra vigilant when keeping an eye on Hannah. Thane had already earlier told Hannah and Kyle what was about to take place in the courtroom that day, and to be prepared for possible retaliation. He just wasn't sure when the inevitable war would start.

Apparently, it had already started.

Thane arrived at his law office a few minutes late for his meeting with Iris Robinson. She had said she wanted to talk with him about testifying on her daughter's behalf, and asked him to simply hear her out. Despite being against the idea the second he heard it, he agreed to at least hear what she had to say.

Iris was sitting in the waiting area when he walked through the entrance. He held up a finger and apologized.

"Sorry I'm late. Could you give me one minute?"

He walked over to Letitia, working behind the reception desk.

"I'd like for you to go ahead and lock the front entrance. Anyone who has business with us can knock. I'd rather not allow anyone who shouldn't be here to come in unchecked. Also, anything pressing I need to know with Ms. Robinson?"

Letitia appeared to give it some thought before answering. "I don't know if you consider needing to wash blood off your hands before meeting with her to be pressing or not. Guess I'll defer to you on that."

Thane looked down and saw some dry blood between a couple of his fingers.

"Let me guess," Letitia said, "you cut yourself shaving."

"Well, it did involve a razor blade." Thane turned to Iris. "Actually, just one more minute, if you would."

Thane excused himself and went to the restroom to wash his hands. Standing in front of the mirror, he also noticed a few drops of blood on his shirt collar. He had partial success washing a couple of the spots out with a damp paper towel, and a couple of the larger spots at least turned to a faded pink instead of dark red.

After returning and bringing Iris into his office, he motioned for her to have a seat at his table.

"Thank you for meeting with me," she said. "I know it's a busy time for you, but I really do think it's important for me to testify for Bonnie."

Thane respected Iris's desire to help her daughter. He didn't agree with the suggestion, but at least respected where it came from.

"I understand, but you remember how things went during the interview with Barnes. If I was the only one who got to ask you questions, we could make it work, but unfortunately Barnes would also get to cross-examine you, and he would bring up the interview, making you come across as being unreliable. You would also be opening yourself up to charges of aiding and abetting."

"I thought my immunity deal shielded me from any charges."

"Only if you were completely truthful. Once you tried taking responsibility for Dixon's murder, that deal was off the table."

"I only wanted to help my daughter."

"And that's why Barnes didn't press charges, but if

you go to court to testify, he could always change his mind and come after you."

Iris appeared to consider that for a long time, then looked back at Thane, appearing resolute.

"I'm willing to take that chance."

"But what would you even say?"

"I've been thinking about it. You could bring up the interview with Barnes and what happened there, and you could ask me why I did it. You've done a great job showing the institutional bias that has been protecting men like Dixon, but I don't believe the jury sees Bonnie as anything other than a black hooker, and I want them to see her as a person. As someone's daughter. You said you don't expect to have Bonnie testify. If the jury hears why I wanted so badly to help her, I know that won't cause her to be found innocent, but it might help them decide to reduce her punishment."

"And if you get charged for perjury?"

"If it helps Bonnie, I'm willing to risk it. But to be honest, I can't imagine anything more than a slap on the wrist would happen to me, if that. People would have too much empathy for me to actually be hit with jail time, and I'm sure it helps that my husband is a top detective for the force. I'm confident I'll be fine."

"This is the sort of thing that is done after the verdict is in, before sentencing. That's when friends and family members usually talk about the character of the person who has been convicted. It's not testimony that is relevant to the actual case."

"But you could ask me about the gun and what I did with it. That is relevant to the case, and at the same time I can also talk about Bonnie and who she is as a person."

Thane thought about it, running the various pros and cons through his mind. The advantage of having someone speak about Bonnie as a human being and not just a victim could help sway the jury in how hard they came down on her. On the other hand, if Barnes went hard after her on the stand, the jury could resent her interference in a murder case and end up punishing her daughter for it. He believed the odds were in favor of there being sympathy, although there was no guarantee of that.

"I have to do this, Mr. Banning," Iris said. "Someone other than her lawyer needs to speak for her. Please trust me that I won't hurt your case. I wouldn't do this if I wasn't convinced I can help."

"You also thought you could help with Barnes asking about the gun, yet you accomplished just the opposite."

"I understand that. And I'll do better this time."

Thane thought Iris was right. She struck him as being a strong, intelligent woman, and not someone who would get rattled and go off-script if Barnes played rough. They would work together on what she would say and how to take full responsibility for what she did and why she did it. Thane knew it would be better if he talked about what happened at the interview rather than leaving it up to Barnes. She would have to come across as completely apologetic for her lie and present a picture of Bonnie that the jury had yet to see.

"I'll let Barnes know we're adding you to the witness list. It will either piss him off or make his day, neither of those exactly working in our favor. But I agree with you that the upside outweighs the downside, in part because right now I'm struggling to find any other upside that would help her."

"I appreciate it, Mr. Banning. I promise you I will help."

"But you can't lie anymore, Ms. Robinson. You simply can't."

"I know. I promise I won't lie." She then reached across the table and took one of Thane's hands and held it tightly between both of hers, looking deep in his eyes as she spoke. "And as you question me on the witness stand, I hope you remember I always keep my promises. Always. It's important you remember that."

47

Thane got home after Hannah, which meant it was his turn to make the post-work cocktails and take them out to the backyard where Hannah already waited. Or at least a cocktail for him. She would be getting a glass of seltzer water, but he put a lemon slice in it to fancy it up a bit.

When he went out the sliding glass door, he noticed Hannah's chair was positioned to the side a little more than usual, allowing her a peripheral view of the sliding glass door leading out onto the deck. Usually their chairs faced directly away from the house. It bothered Thane that she was now having to think like that.

He kissed her hello, handed her the seltzer water, and saw her looking longingly at his old fashioned. He knew he should start drinking seltzer water in solidarity with her, at least when she was around, but damn, he needed something stronger after his day. He lowered himself into his Adirondack chair, feeling as though it might take a tow truck to get him back out of it. He was exhausted and wished he could spend the rest of his week there in his backyard in his lawn chair.

"Tough day?" Hannah asked.

Thane summoned enough energy to at least shake his

head.

"That's one thing about spending time in prison, you find it's awfully tough to complain about pretty much anything else. A bad day out here is usually a day in Candyland compared to being locked up, although today was pretty damn close to being that bad."

She reached over and squeezed his arm, a simple act that always touched his heart.

"Kyle seemed to be on high alert today. Any repercussions or threats from Stick yet?"

"I haven't heard from him," Thane said, not exactly lying. He didn't see any reason to share with her the specifics from the parking garage. She knew she needed to be extra vigilant until all this played out. What bothered him was not knowing how it would play out.

He told her about his conversation with Iris and the plan to call her as a witness. He also talked about the woman's effort to take the blame for the murder and how she broke down trying to convince Barnes that her daughter was a good person. Thane respected Barnes for not punishing her for that lie. He knew Barnes was a father and empathized with her desire to do whatever she could do to help her child, but Thane wasn't sure how far that benevolence would go. He sensed it wouldn't go much further.

Talking about Iris made Thane think about her husband. It struck him that he hadn't heard from Struthers lately, nor had anyone reached out to him to let him know the detective was asking questions. He wasn't sure if that was because Struthers was doing his work behind the scenes or if Struthers had paused the investigation to give Thane the bandwidth to focus on helping his daughter.

"Will her testimony help?" Hannah asked.

"It could. Intellectually, they know Bonnie is someone's child, but that's different than feeling it emotionally. Also, they may assume Bonnie comes from a family of drug addicts or criminals, and seeing Iris might help them see Bonnie differently. They may take Iris and her testimony into consideration when sentencing her daughter."

He wasn't sure how Barnes would handle Iris as a witness. Barnes wouldn't want to be too harsh on her, which could generate more sympathy for her and less support for the state, but he would certainly bring up her lying to show she had gone over the line trying to help her daughter.

"She just can't lie on the stand," Thane said. "If she does that and the jury learns about it, she will only hurt Bonnie's cause."

"Do you think she will?"

"No, I don't. She promised she wouldn't, and she went out of her way to make sure I knew she always keeps her promise. I guess she wanted to make sure I believed her, but it seemed to be important to her that I knew that. She's right to sense my reluctance, though."

They sat a while longer in silence, each of them looking out at the trees that lined the back of their property. Finally, Hannah spoke.

"Are you still looking to take time off after this trial? Stay home with me and the nameless one?"

Thane smiled. "Yes. I'll be here so that I can be totally helpless and clueless around you."

"Great. We can do that together." She smiled, before turning more serious. "And you're looking to stay out of the newspapers for a while?"

"Once again, for the record…"

"I know, I know. I'm the one who got you into this one. And I understand it's hard to not help someone in need."

"It is, at that."

"But we need a little help as well."

"Just because I'm struggling to assemble a baby crib?" Thane asked, smiling, but he saw Hannah didn't respond right away. Nor did she smile.

"We need to talk about whatever it is that's going on with you. Or with us. I don't mean to imply it's all on you, but you're the one who has gone through the most traumatic experience. And if this is simply the lingering impact of that experience, then I'll understand. But it feels to me like there's something more going on, and I'd like us to be able to get it out into the light. And I recognize now's maybe not the best time," she said as she looked down at her stomach, "and it's not as though we don't have some other things going on, but I think it's important we figure it out."

"This case will be over soon, at which point I'll do whatever I can to try to help you understand. I'm struggling, I know that." He finished his cocktail. "And I've been talking with a therapist."

Hannah again reached over and held his arm, but this time she didn't let go.

"Has it been helpful?"

"It's good to have someone to talk to about all this." He felt Hannah's grip tighten a bit on his arm. "I didn't mean it like that. I know I have you. I mean it's good to have someone I can talk to whose opinion of me isn't as important to me."

"I'm glad you're talking to someone. I'm hopeful you'll be talking to me, too."

They returned to their silence, which wasn't as comfortable as it had been, although Thane felt relieved after telling her he had been seeking therapy. He wanted to be done keeping secrets, and perhaps this represented one small step toward having the larger —and more consequential—conversation that he'd been avoiding.

"Do you think about what you would do to protect our child?" Hannah asked, possibly thinking about Iris, but also perhaps remembering the threat that Stick posed. "Would you confess to a murder you didn't commit to protect our still-to-be-named girl?"

It was a tricky question for Thane. Usually those 'how far would you go' questions were entertaining at bars or at parties, but Thane had already raced long past how far he ever thought he would go, and that was only to try to get justice. Or vengeance. Could he go any further than that while trying to protect his family?

He had been wrestling with that question whenever he thought about Stick.

"I would do anything," Thane said, knowing what that could include, and not being proud of being open to that possibility.

48

Thane was anxious as he sat in the courtroom, waiting for the day's proceedings to begin. Like most any good lawyer, he almost always knew what the witness he called to the stand would say, but he didn't feel confident that would be the case this morning.

He and Kristin had worked with Iris on her testimony. The emphasis would be on Boo as a daughter. As a human being. The types of stories only a mother could tell. Iris appeared attentive and took notes, but Thane got the feeling she already knew what she planned to say.

Thane had expected Boo to be vehemently against the idea of her mother testifying, given how she had even denied Iris was her mother in an effort to protect Iris's reputation, but she said she would defer to her lawyers. Thane guessed Boo was quickly learning that standing up for a principle was all well and good until she realized how bad prison really was.

But Boo also conveyed more energy and interest as they waited for court to be called into session. She had been fairly withdrawn and distant during the proceedings to date, but this morning she looked alert. Even hopeful. Thane wasn't sure why, but he thought it could only help for her to appear more interested in the court session at hand.

Depending how Iris's testimony went, Thane could be calling Boo as his final witness. If it looked as though Iris's image of her daughter had reached the jury, the defense would rest, in part because up until that morning, Boo hadn't exactly conveyed warmth. But if Iris didn't do as well as he hoped, he would consider having Boo testify. He needed to get the jury to see her as a real person—as a victim—and he wasn't convinced he had accomplished that yet. The question of her guilt was all but established, so everything he did now was with an eye toward sentencing.

Judge Miller appeared and the bailiff called the court into session. Thane rose and called Ms. Iris Robinson to the stand.

Iris once again dressed like a top executive. Thane and Kristin believed that the more impressive she looked, the more credible she would appear. This would be important if—or when—Barnes went after her previous misleading statements.

Thane's first questions established who Iris was: the mother of the defendant, and the wife of a top L.A. police detective. Thane could tell she already had the jury's attention, and that a sense of surprise rippled through the jury box.

Iris exceeded Thane's expectations as she talked about raising Boo, which was saying something because he already thought she would do a good job. She told stories of her daughter as a young girl, and Boo's struggle with drugs in high school. She also talked about the challenges that sometimes came with having a police detective for a father.

In contrast to her earlier interview with Barnes, Iris didn't come across as a woman desperately willing to do or say anything to try to help her daughter. Instead, she spoke in a sincere and direct manner. She put her love for Boo on full display, but she also didn't shy away from acknowledging the poor choices her daughter had made in the past.

Before concluding his questioning, Thane broached the issue of Iris's interview with Barnes. He did that last, after the jury had already formed a more positive perception of her. He knew Barnes would try to alter that perspective, but at least Thane could try to set the foundation for how the jury would respond to Iris's earlier perjury.

"Ms. Robinson, not too long ago, you and I met with Assistant D.A. Barnes regarding your possible cooperation with this case, correct?"

"That's correct."

"He thought you had disposed of the murder weapon and wanted your testimony to that effect?"

"Yes, sir. He offered me immunity from all charges if I were to tell him what I knew."

"And you told him that you had the murder weapon in your possession and that you had thrown it into the Pacific while on a ferry to Catalina Island?"

"That's correct."

"And were you being honest about that?"

"I was. I obviously couldn't tell him the gun's exact location, but I could tell him what I did with it."

Thane paused for a moment, letting there be a moment of silence before broaching the more awkward part of the testimony. He wanted to show that while Iris had lied about her involvement in the murder, that didn't mean she couldn't be trusted on everything else she had said this morning.

"As you have clearly shown during your testimony this morning, you love your daughter very much."

"She is my world."

"You were upset at what happened to her."

"Beyond upset. As most any parent would be."

"At the end of the interview, you not only said you threw away the murder weapon, you said that you had actually killed Coach Dixon yourself."

Iris only nodded in agreement. Thane could hear a soft murmuring from the gallery at this interesting turn.

"Can you tell the jury why you said that?" Thane asked.

Iris turned so that she could offer her explanation directly to the jury.

"I said I murdered Mr. Dixon because that's exactly what I did. I shot and killed that son-of-a-bitch who hurt my daughter."

The uproar inside the courtroom was as loud as if someone had yelled that there was a bomb in the room, and as far as Thane was concerned, there was. Judge Miller banged his gavel for a solid thirty seconds before the gallery began to quiet. Thane wished it would take the judge another thirty minutes to restore order so he could try to figure out where to go from here.

He glanced back over to Kristin as if wanting to confer with her, but she looked every bit as speechless as Thane.

Thane wasn't sure what to do with Iris's testimony. If he tried to treat it as fact, the jury wouldn't believe anything he said during closing statements. But if he said he had no further questions, Barnes would carve her up on the stand. He could tell without looking that the Assistant D.A. likely had a new glimmer in his eye.

Thane decided to cut his losses and hope that the jury would understand why Iris was still trying to confess to a crime to save her daughter. But he couldn't be seen as trying to perpetuate the lie and, in the process, be seen by the jury as trying to pull a shady tactic to try to get his client off the hook.

Thane turned to Judge Miller, who looked at him as if trying to figure out if he should feel a little sorry for Thane, or if the defense was trying a fast one in his courtroom. Thane's expression must have helped the judge see this was as unexpected to him as it was to everyone else in the room.

"No further questions, Your Honor."

Thane returned to his chair.

Arthur Barnes took a moment before rising, perhaps because he didn't want to appear too anxious to start the questioning. Thane knew Barnes would once again be able tear down any credibility that Iris had shown earlier, and to make the jury see that the mother—just like the daughter—did not deserve their respect. What he didn't understand was why Iris thought this time it would work.

"Ms. Robinson, I appreciate your honesty in saying you would do or say anything to help your daughter. You've amply proven that to be the case this morning."

Iris watched Barnes as he worked his way to his point.

"You requested full immunity for your testimony before agreeing to talk with me, correct?"

"Yes, sir."

"You didn't ask for partial immunity, which would have simply covered your actions related to getting rid of the gun, you requested full immunity, which meant you knew you could admit to anything, and you couldn't be charged with the crime. You made us believe you only knew about the gun, in order for us to be willing to go along with your request for full immunity."

"That's not true, sir. I requested full immunity, but you believed I only knew about the whereabouts of the gun. I didn't imply that was all I knew."

"Be that as it may, now that you've received full immunity, there is no downside to confessing to a murder you didn't commit if it means saving your daughter." Barnes paused, then looked up toward the ceiling as if he had just remembered something. "Oh, wait, actually there is a downside. The immunity deal is only good if everything you said was the truth. Otherwise, not only is there no deal, but you can be charged with perjury."

"I told no lies during my interview with you, nor have I lied today."

Barnes quickly marched back to his table and brought out a folder. He riffled through the pages until he found what he wanted.

"Just to clarify, your daughter called you at 12:55 in the morning, and you answered your phone. And you were home at the time, were you not?"

"I was"

"But the gunshot was reported at 12:50, five minutes before the phone call, not to mention the fact you live at least 15 minutes away from Coach Dixon's home. When I confronted you with that during the interview, you said your daughter is a good person and that I had to understand she had a good heart. You said that you and your husband had let her down and that you were the ones who should be punished. You said you were claiming you killed Coach Dixon only to try to protect your daughter. Those were your exact works, were they not?"

"All of those words are correct except I didn't say I was only claiming to have killed Mr. Dixon to try to protect Bonnie. You inferred that. I did not lie when we talked earlier. I killed that man."

"But the evidence shows otherwise."

"What evidence is that, sir?"

"All of it," he scoffed before pausing.

Barnes looked like he wanted to ask another question in an effort to completely dismiss Iris's claim, but Thane thought the man sensed something wasn't quite right. Iris's demeanor was completely different than during the interview. During their initial encounter, Iris appeared to be grasping at straws to save her daughter. This afternoon, she sounded confident and collected, and Barnes apparently sensed it wasn't in his best interest to continue questioning this witness.

"I appreciate your love for your child, Ms. Robinson. I, too, have children for whom I would do—and say— most anything to help. But the evidence tells us what you're saying simply is not true."

Barnes looked at the jury and all but shook his head to convey his sympathy for the defendant's mother.

Thane now had to decide whether to ask Iris more questions, or to let her step out of the witness box. She looked at him, appearing to be doing everything she could to get him to let her speak more. He then remembered her telling him that it was important that he believed her when she said she wouldn't lie. It was for this very moment. She knew this would happen.

Thane looked over at Kristin, who subtly shook her head no, obviously feeling it was best to have Iris step down from the witness box. He then looked at Boo who, for the first time since her mother began testifying, met his eyes and gave him the slightest of nods. She wanted Thane to let her mother speak. Thane didn't know where things were going to go, but he decided at that moment to trust his client and her mother.

"Redirect, Your Honor," Thane said.

As Thane rose to once again approach the witness stand, Barnes glared at him as if all of this had been orchestrated in advance. Barnes likely thought at first that Thane had been as blindsided as everyone else had been, but now that there were follow up questions, Barnes had to assume all of this was some sort of desperate, planned gambit. Thane agreed with the desperate part, but in no way had he planned it. He was flying blind.

"Ms. Robinson, when Mr. Barnes said the evidence showed you didn't kill Mr. Dixon, you asked what evidence. You have been present during this entire trial, so you have heard the various pieces of evidence against your daughter. Which evidence are you saying should be questioned?"

"Objection," Barnes said. "Defense's question is far too broad. If Mr. Banning has a specific question, he should ask it, otherwise it sounds like he's fishing."

Thane was fishing, along with trying to figure out what he could ask more specifically that didn't run the risk of finishing off his case, but Judge Miller surprised him.

"Overruled," Miller said. "You referenced the evidence, Mr. Barnes, in a broad manner, so the witness may answer the question."

"Thank you, Your Honor," Thane said. Usually when a lawyer said thank you, they were just being formal, but Thane's 'thank you' truly came from the heart.

"Ms. Robinson? Which evidence are you referring to?"

Iris gave it some thought before answering. "Again, all of it. Where to start? For one thing, the prosecution referenced Bonnie calling a burner phone prior to entering Mr. Dixon's house, and he suggested she called her pimp. But it wasn't to her pimp. The phone is mine. I still have the phone, so that can be verified. Given the tensions that sometimes resulted from Bonnie's troubles and her father being a detective, I bought a burner phone that my daughter could call if she ever got into any trouble. I know my husband would never deliberately look at my calls on my regular phone, but I didn't want to take the chance he would accidentally learn of Bonnie needing help."

"And she didn't call when she first got there," Iris continued, "she called after the abuse took place. She called me right after Dixon had done what he did to her. I grabbed my gun and went over there while she got her things together to leave. I then entered the house, turned up the TV real loud, and shot the man. Shot him for what he did to my daughter."

Iris's testimony seemed to be making an impression on the jury, but Thane struggled with not knowing which questions he could ask that wouldn't blow up everything she had just said. He didn't know how far he could push it, but he needed to believe Iris knew what she was doing.

"Anything else?" he asked.

"Yes. I was optimistic the TV volume covered the sound of the gunshot, but Bonnie then said that after calling me she went through the garage and went to the front door as if she had just arrived so she would appear on the Ring camera video. She did that because she knew the police would be able to trace the evening back to her, and she didn't want me to get in trouble. That way the police would find her and not me. Mr. Dixon never had her go to the front door for the very reason of not wanting her to appear on his security video. He always had her arrive and come in through the garage. She had already been at the house and had already been abused before showing up on the security video."

"When I arrived, I went through the garage door, walked into the kitchen, and shot Mr. Dixon. Bonnie and I then decided I would return home. My daughter waited twenty minutes, then went outside and fired the gun in the air to ensure a neighbor would hear it to establish an assumed time of the murder. She then called me to establish my presence at home, then broke the Ring camera immediately afterward to make it look like she had done the killing. But believe me, I'm the one who killed that man."

Iris looked over at Boo, which caused most of the jury to also look over at her. Boo nodded quietly to her mother, confirming this as being true.

Thane didn't want to press his luck. Right now, Iris sounded convincing enough to perhaps sway at least one or two jurors, and that would be enough to at least end up with a hung jury.

"No further questions."

As expected, Barnes rose before Thane had even retaken his seat.

"Your Honor, permission to redirect."

"Go ahead, counselor."

Despite the chaos in the courtroom, Barnes did not appear shaken in the least. If anything, he simply looked angry. Whether angry at Iris for pulling what he saw as a desperate trick or angry at Thane for orchestrating yet another one of his courtroom tricks, Thane wasn't sure, but he knew the man looked mad.

"Ms. Robinson, you testified you would do anything to help your daughter, and now that you have immunity—immunity, I remind you, as long as you're being truthful—you decide to take full responsibility. You are able to toss out a version that I suppose can't be disproved, but it doesn't pass the smell test."

"I can't help that, sir. All I can do is tell the truth."

"Well, that remains to be seen. For example, you were upset your daughter had been arrested for murder. You were upset your daughter was behind bars—at times breaking down while I questioned you—and yet you are just now telling us you killed Coach Dixon."

"With all due respect, I told you during my interview with you."

"But you also made it sound like you were doing this out of desperation. You did that intentionally. You didn't mention anything about your daughter calling a burner phone you happened to have, or about why she broke the video camera, or anything you're saying now. If you expect the jury to believe you now, why didn't you press this issue with me when you had a chance. If you thought it would get your daughter released sooner, why in the world would you leave her in jail until your testimony today?"

Iris looked hard at Barnes, then down at her lap for a long moment. The courtroom fell as quiet as it would have been had no one been in the room. Finally, she looked over at the jury, acting as if Barnes wasn't even there.

"After I graduated high school, I started school at ULA. During my first year, a boy my age who was a baseball major league prospect assaulted me. Star pitcher, and the reason ULA's baseball team was ranked. I won't get into the details here, but what he did to me was inexcusable. Nothing close to the abuse my daughter suffered, but still inexcusable. And yet the university found a way to excuse it. They managed to cover it up, and they managed to silence me, and it has been with me ever since."

Iris paused, as if trying to cleanse her mind of that memory, then turned her attention back to Barnes.

"When Bonnie called me and told me the abuse Mr. Dixon had put upon her, I reacted out of anger. That is on me. I shouldn't have done what I did, but I did it nonetheless. I wanted to call the police—I wanted to call my husband—and immediately tell him what I had done, but Bonnie kept me from doing that. She felt guilty for having put me in that situation, and she tried to protect me. She also knew of my experience in school, and knew that ULA would not want Dixon's name sullied, but she wanted his actions known. She wanted to show how the University, the donors, the athletic department, and the media would rally around and protect this football coach in an effort to keep his actions a secret, just as they had done for that baseball player so many years ago.

"Bonnie and I talked about how I might be able to be granted immunity, so once you offered that, I wanted to tell you everything, and I would have, had you asked, because I knew if I lied the deal would be off, but Bonnie wanted to see this through further. By talking about this in a court of law, she thought the message would be a hell of lot more likely to break through the conspiracy of silence than if I had told you in the privacy of your office because it was possible you might be a part of that conspiracy. So did it hurt me to leave my daughter locked up longer than necessary? Yes, it did, very much, but I'm also so very, very proud of her for taking a stand."

Barnes appeared to be at a loss for how to proceed from there. Eventually, the best he could come up with was to shake his head.

"That's a nice story, Ms. Robinson, albeit a pretty convoluted one. But wouldn't it be nice if there was actually evidence corroborating your story of being at Coach Dixon's house?"

Barnes turned back to his seat.

"There is evidence."

Barnes stopped but didn't turn back toward the witness.

"In the bedroom…" Iris started to say.

"No further questions, Your Honor," Barnes said loudly, trying to talk over Iris.

"I'm saying that in the bedroom, I…"

"No further questions!"

"Objection," Thane yelled. "Prosecution asked the witness a question. She deserves the chance to answer it."

"A rhetorical question, Your Honor."

"A question, nonetheless," Thane responded.

"Then I withdraw the question."

"If there is evidence that supports her story, don't we all deserve to hear it?" Thane asked. "Otherwise, aren't we simply doing what the witness and her daughter said would happen? Mr. Barnes, Ms. Robinson said you might be a part of this conspiracy of silence. You can show you're not by allowing her to answer your question, rhetorical or not. Are you interested in trying to get to the truth, or just to get a win in court?"

Judge Miller looked down at Iris, then at Barnes, awaiting his response.

Barnes stood frozen, appearing to be running scores of calculations through his head. Thane assumed he was weighing whether it was more important to his career to try to win the case, or to be seen as trying to cover up a violent act against a young woman.

Barnes finally waved his hand, indicating that Iris could continue. He sat at his table to hear her response.

Iris nodded her appreciation to Thane, and once again turned to the jury.

"I wanted to respect my daughter's desire to have a chance to bring the behavior of her coach and the university to light, but I worried that when it came time for me to talk about my role, no one would believe me. That you would assume I lied simply to save my daughter, the argument Mr. Barnes is making right now. An argument, I agree, that sounds reasonable. So I left a piece of evidence I thought would be safe from detection, but that I knew where it was."

Iris closed her eyes, as if speaking the words caused

her pain.

"Before I left Mr. Dixon's house, I put two of my fingers in the pool of blood forming around him, then I went into his bedroom and over to his chest of drawers where I left my fingerprints on the bottom of one of the dresser drawers. I was confident the police would not be checking the bottom of a drawer in the bedroom for evidence, but if you go and look, you'll see they are my fingerprints, and DNA testing will show it is Mr. Dixon's blood."

She opened her eyes and looked one last time back at the jury.

"It was all I could think to do. I wanted to do something that could keep my daughter from going to prison for something I had done."

49

The pieces of evidence Iris Robinson testified to in court did, in fact, turn out to be true. She produced the burner phone linked to the same number that Boo had called the night of the murder.

And the bloody fingerprints were, indeed, found exactly where Iris said they would be. As she expected, the police had no reason to look underneath a clothes drawer in a bedroom when the murder had taken place in the kitchen and they had the suspect confessing to the crime.

Thane recalled Detective Hawkins to the stand to testify as to the accuracy of both of these pieces of evidence. He clearly wasn't happy having to confirm everything Thane asked him in court, but he acted professional about it.

Upon cross-examination, Barnes asked Hawkins if this new evidence convinced him that Boo didn't commit the murder, and Hawkins said it didn't change his mind, although even the jury had to see he didn't sound as resolute in his belief as he had previously. His cockiness had been quieted.

Barnes had to know, as Thane did, that there was now potentially enough reasonable doubt to find Boo not guilty, but neither of them were willing to assume anything was a given.

During closing arguments, Barnes told the jury that Boo had been there the night of the murder, she had motive, she had access to the murder weapon and, most importantly, she said she had done it. It wasn't until the eleventh hour, when things were looking bleak for her, that her mother came up with her confession. A confession that only came about following blanket immunity. That all seemed a little too convenient for Barnes.

His main question for the jury to consider when deliberating was this: would Bonnie Cruise truly stay in jail all those days—and would her mother let her stay in jail all those days—solely to make a point? To make a social commentary? Barnes didn't believe either of them would have done that, and he told the jury they shouldn't believe it either.

When Barnes had concluded, Thane rose to address the jury. To no one's surprise, he reminded the jury of Iris's story, and of the evidence which she provided which backed up her confession. A confession which, for the record, the Assistant D.A. had immediately dismissed during the initial interview without pushing further. He had made an assumption rather than being thorough.

"To say there isn't any reasonable doubt strikes me as requiring too much of a stretch of the imagination," Thane said to the jury. "Even if Bonnie's mother hadn't left her bloody fingerprints at the scene of the crime, there is still enough room for reasonable doubt. But with this irrefutable evidence that she was there the night of the murder, how can anyone say they are certain my client killed Mr. Dixon?"

Thane looked over at Barnes for a long moment before turning back to the jury.

"But the prosecution asks a reasonable question. Why would Bonnie Cruise stay in jail longer than she needed to? And why would her mother let her stay there?

"Bonnie stayed in jail because she felt guilty about having put her mother in a position of killing the man who had abused her. If Ms. Robinson had confessed right away, she would be the one being sentenced to jail, and Bonnie couldn't let that happen. She felt at fault for putting her mother in that situation, and she would not have allowed her mother to confess before getting immunity. I doubt they thought it would work, and admittedly they played the system to bring about such an offer, but at no point did Ms. Robinson lie to get it.

"As for why Ms. Robinson let her daughter stay in prison even after the immunity deal, she did so because she knew her daughter wanted to send a message. A message about the dereliction of duty by the University of Los Angeles. A message about a donor threatening to revoke a scholarship because an eighteen-year-old girl had the audacity to turn down a football star's demand for sex. A message about the police oftentimes giving preferential treatment to people in power."

Thane shook his head, conveying his distaste for what had been uncovered during this trial. He had formed his new law practice wanting to use the money given to him by the city to help people who were up against corrupt systems and organizations, and this case seemed to have it all.

"And do you think the media, in the future, will do a little more digging and not focus on simply trumpeting the virtue of a man solely because he had a winning record?"

Thane looked back at Boo, who sat more upright than she had during the entire case, as though no longer the victim but, instead, the one with the power.

"And finally, to be honest, jail wasn't as bad as Bonnie's time with Cash Dixon had been. People have been willing to endure a lot more than Bonnie Cruise did in jail for a lot less. And so, if the question is why would someone do something like that, I believe you've seen firsthand why. Think about what you yourselves have come to learn during this trial. It is for that reason that I urge you to render a verdict of not guilty."

Closing arguments were concluded by 10:00 a.m., and at 3:15 word came back that the jury had reached its verdict. The gallery was once again packed, with at least a third of the seats occupied by journalists, most of whom were trying to decipher what it meant to have such a relatively quick verdict. Did it not take long because of the defendant's confession or because of her mother's testimony?

Thane noticed that District Attorney Angela Day was nowhere to be seen as court neared ready to be called to order. That wasn't a good sign for Barnes. The failure of this case, should it end up being a failure, would fall solely on his shoulders. Thane believed Angela would have been there to stand by her lieutenant if it wasn't election season and if Barnes wasn't rumored to be planning to run against her. Thane also was quite certain that that rumor was soon going to disappear. Or at least it would if the jury determined he had let Coach Dixon's killer go free.

Iris sat in the gallery immediately behind where her daughter would be sitting. A few minutes before court was scheduled to resume, her husband slipped in and sat behind her, taking her hand in his. When Boo came into the courtroom she offered a half-smile to her mother, then paused a half-step upon seeing her father there. Thane saw Struthers give his daughter a subtle thumbs-up, which caused Boo to respond with a just-as-subtle nod of her head.

Boo took her seat between Kristin and Thane. He marveled at his client's ability to appear disinterested even when facing the threat of spending most of the rest of her life in jail. Previously he had wondered if she had learned to simply assume the worst, and that there wasn't any use fighting back, but he now knew that was no longer a fair assessment of the young woman. She had truly fought back.

Her refusal to accept a far-more-than-generous plea agreement also now made a lot more sense, given her knowledge of how her mother would testify. It seemed like that was always part of their plan. It was still a gamble, but now a gamble Thane better understood.

"You doing okay?" Thane asked her.

"Glad it's almost over. But however this plays out, I want to thank you for what you've done for me." She then turned to Kristin. "I want to thank both of you."

"Just doing my job," Kristin said, although Thane could tell Boo's words meant something to her.

"Nobody's job should entail going up against

someone like Stick," Boo said. "There were scores of ways that that could have been handled, all of them wouldn't have involved you going face-to-face with him, but you got up there and took him head on. I admired that. Also thought it was pretty stupid, but I still admired it. And I appreciated it."

Kristin began raising her right arm from the table.

"You're not going to give me a hug, are you?" Boo asked, straight-faced.

Kristin's arm paused in mid-air before she laid it back down on the table.

"Wouldn't dream of it."

The two women looked at each other, then broke into smiles. Thane realized it was the first time he had seen Boo smile since all of this began. He felt like he was now starting to see the daughter Iris knew and loved.

Judge Miller entered the court and the jury was seated. After the usual preliminary statements, the jury foreman read the verdict.

Not Guilty.

Thane could hear Iris's gasp of relief over the cacophony of reactions from the gallery. There was scattered applause, and a few disgruntled groans, but they were soon all gaveled into silence. After the judge thanked the jury, he told Boo she was free to go. Before rising, he also told her he hoped she would move forward and do something more with her life.

As soon as the judge gaveled the proceedings to a close, Kristin threw an arm around Boo and gave her a hug.

"Sue me," Kristin said.

Boo hugged her back, then rose and embraced her

mother tightly. When they finally broke, she looked at her father, uncertain. Struthers stepped forward and opened his arms and Boo stepped into them. Her embrace wasn't as strong as it had been with her mother, but she remained in his arms and looked content to be there.

After stepping away from her father, Boo turned to Thane. "Thank you again. For everything."

"To be honest, I feel like you and your mother did most of the strategizing with this case. I didn't see much of a way out."

"But you still respected me and listened to me, and that meant a lot. You also trusted my mother enough to let her testify, even though you didn't know for sure what she would say."

When Boo returned to her family, Barnes stepped over to the defense table. Thane wasn't sure if Barnes had any interest in shaking hands or not, so he left that call up to his adversary. It quickly became clear Barnes didn't stop by to congratulate Thane.

"Once again, you found a way to subvert the system. You know, this is the sort of thing that will bite you in the ass down the road. Judges hate it when they feel like a lawyer will do or say anything to win a case."

"If you're referring to the mother's testimony, it caught me by surprise as much as it did everyone else."

"Right," Barnes said, skeptically. "Either way, you once again made my office look foolish."

"First of all, I didn't do anything. Like you, I didn't believe Ms. Robinson during her interview, but I don't know that I would have completely dismissed her claim out of hand as you did, so don't blame me for that."

Barnes picked up his briefcase and headed toward the

exit, throwing back his shoulders in preparation for the peppering he was certain to get from the press outside the courthouse. His very bad day was about to get worse.

As Thane started gathering his material, a hand landed on his shoulder. He turned and saw Detective Struthers standing behind him. The taciturn man extended his hand, which Thane happily accepted.

"Thank you. I know this was an unusual situation for you—for both of us—but I wanted to thank you for what you did for my daughter."

"I'm not sure I did a lot."

"No, your support of them was important. So, again, thank you."

Thane's phone vibrated. He pulled it out and saw a text from his wife. For a moment, he froze, then looked back up at Struthers.

"I'm sorry to have to leave so quickly, but my wife is on her way to the hospital to deliver our first child."

50

Thane ended up meeting Hannah at the hospital. He was afraid he was going to be too late to participate in the birth, but she hadn't even been taken to the delivery room yet when he arrived. The delivery itself ended up being long and arduous, but mother and baby were both fine. Exhausted, but fine.

Hannah apologized for interrupting Thane's victory party. She had heard the verdict on the news, and immediately after began experiencing labor pains. She wasn't necessarily connecting the two events, but the timing was interesting.

After giving birth and being taken back to her room, Hannah returned to the question of naming their daughter.

"We can't be calling her 'To Be Determined' anymore," she said. "The hospital would like it if we could come up with a name. A real name."

"What are you thinking?"

"I was wondering about a compromise. You like the word that isn't a name, Mesa, and I apparently like the name of a Marvel character, Logan. What if we combine them? Call her Megan?"

"Megan," Thane said quietly, seeing how it sounded on his tongue.

"It means pearl. From all of the difficulties we've faced, we were still able to create a pearl. Something beautiful."

"I like it. I almost like it better than Mesa." He looked at Hannah and nodded. "Well done."

After an hour or so of quietly calling out to their daughter Megan, as if she would pick up on her name through repetition her first day, Hannah was finally getting some much-deserved sleep. Thane sat in a hospital chair that was more comfortable than he expected and watched her sleep. He then directed his attention to his daughter, who was now as innocent and unaware as she would ever be in her life. She was also sound asleep, still tired from the move.

Thane was a father. He was now responsible for another human being. Thank God he wasn't doing it alone. He knew he'd be leaning a lot on Hannah to help him figure out what he was supposed to do, but he also recognized all of this was new to her as well. She was just better at hiding her terror, if in fact she was experiencing any. But he already knew the most important responsibilities in his new job description: keep his daughter safe, fed, sheltered, and loved, but as the Bible said, the greatest of these was love.

He knew it was now time to let go of the darkness, the anger, the resentment he felt from prison. He had played fast and loose with the law, to say the least, and had always found a way to justify it, whether it was justifiable or not, but that also had to end. He needed to be the type of father his daughter deserved, and to be the kind of man

Hannah married years ago.

He knew what he needed to do. The question was whether or not he could do it. The man who had set Thane up for a murder he didn't commit was now dead, as was the man who actually killed the young woman. And the District Attorney who let Thane go to jail, even though he knew Thane was innocent, had now been exposed and disgraced.

It was time.

His stomach rumbled loud enough that he was afraid it would wake Hannah or the baby, or possibly both. It reminded him that he hadn't eaten in over fifteen hours, so he quietly lifted himself from his chair and slipped out of the room to find the cafeteria. It was 2:00 a.m., but he hoped the hospital had at least some sort of food available for its night shift.

After devouring something fried that looked like it could be in the same family as chicken nuggets, along with some cold and limp french fries, Thane returned to Hannah's room. She was still sleeping, as was their daughter, but as Thane lowered himself back into his chair, he noticed a small, shiny trinket resting upon the baby's blanket, rising up and down with each tiny breath.

Thane rose and walked over to take a closer look, not having noticed it before, and saw it wasn't a trinket.

It was a bullet.

Thane was grateful Hannah had given birth so soon after the trial was over. He had no doubt Stick was going to seek revenge on Thane—the warning sign had already been given—and at least for now Hannah was fine staying home with Thane and their new daughter. And now that the trial was over, Thane was able to stay home and keep them both safe.

He told Hannah as much as he believed was necessary, including repeating the fact that Stick was not a man to be trifled with and that they needed to be extra cautious until Thane could figure out a way to resolve the situation.

He didn't tell her about the bullet.

They did not go out for walks, which wasn't a problem right away because Hannah was still exhausted, but Thane knew they couldn't stay hidden forever.

He caught himself frequently looking out the window and across the street, looking for anyone possibly casing their home. He thought there was a good chance Gideon was also out there somewhere, keeping watch. He didn't expect to be able to see Gideon, but Stick's crew didn't exactly strike him as being surveillance experts.

Thane also occasionally slipped out the back door after dark and surreptitiously checked out the area for suspect cars or people loitering, but he didn't see anyone.

Thane would have been surprised if Stick came at his family right away. The psychopath would enjoy trying to unsettle Thane for as long as possible before making his move. Thus the leaving of the bullet.

For that reason, Thane decided to make the first move.

He told Hannah one evening that he had to go into the office for about an hour or two, then reminded her to be sure to lock the door and to not open it for anyone.

He had his briefcase in hand when he went through the kitchen and into the garage. The only thing in his briefcase was a Smith and Wesson J-Frame revolver.

He drove straight to the bar where Stick always hung out. If he wasn't there, Thane wouldn't know where to find him, but in that case, he would simply come back another time. Stick had been there every other time Thane was looking for him, although tonight he was going much later than usual.

Thane wouldn't be asking Gideon to join him, even though his friend's presence would have been a huge comfort to him. He didn't want to drag Gideon into something that could result in blood. This was his fight, and Gideon had managed to stay out of trouble so far following his most recent parole. There was no way Thane was going to do anything to jeopardize that.

Thane pulled up in front of the bar and sat in his car for about five minutes. He remembered sitting in the hospital room and silently telling himself it was time to do better. He remembered knowing with certainty that he couldn't keep coming up with excuses to go outside the law when he or someone he loved had been wronged.

And then he remembered the bullet on his sleeping baby's blanket.

He took the gun from his briefcase and placed it in his shoulder holster which was hidden under his sportscoat. He hoped that not only being a lawyer, but also dressing like one, might cause Stick not to view him as a threat, but he was fairly certain a man like Stick didn't make a lot of tactical errors.

He entered and found Stick sitting at the bar, staring at his phone, with a can of Budweiser in front of him. The only other person there was the bartender who looked like he could regale him with eye-witness stories from the Civil War.

Stick looked up and saw Thane's reflection in the mirror. He nodded at the bartender who turned and shuffled out of the room.

"Counselor," Stick said. "I hear congratulations are in order, although I suppose it's best not to get too attached to that little bundle of joy. I'll tell you what, though, that baby is a heavy sleeper."

Thane didn't respond. Prison had taught him that losing your temper usually meant losing your edge. But it wasn't easy not to charge him right then and there.

Stick slowly spun around on his barstool so that he was facing Thane. He leaned back against the bar and looked up at the ceiling, as if contemplating some deep thought.

"Why you suppose people always refer to babies as bundles of joy? You suppose they ain't never been around one? Seems to me like all babies do is cry and kick and shit their diapers. Where's the joy in that? They never say anything funny. They never do anything interesting. I just don't get it."

"We need to resolve things, Stick."

"That's a fact. And I'm planning on doing just that."

"I can't let you hurt my family."

"Then don't let me. Make me earn it. But I told you what would happen if you crossed me, and you blew so far past that line it was as if you wanted to be a bachelor again and were making sure I'd make that happen for you. What your little Barbie doll did in that courtroom is not something that can be forgiven."

Thane regretted how far Kristin had gone to make Stick look bad in court. He didn't regret putting him on the stand—at the time he agreed that was the right thing to do for his client—but they had pushed him further than they needed.

"If you want to come after me, come after me, but leave my family alone."

"Yeah, well, that's the thing, by going after your family, I'm going after you where it hurts the most. Now, that's not to say you might not get cut up a little here and there in the process, but that's just so you'll have a few visible scars to remind you of our time together. But I firmly believe it's the internal scars that hurt the most."

"Is that what your guy with the razor was supposed to do? Leave some visible scars?"

Stick broke out laughing.

"I gotta hand it to you, counselor, you sliced the shit out of my boy's mouth. Even lost part of his tongue. The kid is going to be talking like Elmer Fudd the rest of his life. Goddamn, I had the feeling you could fight, but that definitely exceeded expectations. But I can tell you one thing for sure, you're not going to be able to stop everyone."

"Again, I can't let you hurt my family."

"Then I guess you're going to have to kill me."

"If anything happens to either of them, I'll do that. I can promise you that."

"Well, I respect a promise as much as the next guy, but I also promised you what would happen if you messed with me, and you did it anyway. If you need to kill me afterward, then take your best shot, but many a man has tried."

"Then maybe I need to kill you now."

Stick's smile diminished by a degree or two as his hand slowly moved to the small of his back.

Thane quickly drew his revolver from his holster and pointed it at Stick's chest.

"I'd rather see both your hands, if you don't mind."

Stick paused before slowly placing both hands on his legs.

"For some reason, I don't see you shooting me."

"For some reason, I get the feeling you don't know me very well."

"Ain't you supposed to follow the law? Hell, that's even part of your job title. Lawyer."

"We're all supposed to follow the law. That's the whole idea behind it. But for whatever reason, guys like you feel they can do whatever they want to do, but everyone else needs to follow the rules while they try to stop you. Why do you suppose that is? Why should the bad guys be the only ones who get to ignore the rules?"

"Because we're the bad guys," Stick said, chuckling. "That's part of what makes us bad. You want to start shooting anyone who makes you angry, you can't be calling yourself a good guy. You'll just be one of us."

"Maybe protecting my family makes me a good guy."

"Yeah, keep telling yourself that, but you and I both know your baby gonna end up with a gangster for a father."

Thane pictured Stick standing over his baby in the hospital and placing a bullet on her blanket. He didn't think Stick had the guts to do that himself, but it helped Thane to picture it that way.

He then imagined Stick breaking into their home while he was away and doing unspeakable things to

Hannah.

And he thought of all the violence he had been subjected to while at Forsman Penitentiary and how it had numbed him of trying to take into consideration what was moral and what wasn't. In prison, the name of the game was survival, not morality, and now here he was trying to negotiate his family's survival with a beast.

But he wasn't in prison anymore.

"You can think of shooting me as one last favor to your client," Stick laughed, "because I can tell you one thing for sure, that little bitch is going to be tasting her own blood otherwise, and it ain't going to be fast for her, neither. You can add another billable hour or two on your final invoice to her for saving her from that level of pain."

Thane was surprised he hadn't already pulled the trigger. That in and of itself gave him hope.

He finally put the gun back into his holster.

"I knew you weren't no killer," Stick said.

"I'm going to protect my family, Stick."

"Yeah, so you've already said. In the meantime, it will be a good time to send this to the cops."

Stick brought out his phone and once again played the audio of Thane asking Stick to coerce a witness.

"This will tie you up for a bit. Keep you away from home when you're needed most."

Thane felt like he needed to allow himself one more exception to his moral code, but if he hadn't already shot Stick after his family had been threatened, he wasn't going to do it because of the threat of that audio. But now that there were two different threats to his future with his family...

And then a familiar voice came from behind him.

"I'd like to hear that recording again."

Stick looked at the man as a snarl crept across his face.

"Who the hell are you? And where'd you come from?"

"I'm Detective Vince Struthers with the LAPD, which is reason enough for you to not do anything stupid. And you need to tell the owner of this dump he should keep his back door locked."

Struthers walked past the pool table and into the main part of the bar. Thane realized Struthers had managed to follow him from his home without being detected, which didn't surprise him because all he had been thinking about was dealing with Stick. He wasn't sure how much Struthers had heard, but he had obviously heard the audiotape.

"I'd like for you to come to the station with me and tell me about what it is you have recorded there."

"I ain't working with no cops."

"You just said you were going to send it to the cops. I'm a cop. You picky who hears it?"

Stick thought about it, and a smile once again returned to his face as he looked at Thane.

"You heard the man. He's making me give it to him, so don't be acting like I ratted you out. Us good guys, we work with the cops." Stick turned back to Struthers. "Why can't I talk to you about it here?"

"Because I have a colleague who is going to want to hear it, and I'll want to record it so we'll have a copy. It won't take long."

In a way, Thane was glad it was Struthers who had come across the tape. He had always respected the man, but lately had grown to like him as well.

"Thane," Struthers said, "I'd also like for you to come to the station as well. Can I trust you to follow us there, or do I need to have you ride with me as well?"

"I'll follow you."

Struthers studied Thane, then nodded that he believed him. Thane found it ironic that now that Struthers had at least some hard evidence against him, he finally called him by his first name, rather than his usual insistence on calling him Mr. Banning.

"Alright," Struthers said, turning back to Stick. "If you have any weapons on you, I strongly suggest you take them out and leave them here at the bar. I assume your stuff isn't messed with here."

"Damn well better not be."

Stick stood and looked at Thane, still smiling.

"Always a pleasure, Counselor."

As Stick once again reached toward the small of his back, Struthers told him to take it out very slowly.

"You concerned I'm going to shoot someone?" Stick said.

"Who knows? I heard what you said about Bonnie, so maybe you're concerned I have a grudge against you."

"Who the hell is Bonnie?"

"Bonnie is his daughter," Thane explained, when Struthers didn't answer. "Boo's real name is Bonnie. You remember Boo. She's the one who is going to taste her own blood."

Stick nodded, as if he knew this all along, but Thane could tell the wrist-watch-sized wheels in Stick's head were spinning. His hand moved exceptionally slowly to his back.

"Do you see what he's doing?" Struthers asked Thane.

Thane didn't understand the question, and looked at Struthers quizzically.

"Do you see what he's doing?" Struthers asked again, saying each word slower.

Thane thought for a moment, then figured it out. "He's going for his gun," Thane said.

"Yeah," Struthers said. "That's what I see, too."

At which point Stick also figured it out. His hand stopped moving, but he seemed to realize things weren't going to go down that easily. Thane wondered if Stick would try and take a first shot at Struthers, since he was the one holding the gun, but instead Stick glared at Thane as if he had set this whole thing up. Stick whipped out his gun and began pointing it at Thane, rather than at the detective with the gun, but three shots from Struthers' gun made a strong impression on Stick's chest, and another two bullets hit Stick in the head as he dropped to the floor.

Neither Thane nor Struthers moved at first. Thane remained frozen from surprise, and he had no idea what Struthers was feeling, but the detective wasn't moving either After a moment, Struthers walked over and checked for a pulse, although it was obvious it didn't need to be checked.

Thane thought it revealing that Stick's anger at him was so strong that the thug was more determined to try to kill Thane than to try to take out the detective with the gun.

Struthers radioed that shots had been fired and one suspect was dead. Then he stood over Stick's body and shook his head.

"I don't condone taking the law into your own

hands and carrying out what you feel to be a justifiable execution," Struthers said as he looked over at Thane. "You understand what I'm saying? I don't condone it." He looked down again at the body at his feet. "But sometimes I understand it."

Thane wasn't sure what to do, or even if he should say anything. He thought he knew the detective well enough to know this went against everything he stood for.

"What I don't understand," Struthers continued, "is why you didn't shoot him. The man was threatening your family, all but promising to hurt your wife and your newborn child. And you had a gun. It would have been so easy for you."

"How long were you back there?"

"Long enough to get the gist of the conversation. I figured you were going to kill him."

"Would you have arrested me if I had?" Thane asked.

At first Struthers shook his head, then shrugged his shoulders as if now uncertain. "I don't know. It certainly would have made my job easier. But it's also just as likely I would have bought you a beer." He studied Thane, as if the answer to his questions were somewhere on Thane's face. "I was pretty sure I knew what went down with your former boss and that detective who killed Lauren McCoy, so I assumed you would easily kill this piece of shit, especially given what he was saying about your family. Now I'm thinking, maybe I've got you wrong. I also need to figure out what I'm going to do, personally. This isn't how I operate."

"For what it's worth," Thane said, "he did draw first. I'd testify to that if need be."

"And would you also mention I got him to do it?"

"You didn't make him do anything. He was stupid enough to do it on his own. Either way, whatever you want to put in your report is up to you, but nothing bad will come from me. The man was a cancer."

"He was at that," Struthers said softly, before seeming to remember something.

"Hey, how's your little baby doing?"

"She's good. I'm not sure she totally understands the concept of sleep yet, but other than that, she's pretty perfect."

Struthers offered up a rare, albeit sincere, smile. "Yeah, you might as well put away your concept of sleep for what's going to feel like fifty years."

A police siren cut through the quiet night, still several blocks away, but closing fast.

"Be there for her," Struthers said softly. "I didn't do a great job of that. I realize now I put my job and what I thought were my responsibilities ahead of what should have been my number one responsibility, which was keeping her safe. I didn't do that."

"You did tonight," Thane said. When Struthers didn't respond, Thane asked him how Boo was doing.

"She's home with us, at least until she can find her own place again. I think it's going to be alright. Or at least it's going to be better now," he added, looking at Stick.

Struthers walked back over to the body, took a handkerchief out of his pocket, and used it to remove the phone from Stick's shirt pocket.

The phone screen was locked, so Struthers held the phone up to Stick's face, but it didn't unlock due to the blood running down Stick's face. Struthers grabbed a bar rag and wiped enough blood off Stick's face to unlock the phone. He found the recording of Thane, and as it was playing, he hit a button which announced the deletion of the recording. He returned the phone to Stick's pocket. Blood had already recovered much of the man's face.

"I'm taking myself off your case," Struthers said. "I don't know if it will be considered a cold case, or if Detective Hawkins is going to ask for it. He's like a pit bull with a bone, but he won't be seeing any evidence from me that could help him."

"Thanks for telling me."

"And do me a favor and thank your wife for me. I don't know if she told you or not, but she's offered Bonnie a job to help out around the shelter. Hopefully this one will work. I'm optimistic."

They heard a squad car screech outside the bar and cut its alarm.

Again, Struthers looked close at Thane as if still totally confounded.

"Why didn't you shoot him?"

When Thane didn't answer, the detective looked at Stick yet again. "For whatever reason, it's important to me you realize this isn't who I am. Not as a detective and not as a human being."

Thane walked over and stood next to him, looking down at Stick's body.

"I doubt there's anyone who understands that better than me."

51

Kristin was still breathing hard as she drove back to her condo after having spent an hour at her Pilates class. There was still a sheen of sweat on her forehead, but she felt like she could have gone another hour at full force without breaking pace. As good as the workout always made her feel, it didn't come close to the feeling she got from the call right before class began.

Thane called to tell her what had gone down the previous evening with Stick. She didn't hear everything clearly at first. Just hearing Stick's name caused her insides to seize, and when she heard the words 'Stick' and 'shot', she initially thought Stick had shot someone. And then she thought Thane had shot Stick. That scared her, because even though she had great respect for Thane and thought him to be a moral person, for some reason deep down she sensed he might have the capacity to go and shoot Stick in cold blood. She was relieved—and more than a little embarrassed at herself—when she asked him to repeat what he had said, and she realized that an LAPD detective had shot and killed the son-of-a-bitch.

She wasn't embarrassed at all, however, at the wave of relief washing over her, knowing this man was out of her life. Nor did she try to tell herself she shouldn't take joy in another human being's death. Oh, no, she took joy. A lot of joy. And she embraced it. She didn't let herself think too often about the time Stick had forced his way into her apartment, but the recollection wasn't nearly as traumatic now, knowing the man had five bullets in him.

Apparently, Boo was wrong. The man could be killed.

Her flirtation with going to work for the D.A.'s office stemmed from a desire to put men like Stick away, but Boo's case showed her that she could still take on monsters like him while also protecting their victims. She called D.A. Angela Day shortly after the trial was over, telling her she'd decided to stay where she was. Angela was gracious and told Kristin that, while disappointed, she believed Kristin was making the right decision.

She pulled into her condo's parking lot and instinctively started to scan the area, then caught herself and stopped. As a single woman in L.A.—or pretty much anywhere for that matter—it paid to be aware of one's surroundings, but these past few days she had found herself looking at every car in every parking lot, at every person on every street and in every building, trying to discern whether they represented danger or not. Today, she simply got out of her car and entered her condo complex.

When the elevator reached her floor, she didn't peek out into the hall before stepping off the elevator. Unlocking the double lock on her door, she wondered whether she would now go back to only using the main deadbolt.

She walked into her condo and dropped her gym bag on the floor, then took a deep breath as she looked around her home. It was quiet, secure, and peaceful, just like it used to be.

She walked over and threw open the curtains. The bright L.A. sunlight filled the room and warmed her face. She stood looking out at the bright blue sky, happy to stand at the window for a long moment, basking in the sun.

Gideon sat pressed against the door in the backseat of the Uber, as if trying to make himself as small as possible, which, given his size, was a hopeless exercise. Alice sat on other side of the seat, apparently unaware of Gideon's discomfort. Unaware, or at least willing to not call attention to it.

He had been at the diner the previous afternoon for lunch, and Alice congratulated him on his win in court. Telling him well done, as if he had been the one standing up there talking to the jury. She told him she respected anyone who stood up for the underdog.

He thanked her and told her his sister Pearl was having a congratulatory dinner for him at their house on Saturday night. She said that that sounded nice, at which point Gideon, without thinking, asked her if she'd like to go with him. To his surprise, she said she'd love to.

Gideon didn't know what was supposed to happen at that point. Was he supposed to pick her up? That would be hard, given that he didn't drive, but maybe the Uber driver would take him to pick her up and then take them to his sister's house. Did Uber drivers do that? He didn't know why not, since what did it matter to them who they took and where, as long as they got paid?

And now there he was, in the backseat of an Uber, sweating like he was sitting in a sauna. He knew he should be trying to carry on a conversation, but he was afraid if he opened his mouth, something foul would come out. Or at least something embarrassing.

When he went to Alice's door—the Uber driver having diplomatically suggested he do that rather than have the driver honk for her—she answered looking beautiful. Gideon had only seen her in her waitress outfit, and he was caught off-guard seeing her dressed up. It was all he could do to keep from saying 'whoa' out loud, although he said it to himself. At least he hoped he didn't say it out loud.

And she even smelled good. She'd obviously put on some sort of perfumy thing that wasn't too strong. The scent made him want to sit closer to her, although he was too nervous to try that. Working at the diner, she usually smelled like french fries; not that he didn't also find that attractive.

In the car, he looked down at the floorboard and noticed Alice's shoes were a lot nicer than the ones he had complemented the last time at the restaurant. He wondered if he should also compliment these, but decided he didn't want to come across as a one-trick pony, even though that was his only trick.

The driver pulled up in front of Pearl's house. Gideon got out and thought perhaps Alice had realized she'd made a terrible mistake and was telling the driver to take her back home, but then he realized she was waiting for him to open her door. Or it was stuck. Whatever the case, he hustled over and opened it for her, feeling like a classy doorman at an expensive hotel.

As they walked up the front steps, Pearl opened the door. Gus stood behind her with a big smile on his face.

"Alice, this is my sister Pearl. And you've already met Gus."

Pearl stepped forward and gave Alice a big hug, beaming an even larger smile than her son's.

"Very nice to meet you, Alice. Please, come on in."

She led Alice into the house. Gus looked up at Gideon and held out his fist for a fist bump.

"Uncle Gid. You smooth dog."

Gideon made a fist as well, but held it up in threatening manner

"Don't make me hurt you, boy."

But Gideon smiled and tapped fists with Gus as he entered the house after his date. A real date.

52

Thane sat across from Jenna Kennedy, his therapist, for the first time in over a month. At first, the trial had forced him to clear his calendar of other commitments, and after that he stuck close to home while Stick remained a threat to his family. Now, he was not only able to make his appointment; he actually wanted to talk about how he was feeling.

They talked about life as a new parent, and they shared stories of sleepless nights and frayed nerves. Jenna had a much larger pool of stories to pull from, being the mother of four, but she promised Thane his time would come.

"How have you been doing since we last spoke?" Jenna asked. "I sense more of an openness from you. Maybe even some optimism?"

"I'm feeling better. Winning the case I've been working on is certainly a relief, and obviously the safe delivery of our child was a huge weight lifted. Both of those had me preoccupied."

The absence of Stick also had a major impact on Thane's demeanor, but he kept that one to himself. The danger he had presented had consumed Thane.

But the biggest reason for his optimism was the fact that he hadn't shot and killed Stick, even though he would have easily been able to justify it to himself. In fact, he believed he had a far stronger argument for killing Stick than he had for setting Lauren McCoy's father on Thane's former boss and the disgraced detective who had killed her.

He hadn't been sure how he was going to protect his family from that sociopath, and even though there was nothing more important to him than Hannah and their baby, he had nevertheless put away his gun. He had wrestled with the morality of what he wanted so badly to do and had ended up on what he felt was the true moral side of that equation.

All of that gave him hope that perhaps he was making progress getting back to being the man he was before being sent to prison.

As he shared his sense of optimism—without all the details—he knew the question she would have for him.

"You've talked about being more open with your wife," she said, as expected. "Do you feel like now is a good time to tell her whatever you've been holding inside all this time?"

It took Thane a long moment to try to come up with an excuse that didn't sound too much like an excuse, although he knew he would fail in that regard.

"With the baby, and all of the big changes that that brings, I'm thinking I should wait at least a little while until things settle down more."

"Yes, maybe when the child is two or three. There's so much less going on then. Or even better, when she becomes a teenager. She'll be staying inside her bedroom a lot anyway, which will give you even more time to talk with Hannah."

"I didn't think therapists were supposed to be sarcastic," Thane said, smiling.

"What in the world gave you that idea?"

"You believe I'm just coming up with an excuse to delay talking with her."

"I'm pretty sure you and I both know that's an excuse. What are you really feeling?"

Thane didn't push back about thinking it was an excuse, although he did know that what he was going to be telling Hannah could totally shake her world to the core, and doing that not long after bringing home a newborn might not be the best timing. He knew Hannah very much wanted him to open up, but then again, she also didn't know the magnitude of what he had to say.

"I'm a little scared."

"Let's talk about what could happen. When you envision telling Hannah what it is you want to tell her, what is the worst-case scenario that plays out in your mind?"

The worst thing would be Hannah looking at him like he was a creature she didn't recognize. A monster she didn't want to have around her child, or around her. He had lost her for the five years he had been in prison, and he knew he couldn't survive losing her again.

"The worst scenario is her not wanting to be with me anymore."

"And what is the best scenario that plays in your mind?"

Thane didn't have to think too hard about that.

"The best scenario is that when I'm done telling her, she takes me in her arms and holds me and tells me she loves me and it's going to be alright." Saying that aloud almost made his voice crack.

Jenna let that sit for a minute, giving him the opportunity to continue envisioning that scene playing out.

"Deep down, what do you believe you should do?"

"I should tell her," Thane said. It wasn't even a question.

"And do you feel you're now in a place where you'll be able to do it?"

He wasn't quite as quick to answer this question, although he was almost as confident when he did finally reply. "I do."

They again sat in silence. Jenna obviously knew she couldn't tell him what to do. He had to make the decision.

The problem was he was scared. Very scared. But he also knew maybe that was the type of fear a moral person could confront.

53

Thane sat in his usual place on the floor with his back against the far wall in the nursery, watching his baby daughter sleep. Her crib still had not collapsed, but Thane looked like he was ready to leap into action at any moment should it start looking unstable. A soft blue light near the crib was the only source of illumination in the room, which gave it a magical feel as if the baby was being protected by a wizard.

Hannah passed by the door and stopped to watch her husband for a minute before coming in and joining him. She lowered herself to the floor so that she was sitting next to him, then joined him in gazing at their daughter. Finally, she broke the silence.

"So, whaddya think?"

Thane shook his head. "Remember a couple of years ago when I tried learning how to make bread?"

She smiled. "That's what's running through your mind? But yes, I do remember."

Thane continued studying their baby in amazement.

"I never could make an edible loaf of bread, but somehow I was able to help make a perfect human being. How is that even possible? Shouldn't the second thing be so much harder than the first?"

"Maybe it's because when you were trying to make bread, you never let me do the majority of the work."

Thane nodded, agreeing with that assessment. He then looked at Hannah.

"I understand you offered Boo a job at the shelter."

"I did. I think she's going to do well there. She's very protective of other women who have been dealt a bad hand."

"Do you have concerns as to whether or not she truly is the one who killed Dixon?" Thane asked. "Or do you feel fairly certain it went down as her mother said?"

"I don't know. I don't see her posing a threat to anyone at the shelter. She just needs a chance to get her life back together." She took Thane's hand. "Do you think she did it?"

"I don't know, but if you made me guess, I'd say yes."

"Why do you say that?"

"I read the police reports. In the interview with the police, the same neighbor who called in the gunshot at 12:50 also said he heard a TV blasting at top volume for a brief moment just a few minutes after midnight. He said it was unbelievably loud and he was getting ready to go out and see if he could tell where it was coming from, but then the sound was turned down."

"Which means what?" Hannah asked.

"Again, I'm just speculating, but I believe Boo turned up the volume to cover the gun shot. I think she then called her mother to tell her what she'd done. That first call to Iris's burner phone came not long after the TV was playing so loud. She wasn't calling her mother to tell her she had just been abused. She called to say she had shot a man. Everything else probably happened as Iris said it did. She went over to Dixon's house. Boo appeared on the Ring video and then broke the doorbell. That's when Iris would have left her fingerprints. Boo then let her mother drive back home before going outside and firing the gun into the air to help ensure someone would hear it in order to establish the false timeline, calling her mother immediately afterward so that Iris had an alibi. Or at least that's what I'm guessing happened, because no one else reported a loud TV after Boo made her first call. It also explains why it was turned up so loud for such a short amount of time. They did all that in an attempt to try to game the system."

"That makes sense," Hannah said. "I had trouble seeing Iris going over there and shooting that man, however much she would have wanted to. But I also know you never know what a person could do. Why do you suppose the police didn't make that connection with the timeline?"

"Because their suspect said she did it. Cops don't usually feel the need to drill down too deep when you have someone saying they did it."

"So, Boo killed the man," Hannah said, more to herself than to Thane.

"Knowing what I think, would you still have offered Boo the job?"

"Yes," Hannah said without having to think about it. "I already thought there was a good chance she did it. I just think it was a unique situation. I don't condone it, but I sort of understand it. I do still believe she's a good person and worth helping."

After a moment, Thane noticed Hannah turning to him, concern on her face.

"Thane, what's wrong?"

He wasn't sure what she meant until he noticed his view of the crib was being blurred by the tears in his eyes that he didn't even know were forming. Soon they were running down his cheeks. He tried to turn away from her, but she put her hand on his face and turned it back toward her.

"Baby, what's the matter? What's going on?"

Thane held up his hand and tried to regain control of his emotions. At a minimum, he was finally able to stop the tears from flowing.

"It's not that," Thane said. "It's just—you've been saying for a while that we need to talk, and you're right. You're right, my therapist says you're right, and I know you're right. I just don't want you to think I'm looking to talk to you now because of what you just said about Boo. About you sort of understanding what she did."

"I won't think that. I can tell you've been getting closer to opening up."

Thane hadn't envisioned telling Hannah his story in the same room as his daughter. He wanted to reach over and take Hannah's hand, but he was frozen in place. He couldn't get up. He could barely move. He knew the best he would be able to do was to finally speak the horrible truth he had been hiding, but when he spoke, it came out as a broken whisper.

"I did a very bad thing. A thing I'm afraid you'll find unforgiveable."

Hannah remained quiet for a moment, obviously trying to give him space, but finally broke the silence in an attempt to help him tell his story.

"While you were in prison?"

Thane shook his head and whispered, "After."

He felt her sit up a little straighter, as if she hadn't been expecting that answer. After another long moment of silence, he continued.

"I was framed for the murder of Lauren McCoy."

She looked at him quizzically. "I know that, baby."

"But you didn't know that Joseph had been scheming with Lauren on that big project I'd been working on. And that she was starting to blackmail him. And that Joseph had worked with that detective, Gruber, who the D.A. finally admitted had killed Lauren."

He could see Hannah trying to take all of this in, before she finally put the first part of it together.

"Are you saying Joseph had that young woman killed?" She looked shocked, and then her eyes grew even larger as more pieces fell into place. "Wait a second. Are you saying that Joseph is the person who framed you?"

Thane nodded. He then looked away and began telling her everything. How he had figured out who had murdered Lauren, and how Joseph had hired Gruber to kill her. About talking with Lauren's father and setting into motion their plan to not only get justice on the man's daughter, but also Thane framing his own client in order to expose D.A. Stone's knowledge of Thane's innocence. And about Joseph coming to his office that final night to kill Thane, but Lauren's father being there to greet him.

The tears started again, and they came even harder. From the time Thane went to prison up until now, he had only cried three times. There was his first night in Forsman when the gravity of his new life hit him, and then his first night back with Hannah after having been released from prison. The third time was at the birth of his daughter. But now the tears that were flowing were more than enough to make up for the many previous years.

"I'm sorry," Thane said, still unable to look at Hannah. "I'm so sorry. I'm so sorry," he said over and over, trying to find another way to express what he was feeling. "I recognize I'm not the man I used to be, but for the first time since being released, I finally believe I'm back on the road to getting there. I feel like there is actual hope." He paused, as if arguing a lost case. "I'm so sorry," he said again, returning to what he felt the strongest.

He finally turned toward Hannah, willing to risk seeing her reaction to his confession. To see if she was looking at him in horror, or if it looked as though she was getting ready to get up and flee the room.

Instead, she was also crying and looking deep into his tear-filled eyes.

She then opened her arms, and Thane let himself be embraced by them.

ABOUT THE AUTHOR

Photo by Sabrina Hendricks

Michael Cordell is a Silver Falchion Award-winning novelist, playwright and produced screenwriter. His first novel, *Contempt*, was a Top 10 Amazon Kindle legal thriller. He has sold three screenplays to Hollywood, including *Beeper*, an action-thriller starring Harvey Keitel. Michael currently lives in Charlottesville, Virginia, where he has taught screenwriting for over fifteen years.

CONNECT WITH MICHAEL CORDELL

Sign up for Michael's newsletter at
www.michaeljcordell.com/newsletter

To find out more information visit his website:
www.michaeljcordell.com

Facebook:
www.facebook.com/michaeljcordell

BOOK DISCOUNTS AND SPECIAL DEALS

Sign up for free to get discounts and special deals
on our bestselling books at
www.TCKpublishing.com/bookdeals